— PRAISE FOR —

Songs for Ivy

"I thoroughly enjoyed Carlos's track. Another very sensitive and human song. So much talent. I loved the sensitivity in the stories and through the lyrics. The song about losing his leg brought me to tears actually. Yet, there was hope in the music and words. Carlos uses his personal life tragedies and observations in his songs to say, *c'est la vie,* and that we must acknowledge our pain but then go on to gain strength from it."

—*Rose Weaver, MFA actor, director, producer, writer*

"I loved the way Ivy came to understand her mother and her father's love for her mother through Jake's diaries. There are no villains in the novel, just people with backgrounds that make them acceptably flawed! Great novel!"

—*Dr. Nancy Carriuolo, 2008-2016 President of RI College*

"As I read this lovely book, I was immediately caught up in the lives of these unique and very believable characters. I found myself wanting to know how things would work out for all of them, unhappy when things didn't go well, disappointed in some of their life choices and, overall, enchanted with them all. This is an amazing achievement. Throughout much of it I wondered how the lives were going to intertwine, how their issues would be settled, and what they would be achieving. They were nicely complex characters and there were plenty of surprises as I read. As soon as this is available for purchase I will certainly be the first in line."

—*Judy de Perla, English teacher (40 years), theater director for youth theater, currently co-founder and director of JDP Theatre Co.*

"A shout out for the author for channeling through his x-ray vision the characters in his first novel. Young and old, strong or weak, rich or poor, healthy or sick they all share the human experience. Through their love, friendship, and compassion, he gives the reader and his characters a glimpse of JOY. Through song, Jake is able to convey, pain, angst, powerlessness, tenderness, acceptance, and gratitude. In this insightful process, he heals his body and his soul. *Songs for Ivy* is a tribute to the arts as medicine for the spirit."

—*Gladys Corvera-Baker, LICSW*

Songs *for* Ivy

A Love Story of Hope and Resilience

a novel by

CARLOS K. BAKER

Songs for Ivy

Produced and printed
by Stillwater River Publications.

Visit our website at
www.StillwaterPress.com
for more information.

First Stillwater River Publications Edition

Library of Congress Control Number: 2020917965

ISBN: 978-1-952521-53-9

1 2 3 4 5 6 7 8 9 10
Written by Carlos K. Baker
Published by Stillwater River Publications,
Pawtucket, RI, USA.

Publisher's Cataloging-In-Publication Data
(Prepared by The Donohue Group, Inc.)

Names: Baker, Carlos, 1974- author.
Title: Songs for Ivy : a novel / by Carlos Baker.
Description: First Stillwater River Publications edition. |
Pawtucket, RI, USA : Stillwater River Publications, [2020]
Identifiers: ISBN 9781952521539
Subjects: LCSH: Brothers and sisters--Fiction. | Diaries--
Fiction. | Premature death--Fiction. | Families--Fiction. |
Substance abuse--Fiction.
Classification: LCC PS3602.A5852 S66 2020 |
DDC 813/.6--dc23

TEXT SET IN ADOBE CASLON.

To my mama, papa, and brother.

– 1 –

With her school backpack over one shoulder and volleyball bag over the other, Ivy stepped into the elevator and rode the thirty-seven flights down from the family's penthouse apartment that she called home. She knew exactly who would be waiting to greet her in the lobby when she stepped out of the elevator; this had been her morning routine for the last three years of her life.

It was Monday morning, which meant Vladimir "Bugs" Bugaychuk, whom Ivy called Mr. Bugs, would be standing at the concierge desk wearing his black suit with gold buttons and a dark red tie, the uniform all employees at the Boston Omni Hotel were required to wear. Bugs, originally from St. Petersburg, Russia, had lived the last forty-five of his fifty-five years in the United States but had never been able to lose his harsh Russian accent. If the truth be known, Bugs didn't have any interest in ridding himself of his accent. He was proud of his heritage and felt if he was not able to live in his hometown of St. Petersburg, the least he could do is speak the English language like a true Russian.

In his mother tongue Mr. Bugs would say, *"Dobroye utro, Miz Miles,"* which meant "Good morning, Ms. Miles." Ivy would reply, *"I ochen' giod utro uoubas khorosho,"* which meant "And a very good morning to you too."

When Ivy first moved into the Omni at twelve years old, she had searched the internet to learn this Russian phrase. Of course, this was the full extent of her knowledge of the Russian language, but it meant the world to Bugs that she had learned this little piece of his mother tongue. He was reminded how truly special a girl Ivy was every time he heard her speak those words. Like most everyone who knew her, he marveled at the fact that after the heartbreak and loss Ivy had gone through so early in her life, she had turned out to be such an amazing young lady.

As Ivy stepped out of the elevator, there was Mr. Bugs as expected, but standing next to him was the hotel manager, Mr. Pierce, who was clearly stressed over dealing with what looked like a difficult hotel guest. The woman doing the complaining looked to be in her late thirties and judging by the tone of her voice, body language, and facial expressions, the woman was unhappy about something. Particularly striking was the fact that the woman must recently have had lip augmentation injections, because her lips looked to be three to four times the size of what human lips are supposed to be. Ivy had the amusing thought that perhaps the woman was complaining that while asleep in her room, she had been bitten directly on her lips by a swarm of wasps. Ivy made eye contact with Bugs, and judging by the slight smirk he flashed, wondered if he was thinking the same exact thing.

So, on this particular morning, Ivy didn't get a chance to talk with Mr. Bugs. However, as she was walking toward the exit, he was once again able to sneak a smirk, and the most subtle of a wink which said as much to her as any of his words could.

Ivy exited the lobby through the spinning doors and into the waiting Lincoln Town Car. She and the driver exchanged good mornings, and, as she did every day to pass the time during her commute, Ivy took out the book she was currently reading. For the last week it was *The Bluest Eye* by Toni Morrison. She became so engrossed in the story that it felt as if she had only just begun reading, yet after nearly twenty-five minutes, they arrived at her school.

– 2 –

The views from the top floor of the most prestigious and expensive building in Boston, the John Harlow Towers, were spectacular. Alan Miles and his partner Harry Begosian had moved their law firm into the office space over fifteen years earlier and were among the most sought-after lawyers in their field of expertise, yet all but one of the eleven junior partners had long since left and only Alan's long-time assistant Cathy Bradford remained. There were dozens of empty offices and conference rooms that were rarely, if ever, used.

Regardless, the firm had no intentions of hiring more employees to fill the office nor plans to move to a smaller office any time soon. Instead, Alan and Harry continued to work together as a two-man team and used temporary help with research and overflow. Even so, over the last 30 years Miles & Begosian was one of the highest-earning law firms in the country.

Alan was sitting in his office busily reviewing papers, ignoring, as he always did, the sweeping view of the city below.

"Morning Alan, morning Cathy, and how are we doing on this beautiful Monday?" said Harry as he strolled into the office.

"Good morning, Mr. B, all is well, thank you," Cathy replied.

"How is your mother doing with her breathing? I spoke to Dr. Berdych and he told me you had brought her to see him and he sounded quite optimistic that he would be able to help her," said Harry.

"After having problems with her breathing on and off for the last two years, it's now been over three weeks without any issues at all. Dr. Berdych is a miracle worker. I understand there was a six-month waiting list, so thank you again for helping get her in so quickly," replied Cathy.

Still buried in a transcript from a former case, Alan continued reading as if he was not aware Harry had walked in his office. Harry looked at Cathy, took a dramatic deep breath, and said, "Cathy, after all these years of working together, one would figure you'd have taught your boss the fine art of multitasking by now. I could ride into this office buck naked on a unicycle while juggling chainsaws and Alan wouldn't know the difference." Harry smiled, amused with himself.

"Morning, Harry," replied Alan without looking up.

"Now Alan, you didn't waste an absolutely beautiful crisp and sunny April weekend sitting in this office buried in law books, did you?" continued Harry. "I assume you were aware that our very own Boston Red Sox played a double header against the defending world champions this past Saturday night."

Alan didn't bother to look up. "Harry, I cannot imagine you would think after all these years that I have any interest in some baseball match! I don't have time for fun, as someone has to prepare for this case, and I know for damn sure it isn't going to be you."

"Alan, let me first say that they are called baseball *games*. Tennis players play matches, baseball players play games. It fascinates me that you don't know this fact, as intelligent as you make yourself out to be." Harry sat down in one of the large leather chairs in front of Alan's desk before continuing. "Now, as far as fun, in all the years I've known you, aside from your lovely wife Clara, and that was only when she begged, you never made time for anything but work. Work is all you know. You wouldn't know fun if it snuck up, gave you an atomic wedgie, and slapped you on your bare ass!" Harry sat back with a self-satisfied smirk.

That last statement finally forced Alan to quickly look up at Harry, which sent a shot of pain through his back.

"Atomic wedgie, what in the hell are you talking about, Harry?"

"The fact that you don't know what an atomic wedgie is once again goes to show that you're not as smart as you claim to be. For your information, an atomic wedgie occurs when the participant on the giving end, generally bigger and stronger than that of the participant on the receiving end, pulls from the back the strap of the receiving party's underwear until it rips completely off, causing significant pain to the rectum and scrotum area. Would you like me to demonstrate?" asked Harry.

This was the usual interaction between the partners, but even after 20 years it made Cathy every bit as uncomfortable to hear Harry speak to her boss the way he did.

"But I digress. Alan, you have been wasting your entire life burying yourself in work and forgetting or not bothering to look up and live. When was the last time you spent more than five minutes with Ivy? And what is with your color today? You seem to have taken the color of a blanched almond, for Christ's sake. Judging by the face you made when you looked up at me, I am assuming you're still experiencing back pain. And I am also assuming you haven't yet bothered to make an appointment to have it checked? I sent you the contact information of a wonderful doctor who I know from my country club, who happens to have an office just around the corner. He offered to make time for you whenever it's convenient, and he even agreed to come up here to the office if that's easiest for you." Harry turned to Cathy and said, "I assume you gave that information to your boss some time ago."

As Cathy was about to respond, Harry cut her short.

"Cathy, I sincerely hope that Alan remembered, but I trust you're aware that tomorrow is Ivy's sixteenth birthday. Have you arranged some sort of gift for Alan to give to her?"

"Yes, of course, Mr. B. I ordered a handful of items from the new line of Nike sports outfits, as well as several books from the *New York Times* bestseller list that Ivy would enjoy reading. I had them all professionally wrapped and will have them brought over to the Omni, where they'll be waiting for Ivy when she gets home from school later today," replied Cathy.

"Cathy," said Harry, as he handed her a beautifully wrapped box, "could you see that Ivy gets this gift from me as well, and please give me a moment to speak with your lovely boss alone?"

Cathy took the gift and quickly and happily left the two alone in Alan's office.

Alan was very much aware of what Harry wanted to speak about and he was not looking forward to the conversation. He pushed his chair back from his desk and gingerly stood up. With one hand on his lower back and the other in his pocket, he blankly stared out the window.

"Alan, I'm assuming you're planning to personally give the box to Ivy tomorrow?" said Harry.

"Harry, I think perhaps you drank one too many martinis last night while watching the baseball match, because it is of no business to you how I raise my daughter. Ivy will get the box one way or another."

"Alan, let me once again remind you that in the wonderful sport of baseball, the most beloved and popular pastime in this country, there are no matches, they are called games, Alan, games." Harry paused to crack his knuckles, something he knew particularly irked his partner. He continued. "As far as martinis, I could drink all the vodka in Russia and still know that you haven't had anything to do with raising Ivy since the day she arrived on this earth. In fact, Cathy has done more parenting of Ivy than you have and that is only because she's picked out every Christmas and birthday gift that Ivy has ever received from you!"

Alan turned back to his desk, slid open the top drawer and took out a small key. While trying his best to ignore the back pain he had been having for the last several months, he gingerly reached down to unlock the bottom drawer of his desk. He took a deep breath, opened the drawer, and saw the box that he had placed there nearly fifteen years earlier. He saw his first-born son Jake's handwriting and was immediately struck by the thought of how weak Jake must have been at the time he had written directly on the plain brown paper bag he had used as wrapping paper. It still amazed him that Jake had somehow found the energy to wrap the box just days before he fell into a coma from which he would never wake.

Alan took the box out of the drawer and, handling it as if it were some sort of breakable object, placed it gently on the desk. He felt the familiar pang of guilt from the fact that he had never found the right time or manner to talk to his daughter about the past. It seemed to him it was just yesterday that he had buried his first-born son and less than one week later his wife Clara, but more than fifteen years had passed.

"Hard to believe it's been so long that she's been gone. Life sure seemed happier back then," said Alan somberly.

"Alan, you were no happier when Clara and Jake were alive than you are today. The fact is, I've known you for forty years and I have never once seen you happy. Remember the night we graduated high school and we organized that big party over the ridge behind the athletic building? High school was finally over, no more studying for finals, no more pressure to maintain a perfect 4.0 grade point average, no teachers or parents...only freedom. The entire senior class was at that party, except for Alan Miles. If I remember correctly, and I have been told that I have quite the memory, you were rewriting the final term paper in which you had received a perfect A+, because you felt you had not defined your position clearly enough."

Alan thought about the last time he saw his wife Clara alive. It was less than a week after Jake had lost his long fight against cancer. Clara had been fighting headaches for the last months of Jake's life, but she assumed they were stress related and hadn't bothered to see a doctor. Together she and Alan sat at the breakfast counter in the kitchen; Clara looked as if she hadn't slept in days. After taking several sips of her coffee, it was clear that she was once again suffering from a migraine. Clara took two aspirin and let Alan know she was going to lie down and close her eyes until the migraine passed. He asked if he should send one of his assistants to the apartment in case she needed anything, but she insisted she'd be fine and he didn't bother to argue. And so, Alan left to go to his office, where he immersed himself in his work.

When he walked through the door of the Omni at 9:30 p.m., he was concerned to find all the lights still off in the apartment. Quickening his pace, he walked directly to their bedroom and knew at once by the manner in which her arm hung limply off the side of the bed that Clara was gone. Alan suspected the headaches and migraines were likely the result of a blood clot in her brain and she had died of an aneurysm. He calmly walked over and checked for a pulse, but knew by the temperature of her skin that it was too late. He thought to himself, now he alone would have to care for their daughter Ivy.

"Alan, where are you right now?" asked Harry.

"I'm thinking about the case and how we're going to convince a twelve-person jury that what the government is asking of our client is simply not within the legal boundaries of our constitution," Alan replied.

Harry looked at Alan and as if reading his mind said, "Clara was a good woman, Alan, and Jake was a good boy. Maybe things would be different if they were still here, but they're not, and you're letting life pass you by."

Harry gently picked up the box and smiled as he recognized Jake's handwriting. "Alan, this is the one gift you should not ask Cathy to give to Ivy. Ivy may have questions that need to be answered." Harry turned and walked out.

– 3 –

For the past sixteen years, Sophie and Ivy had been best friends, and Sophie's parents, Jimmy and Nancy Pham, were as much parents to Ivy as they were to their own daughter. The couple was born and raised in Laos and had come to the United States in their early teens. They met while Jimmy was working as a cook and Nancy a waitress in a small Chinese restaurant in Boston. It had now been over twenty years since the day they got married, and aside from the few nights Nancy had spent in the hospital after the births of their two children, they had never spent a night apart from each other. With the little money the young couple managed to save, they were able to open their own take-out only Chinese restaurant, which they named The Golden Dragon.

It was at the second, slightly larger location of The Golden Dragon restaurant that the couple came to know Ivy's mother Clara. Clara would often come into the small restaurant to pick up wonton soup and vegetable fried rice for her then fifteen-year-old son Jake, who was at that time receiving chemotherapy treatment. For whatever reason, only the food from The Golden Dragon would stay down in his battered body. When they first met, Nancy would sit with Clara, listening to her talk about Jake's illness and how hard it was to watch her son suffer. It was not long after they had met when they realized they were both unexpectedly pregnant. The women eventually began seeing the same doctor and ultimately gave birth in the same hospital in Boston less than a month apart.

Whenever Jake was in the hospital, Clara chose to spend nights sleeping on a chair next to his bed. Only eight weeks after Ivy was born, Clara began leaving her daughter with the Pham family instead of with one of the several full-time nannies Clara could choose from. For Jake, as the first twelve-month protocol of chemotherapy was coming to an end, it was clear that the treatment was not having the effect for which it was designed. Instead, the tumors aggressively spread and attacked Jake's entire body. Ultimately it was decided that there were no viable options for Jake, and the doctors gave him three to six months to make memories with his family.

Ivy began spending most days and nights at the Pham household. Nancy made daily visits to the thirty-seventh-floor penthouse apartment at the Omni Hotel to give Clara time to spend with then three-month-old Ivy and two-month old Sophie. Nancy knew how important it was to give Clara a break from the stress of watching her boy suffer, and would insist she get out of the penthouse apartment even if for only ten minutes of pushing the girls in a double stroller. As a result, Nancy often spent time alone with Jake. She listened to Jake talk about the pain he was experiencing in his back, lungs, hip, and stomach.

She never forgot one particular day, when he explained to her about the phantom pains he often experienced in the foot and knee of his amputated left leg. He described these phantom pains as if someone was putting a nail through the bottom of the foot and knee that were no longer part of his body. On another visit, Jake played guitar and sang several songs he had written, which was something he had never done for anybody other than his mother. In the last month of Jake's life, Clara was overwhelmed with trying to keep him as comfortable as possible, which could only be done using large amounts of opiates. During this time, Nancy made sure to visit with Ivy and Sophie, knowing how important it was for Clara to be reminded she still had her young daughter to live for.

After Clara's sudden death, it was clear that Alan would not be able to take care of Ivy alone. Alan, who had never before met either Nancy nor Jimmy, personally went to The Golden Dragon to ask the Pham couple if then nine-month-old Ivy could stay with them until he got the funeral arrangements in order and could figure out who would take care of Ivy. The couple assured Alan that after having Ivy living with them on and off for the last eight months, she had become a part of their family and was welcome to stay for as long as needed.

This conversation was essentially the only interaction they ever had as it pertained to Ivy and her care. Instead, over the years since having that short conversation, Alan used his many business and political connections, as well as his financial wealth, to help the couple grow their business, as his way to give back for raising his daughter.

Jimmy and Nancy both very clearly remembered the day a team of three men walked into their small restaurant and announced they had been paid in full by Alan Miles and had flown in from Chicago specifically to meet with them. The men explained they were from a consulting firm that specialized in building and designing large buffet-style restaurants and had been assigned to assist them in opening what would be Boston's largest and most modern Chinese food buffet. They were told Alan Miles had already purchased the building site, all plans and drawings were prepared to be looked over and approved, and that all the necessary licenses and zoning certifications from the state were in order.

Alan also had had a large and reputable law firm from New York draw up the appropriate legal documents. These documents stated that the Phams would be one-hundred-per-cent owners of the new business.

The first restaurant was wildly successful and every thirty-six months thereafter, the team of consultants contacted Jimmy to inform him that when he and his wife were ready, the preparations for a new location were finished and was once again waiting for their approval. The couple now owned four, soon to be five, Golden Dragon Buffet restaurants located throughout southern Massachusetts, and had attained more wealth than they had ever dreamed. Regardless of how successful or stressful the restaurant business was for the couple, they never allowed it to affect their love of family and of spending time with Sophie and Ivy.

Ivy had spent her entire life up, until the age of twelve, with Sophie and the Pham family. Once a month, Nancy made arrangements with

Alan's assistant Cathy to visit the Omni apartment with Ivy and Sophie. The three of them would ride to the thirty-seventh floor, where breakfast would be waiting in the formal dining room of the penthouse apartment. Although Alan was never at home during these Saturday morning visits, Ivy cherished these times, as she always considered the Omni her home. The girls would quickly eat breakfast and rush to get changed into their bathing suits and the long white robes and slippers that were waiting for them. Then, off they would go running through the hotel to enjoy the beautiful pool and sauna.

Several times a year, Ivy and Sophie also accompanied Jimmy and Nancy to Ivy's father's law offices, where they had meetings about the restaurant. These were the only times in the first twelve years of Ivy's childhood that she had any contact with Alan. The interaction was limited to a handshake and usually something to the effect of, "Good morning, girls, Cathy has hot chocolate waiting for you in the conference room. I should not need Jimmy and Nancy for more than thirty minutes."

Nearly every time Ivy visited the law office, Alan's partner Harry went out of his way to talk with the girl. He asked about whatever was going on in her life at that time, whether it was dance, horseback riding, karate, or volleyball. Harry did not just ask the girls about their lives, but showed a sincere interest in whatever the girls had to talk about and he often shared with them stories that somehow involved Clara and Jake. For Ivy, it was exciting and special to hear new stories about her family. Harry had a way of bringing their memories to life when he talked about them, and Ivy always looked forward to those conversations. As their visits were ending, he often whispered to her, "Don't you mind about your father. I have known Alan for a long time and he is not exactly what you would call a talker."

Ivy, like her mother, was by nature a very accepting person. She never questioned the lack of emotions her father showed. She simply accepted Alan as he was and happily took whatever little he offered, which was indeed very little.

It was only when Nancy and Jimmy announced that they were expecting their second child that Ivy, by herself, made the decision she would move full-time to the Omni apartment. She felt the Pham family deserved to start a new life with the baby without her being in their home. So at just twelve years old, Ivy informed Jimmy and Nancy that she had decided to move into the hotel and asked them to tell Cathy the news. Ivy never discussed the decision with Alan and in the three-plus years, had yet to discuss much of anything with her father.

Alan rarely came home for any reason other than to sleep once or twice a month. Alan arrived home quite late in the evening, normally past 9:00 p.m., and with a simple "good night," he went directly to the wing of the apartment that contained his office and the master bedroom. Ivy was never sure if he went directly to sleep or if he had more work to do at his desk. However, she strongly suspected, and correctly as it turned out, her father would continue to work into the early hours of the morning.

Jimmy and Nancy continued to act as Ivy's guardians for any parental issues such as school, doctor, dentist visits, etc., and Ivy used the car service for any transportation needs. She ordered the majority of her meals from the hotel restaurant but also had access to cash in her bank account with which she would shop for fresh fruit and whatever else she might need at the grocery store.

– 4 –

Walking out of the locker rooms after having finished volleyball practice, Ivy and Sophie were greeted by Sophie's father, Jimmy, waving not just his hand, but his entire arm and shoulder from one side to the other. He was the only parent that came and sat in the stands nearly every day to watch the last thirty minutes of practice. This was when the girls were finished with all the drills and exercises for strength training, technique, and strategy, and the coach would have the starting six players scrimmage against the remaining six girls. Jimmy did not know much about the game of volleyball, but simply enjoyed seeing how focused the group of girls could be when on the court while playing the sport they all shared a passion for. He especially enjoyed watching Sophie, Ivy, and the rest of the team change from that focus and intensity throughout the practice, to just being young women smiling and laughing the moment the practice officially came to an end.

Jimmy cherished every single moment he got to spend with Sophie and Ivy. He was very aware that their childhoods were quickly coming to an end and in less than eighteen months, both would be off to college to begin their lives without him and his wife. The girls walked over to where he was waiting and he gave both of the girls a hug and a kiss on the forehead. Kissing Ivy on the forehead was not quite as easy because she was now 6'2" and Jimmy wasn't more than 5'5". This type of interaction with a parent in most cases would mortify other teenage girls; however, both Sophie and Ivy knew how sincerely loving a person Jimmy was and both were happy to be on the receiving end of his affection.

"Hello, my girlies," Jimmy said with his heavy accent. "How was your day?"

"I played terrible today. I could not pass the ball at all," complained Sophie.

"You always say that, Sophie. You did fine today, stop being so hard on yourself," said Ivy.

"Well, the part of practice I saw, you all looked like you were having fun, and that's why you play sports, right?" asked Jimmy.

"Mr. Pham, you know your daughter is a perfectionist and if she doesn't pass every single ball perfectly to the setter, she thinks she had a bad day!" said Ivy.

"Well, I thought I played terrible, but Ivy, you were crushing the ball today! I have never seen you hit the ball so hard before!" said Sophie.

"Yeah, Soph, I seriously think I grew again this past month. It may have been just one centimeter, but every time I get taller it seems to throw my timing off. But it sure felt right today," replied Ivy.

To take the focus off herself, Ivy quickly changed the subject and asked, "How is the new restaurant looking, Mr. Pham? Will you be able to have the grand opening next week as planned?"

"Always delays but open on schedule we will," answered Jimmy.

"This is the location near that big mall in Brookline, right, Papa? Oh, and can you please stop talking like Yoda, it is totally weird!" said Sophie, causing the three of them to laugh.

"Yes, in Brookline, but that is not so important. What is important is that Ivy will have a birthday tomorrow. If you don't already have plans, Ivy, you are welcome to celebrate with us this weekend. We can order Chinese takeout, I know a great restaurant that have best General Tzo's Chicken!" Jimmy said, laughing at his own joke, which he often liked to do.

"Sounds like the perfect way to celebrate," said Ivy and continued, "General Tzo's chicken with the Pham family? It doesn't get much better than that, Jimmy!"

Ivy was sincerely excited at the plans to celebrate with Sophie and her parents for her birthday, but of course could not help but feel a pang of sadness in her heart knowing she didn't have her mother and brother with her. In his new pickup truck, Jimmy pulled up to the main entrance of the hotel to drop Ivy off. Normally, Ivy would be driven home by the same car service that brought her to school in the morning. But today, the day before Ivy's sixteenth birthday, Jimmy decided he wanted to drive her home himself.

"Thank you for the ride, Mr. Pham," said Ivy, before hugging Sophie, who had stepped out onto the curb to move from the backseat to sit in the front with her father.

Ivy walked toward the entrance and turned around one last time to wave before heading through the spinning doors into the lobby. As he always did, Jimmy had a heavy heart as he drove away, leaving Ivy at the hotel and knowing Alan would likely not be home.

While riding in the elevator, Ivy looked at her reflection in the mirror and while running her hand through her hair, still wet from showering, saw sadness in her eyes. She knew of course she was feeling this way because in all likelihood she would be waking up on her 16th birthday alone. She couldn't help but feel a little hope that her father had come home early that afternoon, and perhaps even be in a mood to have some sort of short conversation. Of course, as Harry had reminded her many times, her father was not a talker. In fact, he had never once in her life made any sort of small talk.

As she opened the front door, Ivy could not help but feel disappointed that the apartment was indeed empty. Ivy surprised herself by shrugging her shoulders and saying out loud, "Oh well!"

She thought how different it was the few times in the month Alan came home to sleep and how she always felt a certain feeling of discomfort when her father was home. The discomfort was not on Ivy's part; she actually felt more at ease when he was near. Even if he was in his office with the door closed, she somehow felt like she could breathe a little easier and sleep a little more soundly than she normally did. The discomfort she felt was in fact for her father, because she could sense his uneasiness through his inability to even look her in the eyes. Above all else, she thought she could sense his fear that she would ask about the past. She knew instinctively how difficult it was to allow himself to feel anything for anyone, and she pitied him for bearing that burden. She assumed it was as a result of losing his first-born son and his wife, but the truth was Alan Miles had always had difficulty showing any emotions to anyone. Aside from his wife Clara, who had never won his heart the way she had hoped, Alan was only truly devoted to one thing, and that was of course his work.

As Ivy walked past the living room, she saw a mountain of gifts piled on the couch as well as several smaller gifts lying on the coffee table in front of the couch. She could see there was something different about the shoe box-sized gift that was on the coffee table. Ivy knew by the way it was wrapped that it had not been done by an employee of a fancy shop or department store. Instead, it was wrapped the way Sophie or her parents would wrap a gift. She first picked up the note that was written on the stationary paper from Alan's law firm and recognized her father's neat and precise handwriting.

Ivy,

Included in these birthday gifts is a box your brother left with your mother several weeks before falling into a coma and passing. He had left instructions with your mother to give this box to you on your sixteenth birthday. I will be in Washington D.C. for the rest of the week. I had Cathy arrange to have these birthday gifts brought to you a day early. You will notice of course there is also a gift from Harry.

Alan

Ivy moved aside the several fancy wrapped gifts and picked up the box with the handmade wrapping paper. With tears in her eyes, she was unable to read the words written on what appeared to be a brown paper bag that was used as wrapping paper. She wiped the tears from her eyes and read.

To: My Baby Sister Ivy
From: Your Big Brother Jake

Ivy stood still and almost felt as if she was somehow dreaming. She held the box in her hand and kept saying out loud, "Your Big Brother Jake."

The idea that Jake had left something for her was both exhilarating and frightening at the same time. There were so many questions that she had had for so many years, and this gift could contain many of the answers. Ivy carefully removed the tape, making sure not to damage the brown bag, and was left with a red Nike shoe box in her hands. She took a deep breath and slowly took the top off the box. In the box was a wire-bound notebook and a CD in a clear case with a note taped to it that said,

Ivy, please do not yet listen to this CD. First read my journal for instructions.

Ivy picked up the CD and read the words her brother had printed in block lettering, **Songs for Ivy**.

Ivy laid the CD back down in the box and took out the notebook. As she flipped through it she saw that each page was filled front and back with writing in essay form as well as what looked to be poem form. Her heart was pounding, she could feel her face flush warm with excitement. Ivy began to think that what she held in her hands was going to give her a whole new perception of who she was, and from where she came.

– 5 –

Alan's limo pulled up to the small and very private airstrip on the outskirts of Boston's Logan Airport, where he boarded the private jet that would take him to Washington, D.C. He was feeling a deep tiredness in his bones and an ache in his back as he had never experienced before. He had never questioned the importance of his work, as he had always believed in it—that creating new legal realities pertinent to the technology that had entered our lives over the last thirty years was his calling. It was only recently that Alan began to realize that the "heavy lifting" of this work was done. He and Harry had helped lay the foundations and structure of the legal landscape, both nationally as well as internationally. There would always be new challenges that would arise as newer technology came about, but he saw that what remained was mostly maintenance.

It reminded him of an event in history he had learned about in high school called the Texas-Indian wars. In the early nineteenth century, as the first wave of European-American settlers moved into what was then Spanish Texas, the newly arrived "Anglo-Americans" began a brutal war against the native Indians, to bring what the "whites" thought of as peace and stability to the land. The most famous of the fighters were the Texas Rangers. These men were not US Army, US Militia, US National Guard, or any true US Police force. They were described as "one of the most colorful, efficient, and deadly band of irregular partisans on the side of law and order the world has ever seen."

These Texas Rangers were not part of the establishment, but rather outsiders doing the dirty work for the establishment. This feeling of being an outsider was one that Alan could identify with well, because he had never in his life felt like anything but an outsider. Once the Rangers had fought and killed all the strongest Indian chiefs and destroyed all the other capable Indian fighters, the "Anglo settlers" could then safely begin to freely move throughout Texas. Alan imagined it was then only small pockets of resistance that any sheriff or lawman with a rifle and a horse could defend against.

Alan felt like his fighting days were numbered. He had not chosen to focus on this particular area of law by chance. Like Steve Jobs, Bill Gates, Larry Ellison, Michael Dell, and a handful of other brilliant minds, he too recognized, early on, the power and influence computers and technology would have on the world. Alan and Harry had both suspected correctly that virtually an entire set of new laws, rules, and regulations would be needed in order to cope with and enforce the ever more complex intellectual property issues. Now that the smoke had cleared and the lines had been drawn, and the national and international legal issues were for the most part settled, the fire Alan had always felt in his belly was no longer burning; only smoking embers remained. The question he now faced was, what would he do if he no longer spent all his time sitting at his desk working?

Alan often wondered what the Texas Ranger captains had done after having chased the fiercest and most feared native Indian chiefs and their tribes around the mountains and open plains of Middle America for twenty years of their lives. After wiping out the Comanche and the Kiowa, where did the most famous and successful captains of the Texas Rangers ride off to? Did they simply then retire back from where they came, to live out the rest of their lives as normal citizens? These Rangers believed they had been living a life with a mission and that the work they were doing had been of such purpose and such importance, that they were making the world a better place. What did they do when their skill sets were no longer needed? What did they do when the work was done? Alan had not learned the answer to those questions in his eleventh-grade history course.

He leaned his chair back as far as it would go and tried his best to find a comfortable position for his aching back. At just over twenty-thousand feet above southern Connecticut, Alan Miles closed his eyes and quickly fell asleep.

– 6 –

Ivy took a deep breath, opened the notebook, and saw a loose sheet of plain white paper inserted within. She was struck by how different the writing seemed—much less neat and seemingly shaky. Ivy knew at once that her brother must have written the last journal entry on this piece of paper near the end of his life. She began a journey she never imagined she would be taking, that of meeting her older brother.

My baby sister Ives,

I am writing what will be the last entry into this journal that I have been keeping for you over the last four months. It was at that time when I finally faced the reality that I wasn't going to be able to defeat this damn monster that is eating me from the inside out. This monster is made up of my own cells, which in itself is difficult to comprehend. So actually, in a strange surreal kind of way, I will be committing some sort of bizarre-o suicide! That is quite a concept for this fifteen-year-old to wrap his brain around, Ives!

I made a goal with myself to at least live to see my sixteenth birthday. Unfortunately, my birthday is more than two weeks away and I am not sure I will make it. I know now that I'm on my last leg and have one foot in the grave (which is rather ironic being that I only have one leg and one foot).

The truth is it doesn't really matter anymore. In fact, it is probably best that I croak sooner than later. I know that croak may seem like a rather crass word, but I have stopped treating death with any romantic notions and see it for what it is, the moment I cease to exist...and there is nothing romantic about that.

If for no other reason, me being gone should at least allow Mama to get some much-needed rest. I worry more about her than I do myself these days. She always looks so tired, I'm not sure if she has been sleeping at all these last weeks. Even more worrisome are the headaches she has been getting for the last months. Although she would never admit it to me, I know they have been steadily getting worse, but because she is so focused on me, she hasn't been to see a doctor. I feel guilty to be the cause of her stress and sadness. I know when I am gone it will be even harder for her, which of course breaks my heart, but what can I do? Absolutely nothing.

I just took an hour nap but I'm back. I now need a cocktail of meds to keep the pain bearable and as a result doing pretty much anything makes me so tired these days. Ives, I can imagine what I am about to write may sound counterintuitive to a healthy young woman like you hopefully are, but it is actually a relief that the end is near. I don't want to fight anymore. I don't want to feel sick anymore. I don't want to have pain anymore. I don't want to struggle to catch my breath every time I even try to sit up in bed anymore. I don't want to be the cause of our mother's sad and tired eyes, and keep her from having a life outside of me and my monster. Dying is all I have been doing for almost eighteen months now and I no longer want to do it. I am simply tired of dying. What a strange sentence that is, right, Ives? But that really does say it all.

In a book written by John O'Hara that I have read three times (yes, I am a total book nerd) called Appointment in Samarra, *the main character Julian is driving to his home where, although he does not know it at the time, he will end his own life. The author wrote this great line that Julian says to himself while in the car:*

"I'm too tall to run away, I'm sure to be spotted."

The first time I read the line I was not exactly sure what it meant, but the line itself made an impression on me. After reading the book a second and third time and having thought about it quite a bit, I imagine the author is expressing how when we are anywhere we don't want to be, it feels like we are locked in a prison. Whatever it is that we are running away from or trying to escape from always finds us. In the end, we can never run away from the fear, pain, and sadness that take place in our minds...we are always "sure to be spotted."

Until I accepted that the cancer was going to kill me, I too was a prisoner. I didn't want to be sick and face the fact that I was most likely not going to survive. I didn't want to be living in a body that was literally killing me. I was always running (which isn't easy with one leg) to the next "magic" therapy that was surely going to cure me. I started to realize that no matter where I turn, if all I see are prison walls, then why bother running? I decided that I was not going to allow the cancer to take me while sitting in the corner on a dirt floor, starving, with a long, bushy, dirty beard, in some secluded cave in the desert. OK, like WOW, that is quite a visual! Of course, I haven't left the apartment for anything other than doctor's appointments in months, and although I do indeed have some peach fuzz on my head, I am far from being able to grow a beard of any sort. But you get the point I hope. Now please allow me to continue with this completely unnecessary metaphor. Where was I? Oh yes, when the executioner finally comes to parade me out through the city square for my hanging, I refuse to beg for mercy or go kicking and screaming or dragging my feet (or in my case foot). Instead I will go out with my head held high, content with the almost 16 years of life I am privileged to have lived. Ives, I am ready for the next chapter, whatever the heck it will be!

Of course, don't mistake this with being happy about dying in my early teens. More than anything I wish I could have lived to experience more of life and lived to be a part of our family, especially with you and Mama. Unfortunately, that's not to be. So be a good girl, live a good life, always be Mama's best friend, and please take care of Alan (he needs all the help he can get).

Love you forever and ever Ives, Jake

P.S.

This song is called "Smile." I have been working on this song for about a month or so. I don't have much strength left in my fingers anymore, but I was able to finish a recording just for you. Sadly, it is of course the last song on the CD I made for you.

Ivy read and re-read the last entry in the journal a second and third time, placed it back in the notebook, sat back on the sofa and cried. It was a cry like no other she had ever experienced. Ivy wasn't even aware that people could physically cry in that manner. She had seen actors in the movies or on TV shows sob and wail, but had always assumed it was just the actors "overacting," but here she was doing the same.

On the night before her sixteenth birthday, with her hair still wet and with her volleyball warm-up suit still on, Ivy cried herself to sleep on the couch. As she drifted off, she thought only of her mother and Jake and how much she wished they could be there with her now.

– 7 –

Lisa Kobor had her first experience with alcohol at just nine years old, drinking from leftover wine glasses at a party her mother had thrown at their small apartment in the south end of Boston. She had often wondered why her mother drank wine starting first thing in the morning and ending with her passed out drunk at night. She decided she herself would have to try drinking alcohol to truly understand. The first thing she learned, gagging after every sip, was how terrible and bitter the red wine tasted. After a few more mouthfuls, she also recognized that it made her feel less sad and less worried about her mother than she normally felt. So that night, while lying alone on an old, stained, and bare queen-sized mattress on the floor, Lisa decided it was because her mother was worrying too much about Lisa herself, that caused her to drink. The idea that she was the reason her mother was drunk all the time weighed heavily on her young psyche. As a result of coming to this conclusion at such a young age, Lisa began doing everything in her power to never be a bother of any kind to her mother. She learned how to shop, cook, clean, and do all her homework without asking her mother for any help. She also chose not to have another drink until she was in her late teens, and even then, limited herself to just one glass of champagne at weddings or special occasions.

It had been three years since Lisa's mother died of liver cirrhosis just before her fiftieth birthday. At the time of her mother's death, Lisa had not seen or spoken to her mother in several years, but regardless, Lisa was shocked, saddened, and riddled with guilt that she had not been there for her when she died.

Now approaching her thirtieth birthday, Lisa had been seeing the same psychiatrist since she was sixteen, when the depression and anxiety first began. During the first years, she had tried virtually every antidepressant on the market. For the last eleven years, she had been taking the highest daily dose of a drug called Effexor, which for a while had been the most effective of all the meds she had tried. Her doctor had also given Lisa a prescription to take a .25mg pill of Xanax to help her sleep better.

After years of having never been able to completely shed the fear of panic attacks, with the combined effects of the two drugs, Lisa once again felt normal. Together, the Effexor and Xanax had given her a new lease on life. Lisa had once described to her psychiatrist the effect of the meds as if she had spent years in a dark room and now the shades had been opened to once again allow the sun to shine in. Most importantly, she was finally able to sleep more than two or three hours per night, as had been the case for far too long.

All was in order for Lisa, until, of course, just that single .25mg pill of Xanax no longer gave her the effect she needed. And so as often happens, Lisa began buying Xanax, or "benzo bars" as they are called, on the street, which she could easily get from a dealer in her old neighborhood. She started by splitting the 2mg benzo bar in half and just 1mg per day worked wonders for a time. Now, over a decade later, she was up to six of the benzo bars or the street equivalent of 12mg of Xanax every day.

Lisa had no family and no friends outside of her work colleagues, and hadn't been on a proper date for as long as she could remember. The closest thing she had to a friend was an older Italian man named Bill, the technician who had been fitting her with her artificial leg for the last fifteen-plus years. In fact, in her adult life, she had never been in any sort of serious relationship. The closest thing she had ever had to a real relationship was when she was fourteen years old. The boy's name was Jake Miles and that was during the year where they essentially spent every day together at the Boston Children's Hospital.

The relationship continued for some months following Lisa's completion of chemotherapy. She had even, on occasion, visited Jake at his family's penthouse in the Omni Hotel up until four months before he died.

Jake and Lisa were both diagnosed with osteogenic sarcoma (bone cancer) at virtually the same time. They had gotten their initial surgeries and started chemotherapy within weeks of each other. Her tumor had been found just above her left ankle and she had her left leg amputated just below her knee. Jake's initial tumor was found in his knee and femur bone and he had lost his left leg just above the middle of his thigh. Lisa had been one of the sixty per cent of osteosarcoma patients whose body responded well to the chemotherapy and after twelve months her cancer was in full remission. Jake had not been so lucky.

Lisa still missed him, but that was all in the past now. Jake was long gone, along with Jake's mother Clara, who had been so good to Lisa during those days in the hospital. There were five different drugs in the chemotherapy protocol used at that time to fight against the type of bone cancer that both received. One in particular was a combination of two chemicals, Cisplatin and Adriamycin. Of all the chemicals put into their young bodies, these were especially toxic. The two teenagers would vomit hundreds of times throughout the three or four days after the drug was administered. Some days, Clara ran from one room to the other, only to hold the white curved plastic trays that would be filled with endless yellow bile. Clara always put a cold, wet washcloth on their foreheads, while gently rubbing their backs and whispering that everything was going to be okay.

Lisa's mother couldn't face what Lisa was going through. She couldn't deal with the hospital visits, the surgeries, or chemotherapy, choosing instead to hide in her mind-numbing world of alcohol. Of course, after years of therapy, Lisa was now aware it was very likely that her mother had also been suffering from depression and anxiety and simply used the alcohol to drown out the pain. Lisa sometimes laughed at herself when she thought of how dependent she had become on her benzo bars. Yet day after day, month after month, year after year passed and she found herself simply adding more of the pills just to be able to function. Lisa cringed at the terrible realization that she had become just like her mother.

– 8 –

Ivy woke up with Jake's journal lying open on her stomach. She thought to herself that the manner in which Jake's journal was almost cuddled up with her was symbolic, as it was the way she had wished her mother and brother could have been there with her the night before. As much as she wanted to stay home and read the stories Jake had written for her, Ivy knew she had to get up and get ready to go to school. She was sure both Jake and her mother would want her to keep moving forward, even as an exciting turn of events was unfolding in her life. As Ivy dressed, she remembered she had fallen asleep without listening to the song from the CD Jake had made her. She inserted the disc into the CD player and, following Jake's instructions, jumped to track eight, the last song. As she walked into the kitchen to eat a quick breakfast, she heard the acoustic guitar and for the first time in her life, she heard the voice of her brother. Jake's singing was stronger and more mature than what she had expected and gave her goosebumps. Ivy read along with the lyrics as Jake sang his song:

Smile

Well maybe I'll be gone, won't be walking through that door
But my spirit will live on, more alive than before
So do what you will, there ain't no breaking me

I'll take all that you can give, kill my body but my minds free
Cause I know, I'll be remembered
Yeah I know, you won't forget my love of life
Yeah I know, I'll be right here with you
Every time you smile, think of me and smile

I ain't got but one regret, and that's the pain I'll leave behind
Nothing breaks my heart, like the thought of you crying
So promise me one thing, that your sadness won't last too long
Just look up at the clouds, smile and move on!

Jake's song was the most beautiful and emotional song Ivy had ever heard. She did just what her brother had asked of her in his song. She thought of him singing to her and, with tears flowing down her cheeks, Ivy closed her eyes and smiled.

Ivy had been sure to give herself an extra few minutes so she could share the exciting news with Mr. Bugs and bask in his attention, as it was, after all, her sixteenth birthday!

The elevator doors slid open.

"The birthday girl is here!" Mr. Bugs yelled while practically running over to the elevator with a red bag in his hands. He gave her a big hug and handed her the gift.

"It's just a little something from my wife and me, hopefully it's something you'll like," said Bugs.

Ivy opened the bag and took out a vanilla-scented Yankee Candle, which was, as Bugs knew, her favorite.

"It's enough that you always remember my birthday, but thank you so much for this candle, Mr. Bugs. I love it," replied Ivy.

"Mr. Bugs, you are not going to believe what my brother left me for my birthday," Ivy said, and proceeded to tell Bugs about the journal Jake had left her.

"Wow, that sure does sound amazing, Ivy! I never got to meet your brother or mother, but I have heard stories about how wonderful they both were. You must be very excited to learn more about them both," said Bugs.

"I sure am, but first I have to get to school or the only thing I'll be learning more about is detention! I'll keep you posted as I read through the journal. I'll probably be driving you crazy with all the details every morning," Ivy said and continued, "I'll see you tomorrow morning and I still want to hear all about the Bruins game you saw with your nephew this weekend." Ivy quickly walked to the spinning doors and went out to look for her driver.

Sitting in the back seat of the Lincoln Town Car, Ivy had her phone in her hands and was debating whether or not she should write to her father and tell him about the journal Jake had left for her. She assumed her father knew what the box contained, but realized that if Alan had been as unavailable to her brother and mother as he was to her, there was a very real possibility that he would have had no idea that Jake had been keeping a journal. Ivy also realized that it would most likely cause her father stress, as it seemed that anything from the past was clearly not something that her father wanted to hear or talk about. Just then, Ivy's phone buzzed and she saw that her father's secretary had sent her a text message.

Ivy,

Alan is busy in meetings this morning, but he wanted to wish you a happy birthday! Hope you liked your gifts,

Cathy

Ivy expected nothing more and nothing less from her father. She was still thinking about what types of things she would learn from Jake's writing when they pulled up to the main building of the Lexington Prep School.

That morning, Ivy had a meeting with the school guidance counselor, Mr. Connor, who everyone referred to as Mr. C. It was his job to assist all high school juniors with the college application process. He was an odd but very likeable man. First off, he was incredibly obese. Most students guessed he weighed at least half a ton. For reasons only known to Mr. C. himself, he wore wire-framed round glasses, much like those that John

Lennon had worn towards the end of his life. This specific style of glasses made his already huge head appear even bigger. It reminded Ivy of when she was younger and she and Sophie had a box of Mr. Potato Head dolls they played with. Sophie's father, Jimmy, would sometimes take the Mr. Potato Head's black plastic glasses from the box and put them on his own face. The glasses were so small and tight on him, they looked as if they might shoot across the room at any second. Ivy almost laughed at the thought that perhaps he was going for the Mr. Potato Head look.

Mr. C. always had a white handkerchief in his hand to wipe beads of sweat from the top of his balding head. But it was his narcolepsy that caused the most discomfort for the students. He had the habit of falling asleep in the middle of a sentence, and then only five or ten seconds later, waking up and continuing right where he left off as if nothing had happened. This was jarringly awkward because for those few seconds, one was never exactly sure the best way to deal with the situation.

However, he was a big fan of Ivy, and she of him. He came to each and every home volleyball game. He had also been handling all communications between her volleyball coach and the now dozens of college coaches that had been attempting to communicate with Ivy, hoping she would attend their programs. That morning, he was going to help her narrow down her options to just her top three choices, so he could set up dates for Ivy to visit each of the campuses.

"Good morning, Mr. C. How are you doing this morning?" asked Ivy while thinking to herself how odd it was that he could already be sweating while simply sitting at his desk at 8:00 a.m. in the morning.

"Good morning, Ms. Miles, I am doing great, thank you. I noticed while looking over your folder that you have a birthday today. Happy Birthday!" said Mr. C. while dabbing the sweat from his head.

"Thank you! Yup, I turn sixteen today." Ivy smiled.

"I am assuming you need to get to class, so let's get down to business, shall we? Now, did you get a chance to narrow down your college choices? Last time we spoke you were going to try and get it down to your top three choi—"

Suddenly, he closed his eyes, and his head tilted ever so slightly forward, creating a fourth chin. He began to snore quietly. Ivy had spent enough time with him not to be shocked, and she mentally prepared to hold him up if he somehow began to tilt to one side or the other. Ivy felt there was a good possibility that she would not have the strength to support him and could possibly end up pinned under him. She imagined the headlines on the local news, *Star High School Volleyball Player Crushed to Death by Obese Guidance Counselor*. But just as quickly as he had fallen asleep, he awoke and continued where he had left off, "--choices of colleges and volleyball programs so we can set up a campus tour and visit with the coaching staff and team."

Ivy acted as if nothing out of the ordinary happened.

"I've gone over all my options dozens of times, and with Sophie Pham and her parents we even did a "Pros and Cons" list this past weekend."

Mr. C. nodded encouragingly and Ivy continued.

"In the end, I've decided that I do indeed want to leave the Northeast and go somewhere that is warm all year round for my college career. I know some people may be disappointed that I won't be staying in state for college, but I just think it's best for me to live somewhere completely new."

He looked dangerously close to falling asleep again, but Ivy continued.

"If possible, I would like to stay on the East Coast, so two of the colleges on the list are in Florida. Of course, living on the West Coast would also be amazing and so my other choice of schools is in Northern California. The college must have a biology or pre-med undergraduate program as I'm hoping to go to medical school after finishing my four-year undergraduate degree."

Mr. C. looked at Ivy with admiration but not surprise. He beamed with pride to have the opportunity to assist in the future of Ivy S. Miles; she was clearly special. What made her even more special, he thought to himself, was the fact that she didn't even realize how special she really was. Academically, Ivy was at the top of her class, one of the top junior year volleyball recruits in the entire country, and of course, happened to also be stunningly beautiful. Yet she lived her life as if she was just a normal teenage girl. He had been working as a college guidance counselor for nearly a decade now and had never before had a student with such promise.

"Okay, Ivy, sounds like you have put a lot of--" Ivy counted approximately six seconds of snoring "--thought into this exciting next chapter of life. I will speak with your coach and have him get in touch with all three of the programs to let them know the good news. The next step is to coordinate dates on the calendar to visit each of the campuses. Now get going to your English class, or we're both going to have to answer to Mrs. Sullivan," Mr. C. said, only half joking about the English teacher who was in her last year before retiring and who was known to be a stickler with time.

"I wholeheartedly agree, Mr. C. I have a volleyball game this Saturday and don't want to risk spending the morning sitting with Mrs. Sullivan instead! Thanks for all your help," Ivy said as she got up and walked to the door.

"That's what I get paid to do, Ivy." Mr. C. watched his favorite student leave his office.

– 9 –

Ives,

So it's been about fifteen months now since our lives changed so drastically from one day to the next. I had been having poor circulation in my left foot, kind of like the "pins and needles" feeling you get when you sit the wrong way for too long. Every once in a while, I also noticed that I didn't have as much strength in my left leg as the right one. One day after school, Mama and I stopped at a walk-in clinic around the corner from the Omni. I explained to the doctor on call about my foot and knee pain, and although he didn't seem particularly concerned, he ordered an x-ray, as he noticed that my knee was swollen. About fifteen minutes later, the doctor returned and I immediately knew something was not right. He placed the x-rays on the viewer, and explained there was an abnormal growth in my femur. He informed us that he would make a phone call to a colleague at the Boston Children's Hospital for further testing. He never mentioned the word tumor or cancer, but it was clear that whatever he saw on that x-ray worried him.

Mama and I were so shocked by this turn of events I'm not sure we even asked any questions. It's a bit of a blur actually, but I think we both heard in his voice that the situation was very serious.

The following week, I was admitted to the hospital and from that moment, my new life as a full-time cancer patient began.

About six months ago, I was sitting up in the bed in my single hospital room just days after having a surgery called a thoracotomy. This was three months after they had found the initial tumor in my knee. The surgery was to remove four small tumors they had found in my left lung. Ives, of all the surgeries I've had, that one was the most brutal! As bad as it was to have my leg amputated to the middle of my thigh, which was not exactly a barrel of laughs either, at least then I could always breathe normally. But after the thoracotomy, all I wanted to do was cough, because apparently, that's what your body wants to do after having your chest and lungs cut open! Every time I coughed, it felt like someone was smashing me in my chest with a hammer. The irony, of course, is that the nurses actually wanted and encouraged me to cough, because that helps to clear the fluids that build up in the lungs. The nurses gave me a little plastic breathing device to use, which helped with clearing the fluids that accumulate in the lungs. I did as I was told, like a good patient, and kept sucking into this plastic hose, so that when I did it hard enough, I moved a white little ball up and down. The nurse told me that I should think of it as a game. Fun game, right? Those nurses sure know how to have a good time!

As bad as that may sound, it actually got worse. For the first three days after surgery, I had two plastic tubes that were running inside my lung. One to drain the lung of any blood and fluid, and the other to keep the lung inflated. On the fourth day, the tubes had to come out. The doctor on call that day had forgotten to mention that removing the tubes would leave me short of breath. He didn't think to explain that it would feel like I got the wind knocked out of me and I would not be able to breathe normally for few minutes! If he had shared this gem of knowledge with me beforehand, it wouldn't have been so scary. Out came the tubes... and I started to panic. Mama says it was only for a few seconds that I was struggling to catch my breath, for me however, it felt like days.

That was the first time that I actually thought I was going to die. I didn't see my life flash before my eyes like you see in the movies, but

I do remember thinking, "This is it, this is how it is going to end for me! And poor Mama has to watch me die right in front of her eyes!" But I survived, obviously, and only one week later I started getting the chemotherapy treatments again.

Unfortunately, even after eleven months of chemotherapy, the doctors found several larger tumors in my right lung and decided to remove the entire lung. Luckily, the days after weren't nearly as bad as they were the first time. Maybe because I knew what to expect or by then I was better at dealing with pain, I don't know.

So now I am down to one leg and one lung. They have since found tumors in my hip, stomach, and lymph nodes and it has been decided to stop the treatments and face the reality that the monster is going to win the war.

I should mention that this is the first entry of a journal (I find calling it a "diary" sounds so ten-year-old-girl-ish so journal it will be) that I am writing just for you, in order to share and document the time I have left. Up until a few months ago, before it was clear that the tumors had begun to spread, I was sure I would survive and was still planning on growing old with you and Mama and Alan. Of course, there is always the chance that by some miracle the tumors could simply disappear, but that is probably not going to happen. So, assuming my story does not end up "happily ever after" like in the movies, I figure I will keep this journal for my baby sister to get to know her big bro through my own words. So that was my first entry in this journal and I am finito!

I love you Ives!

– 10 –

Alan arrived and checked into the Executive Suite on the top floor of the Ritz-Carlton in Washington D.C., the usual space that he and Harry had been using for the past two decades when working in the nation's capital. The shooting pain in his back was causing him tremendous discomfort and Alan sat awkwardly at the oversized dining room table, attempting to find a comfortable position. He continued to pore over legal documents as he had been doing for the past four hours, checking if there was anything he had missed about the case for which his first meeting was scheduled the following day.

"Alan, do you remember the judge that gave us such a hard time during the intellectual property case we handled for IBM back in... what was it, 1996 or 97?"

Alan looked up to see that Harry had entered the room.

"He was the judge that kept calling you Al regardless of how many times you corrected him that you go by Alan," Harry continued, laughing at the memory. "That cracked me up. He just kept on with Al as if he could care less!"

"Judge Philips, the Honorable Judge Michael Philips," mused Alan.

Harry continued. "He was an eccentric man, but an absolutely brilliant judge." Alan nodded in agreement before Harry went on.

"That was an incredibly tedious and detailed case and yet Judge

Philips never missed a beat. He followed every twist and turn. Particularly during the three weeks that we called to the stand several of world's most brilliant minds to argue their positions on the difference between time complexity and space complexity and the efficiency of algorithms. I remember thinking there is no way in hell Judge Philips will possibly be able to comprehend all this information. Yet after the last experts were called, the Judge succinctly and perfectly summarized the two opposing positions better than even you or I could have."

"It was absolutely brilliant," agreed Alan. "I wonder if he's still hearing cases?"

"Well, judging by the fact that Judge Philips is dead, I'm going to guess he no longer presides over any court proceedings!" said Harry.

"Judge Philips is dead?" said Alan, surprised. "Why, he couldn't have been much older than you and me."

"People die at all ages, you of all people should know that," said Harry.

"What was it that took him, heart attack?" asked Alan.

"The good judge hanged himself in his garage. Evidently, he had been struggling with depression for years," said Harry, sadly.

"Now why in hell would a man a brilliant as Judge Michael Philips go and hang himself? They have medication for those types of issues these days. That's not fair to do to his wife!" said Alan without thinking.

"Well, Alan, if a man is thinking about hanging himself, I can't imagine he's thinking clearly about what is or isn't fair to his wife. He also had three children, the youngest still in his late teens. Now, I've never been in a dark place like that myself, but I understand there are those who just don't see any other way out," said Harry.

Slowly, Alan stood up and used a hand to steady himself. He put his other hand on his back. He had found that applying pressure eased some of the pain he was experiencing. Alan walked across the room and took two glasses from the bar. With the large metal scoop, he filled both glasses with ice and opened a new bottle of Glenlivet 18 Scotch.

Wordlessly, Alan and Harry stood and drank their scotch while reflecting on their respective lives, each searching for the answer to why such a well-respected and successful man like Judge Philips would possibly take his own life.

– 11 –

Lisa was down to her last four benzo bars. Her dealer for the last five years, who she knew only as Cheech, had not returned any of her dozens of calls over the last several days. Although Cheech had never before had any trouble with the law, that Lisa knew of, she assumed he had been arrested and was now in jail. Lisa always bought 150 of the 2mg benzo bars at a time. Because of the volume and consistency of her purchases, Cheech only charged Lisa his cost, which was $4.50 per pill instead of the normal $6-7 price from his other customers. Lisa was already feeling more anxiety than normal at just the *thought* of running out of her drug. She knew of sites on the internet where she could buy all types of pills, but she had also read that much of what those websites shipped were fake. Lisa thought about going down to the club area in Boston where the young hipster crowd partied and where she had heard benzo bars could easily be purchased, but just the thought of walking around Boston asking strangers if they knew where she could buy illegal pills made her flush with anxiety.

Lisa knew she could call her psychiatrist and tell him the truth, after lying to him for years about her drug use. Confess that all along she had not only been taking the one 0.25mg pill of Xanax that he had prescribed, but had been supplementing it with a daily dose of 12mg of street equivalent.

She had read on the internet how dangerous coming off this particular drug could be and that in some cases could even cause death. And she was sure that she was not yet ready to die. Lisa thought maybe this would finally be the time she would face her addiction and find a rehab facility to help her get clean once and for all.

As stressed as she was at the thought of running out of pills and facing the panic and the darkness, there was also a strange calm somewhere deep down inside her. A calm that was trying to tell Lisa she could not continue with the life she had been living for almost a decade, and that it was time to try and find a way back to normalcy. She had felt empty and worthless for so long, it was almost impossible for her to believe there was any chance for her to be happy, or that she even *deserved* happiness.

With her mind spinning out of control, Lisa took two more pills and closed her eyes, waiting for the Xanax to wash over her, allowing her mind to slow and her body to relax until she fell asleep. She dreamt all night of a frantic search, running through an endless maze of hallways, looking through empty room after empty room for her pills, never finding them, still running, running, running.

– 12 –

Jimmy Pham had worked a long day and was finally leaving the worksite of what would soon be the fifth Golden Dragon location. He had spent the last three hours in final trainings for the new staff. Jimmy was joined by his COO (Chief Operating Officer) Eduardo Takahashi, who had been working with him since opening the second Golden Dragon, now almost nine years ago. Eduardo's great-great grandfather was born and raised in Japan. He had migrated to Brazil in the early 1900s, when, following the abolition of slavery, the Brazilian and Japanese governments created an agreement that gave poor Japanese farmers the opportunity to work on the many Brazilian coffee plantations that were in desperate need of laborers.

By the 1980s, after Eduardo's great-grandfather had purchased several small plots of land for coffee growing, and his grandfather had purchased dozens of larger plots, Eduardo was raised in luxury. His family were now wealthy coffee farmers. Eduardo's father, Rodolpho, was a handsome young man who, because of the wealth his father had inherited and continued to create, had never worked a day in his life. At the time, his American mother Martha had been working on a two-year management assignment in Brazil for Proctor & Gamble. It was common for P&G executives to move all over the world, but because of Martha's nearly perfect command of both the Spanish and Portuguese languages, she remained primarily in South America, and more specifically, Brazil. Martha was assigned management jobs working in different sectors, with the goal of implementing P&G's standards of business in a very different business culture.

While touring his family's manufacturing facility, Martha had met and fallen in love with Rodolpho. The couple started dating and only a few months later, Martha found that she was pregnant. The couple never married, but she was in love with Rodolpho and was happy with whatever little attention he gave her. Martha worked up until the day their son Eduardo was born, and less than a week after giving birth, was back at her high-paced routine of working eighty hours per week.

While his mother continued to move from assignment to assignment for Proctor & Gamble, Eduardo was raised by his grandparents and the many maids and help that lived on and around the family compound. He had a happy childhood, learning the language and respectful culture of Japan while also being influenced by the liberal and carefree Brazilian culture. Unfortunately, Eduardo also grew up watching his father, who was a notorious womanizer, bringing different women home virtually every night of the week. What made things worse was his father's penchant for younger girls, which at that time in Brazil wasn't necessarily illegal. By the time he was nine years old, Eduardo's mother had had enough of his father's cheating ways and left Brazil, taking Eduardo with her.

Between the ages of nine and twelve, Eduardo traveled with his mother, constantly moving, changing schools, and making friends. During those three years, he and his mother lived in Argentina, China, and Mexico before they finally settled down in Dayton, Ohio in order for Eduardo to start middle school in the US. He excelled in his studies and after graduating at the top of his class in high school, Eduardo chose to study restaurant and hotel management in college. After he finished his studies, he moved to the fast-paced world of Las Vegas. As he had seen his mother do all his life, Eduardo was ready to begin working his way up the corporate ladder.

By his mid-thirties, Eduardo was making $150,000 a year as the managing director of one of the largest and highest volume 24-hour buffets in Vegas. He was proud and content with his professional achievements, but less so with his personal life. Eduardo had lived in Brazil with his father's family for the first nine years of his life, and during these formative years had too often seen his father running around with women half his age. Now in his 30s, Eduardo was ashamed that he himself was doing the same. He knew that dating teenage girls, all of whom were a part of the staff that he was in charge of, would sooner or later catch up with him and cost him his job or worse, land him in jail. Yet no matter how many times he told himself he would stop, he would meet a new and younger girl.

While thumbing through a restaurant industry magazine, Eduardo came across a job opportunity to manage a privately-owned Chinese buffet-style restaurant in the Boston area with a second location opening soon. Something told him that it was time to make a change in his life. Although Eduardo had always imagined working in the corporate world and was certain he could never make as much money working for a family-owned business, he also felt that in the long-term, the empty life he was living in Vegas was not what he was meant to do. He feared that if he stayed living in Vegas, he would end up like his father. Eduardo prepared his resume and responded to the ad the next day.

Within the week, he had spoken with Jimmy on the phone three times, each session lasting for well over an hour. The following week, Eduardo gave notice to the casino management and boarded a one-way flight to start his new life in Boston, Massachusetts.

It was on the flight to Boston that Eduardo met his future wife. He had arrived at the airport early and was sitting in the seats nearest to the boarding gate.

After the families with children and people needing assistance had all boarded, Eduardo was the first in line to board. He placed his small carry-on suitcase in the compartment above his seat, took off his sports coat, and carefully folded it and laid it on top of his suitcase. He was buckling his seatbelt and rolling up the sleeves of his white button-down shirt when he looked up and saw the woman he knew at once would be his wife and the mother of his children.

Eduardo had never before thought of whether or not love at first sight could actually happen, but in that moment he knew it was real.

The woman looked to be a bit younger than Eduardo and clearly came from an Asian background. As luck or fate would have it, her seat was in the aisle directly across from his. Without thinking twice, Eduardo leaned over and introduced himself. He discovered that her name was Happy, and after six hours of conversation, as the plane landed at Boston's Logan Airport, she knew that she had just met the man of her dreams.

– 13 –

The last time he had been to his family doctor, Mr. C. was shocked to find out just how heavy he'd become. He couldn't remember exactly how long ago it had been, only that it was before his mother had died, which was five years ago. He knew that his weight at that last visit had been 325 pounds, and he estimated that he'd gained ten pounds a year for the last five years. Mr. C. feared that his weight had ballooned to somewhere near 375 pounds. What he didn't know was that he'd gained closer to thirty pounds a year for the last five years, and he now weighed well over 500 pounds. He knew that he was getting bigger because every year it had become increasingly difficult to get in and out of his mother's old Volvo station wagon. In fact, Mr. C. had grown to hate when strangers stared at what he knew must be the comical sight of him fighting to get in or out of the mid-sized Swedish sedan. Once he actually got in and sat in the seat, in order to get the driver's side door to properly close, he had to rock his body back and forth several times to catch the momentum at precisely the right moment, so he could pull the door shut. It sometimes took him three or four attempts to finally get the door latch to catch. In recent years, he would pretend to be looking for something in the trunk, until no one was around to watch the struggle of him getting into his car.

On his drive in to work every morning, Mr. C. stopped at the donut shop around the corner from his house. By the time he pulled into the drive-thru, the employees had already begun preparing his daily order of two extra-large iced coffees, with extra cream and extra sugar; four sausage, egg, and cheese English muffin breakfast sandwiches; and a box of a dozen donuts. Even though his commute was less than a fifteen-minute drive from the donut shop, all the food was safely in his stomach by the time he arrived. He chose to never eat in front of people, which meant he did not eat in the cafeteria, opting instead to bring an array of junk food, that he snacked on throughout the day.

Mr. C. had always been a big guy. He came from a family of big people and it had never been much of an issue. His father had weighed over 350 pounds at the time of his death, in his early 60s, caused by a heart attack. His twin older sisters were both hovering around 300 pounds, and his mother, at only 250 pounds, was by far the runt of the family. In fact, she had always been the most wonderful and loving mother possible. She loved to cook and bake, and nothing made her happier than watching her family enjoy the meals that she had prepared. Mr. C. and his sisters had had a happy childhood, but both sisters had always felt that their mother favored their brother, which was the truth. Their mother had a special place in her heart for her son, and her daughters resented him as a result. At the time of their mother's death, the girls had not been back to visit in several years, and now Mr. C. had completely lost contact with his sisters, having last seen them at the lawyer's office to learn about their inheritance.

Mr. C. had no interest in moving away from the town where he grew up, because he had never wanted to be away from his mother. After high school, he got his undergraduate and master's degrees in education, choosing to commute rather than stay on campus like most other kids. His mother took care of the house, the shopping, and cooking while working part time as a nurse at Boston Mass General. She was happiest when taking care of her son, whom she adored more than anything in the world. Five years ago, she had felt a sharp and sudden pain in her stomach and knew something was wrong.

Calmly, she drove herself to the emergency room, where she was rushed into surgery. Just as she had suspected, her appendix had burst. The doctors did all they could, but while on the operating table, her body began to shut down and she fell into a coma. His mother never regained consciousness, and less than a week later, she died peacefully with all three of her children by her bedside.

Mr. C., who had never before had to cook or clean, was forced to learn how to live life on his own. He often had food delivered, but was also able to buy groceries without ever needing to actually go into a grocery market. He did all of his food shopping online. He ordered only frozen meals, which simply needed to be put in the oven or microwave. Of course, an average person usually ate one frozen meal, but Mr. C. could eat four or five at a sitting. He snacked on an endless array of chips, candy, ice cream, cookies, and anything else he saw on the grocery store website that looked tasty.

When not at work or at the Friday night school sporting event, he spent every waking minute drinking two-liter bottles of Mountain Dew or Coca-Cola, eating junk food, and sitting in front of his computer alone, lost in the world of fantasy/adventure games. He had an entire social network of what he considered friends or teammates, and became submersed in that fantasy world from the moment he arrived home from work, until the early morning when he could no longer keep his eyes open.

Of course, Mr. C. knew that his weight was completely out of control and that he should try and eat healthier and perhaps do more exercise—or any exercise at all, for that matter. He was also aware that he should clean up the house, as it hadn't properly been cleaned since the day his mother drove herself to the hospital, never to come home again. One side of the two-car garage was so full of trash bags of empty soda bottles and frozen food containers and boxes, that he could no longer even open the garage door. He feared that one day, the bags would come pouring out like in a scene from a cartoon. Yet he never seemed to find the energy to take the trash out to the curb. He often told himself he would make changes to his life starting tomorrow, but tomorrow came and the piles of trash, along with his body, only grew bigger.

– 14 –

As Ivy was driven back to the Omni by the car service, she was thinking about her relationship with Sophie. She and Sophie had been like sisters their entire lives. The girls had shared a bedroom for the first twelve years of their lives. Together they took ballet, karate, horseback riding, and soccer, until finally they had settled on volleyball as the activity they both loved the most.

Recently, however, Ivy felt like their relationship had changed, almost imperceptibly. Several months ago, Sophie began babysitting for her father's right-hand man, Eduardo, and his wife's six-month-old baby boy. So the two best friends had not been able to spend their normal Saturday nights together. But it was more than just not spending as much time together. Ivy sensed something else, but she could not quite put her finger on it. Ivy asked Sophie dozens of times if anything was bothering her, but Sophie just laughed it off, promising that she was fine. Ivy wanted to believe her, but she knew Sophie too well. She noticed how her friend was now very aware of what she ate, careful to never specifically talk about dieting, but no longer eating the sweets or junk foods they had always snacked on together. She had also begun to dress differently, opting for a slightly more sophisticated look rather than the sports clothes she normally wore. Ivy loved Sophie more than anyone in the world and out of respect for their friendship, didn't want to press too hard. She decided to give Sophie her space, reasoning that if something was really going on, Sophie would share it when she felt comfortable.

Ivy's mind turned to her father and the fact that he was not aware of her decision to go out of state for college. She had assumed he would want her to attend Harvard. It was, after all, both his and her mother's alma mater. Ivy had met with the coach of the Harvard women's volleyball team, and if she *were* to stay in state for college, Harvard would be her first choice. But Ivy was absolutely sure that she wanted to spend her first four years of college somewhere that had warm weather all year round, and plenty of beaches for beach volleyball.

It wasn't that she disliked the cold winter season of the Northeast—Ivy actually enjoyed the winter months in New England. It was simply the fact that in Florida, California, or any of the states located in the warmer climates, playing volleyball on the beach was an option all year round, and regardless of not having much beach volleyball experience, Ivy was quite confident that she could easily make the transition and was planning to play on the women's beach volleyball team at whichever college she ended up attending. The Division I beach season was opposite the Division I indoor volleyball season, making participating in both sports an option for any player with the talent and interest.

Ivy thought that perhaps she should send her father a message, explaining to him that she had narrowed her options down to several colleges in Florida and California, but ultimately, she decided against it. She felt that sending him the information would be a distraction, and a distraction was the last thing she wanted to be to him.

Everyone who knew Ivy found it strange that her father had never once seen her play volleyball. Since the age of twelve, when she had begun playing the sport, it was clear that she was a naturally gifted athlete. Of course—she had volleyball in her blood. Ivy's mother Clara had attended Harvard on a full ride volleyball scholarship and had even received an invitation to try out for the US Women's National team during the summer after her sophomore year.

Unfortunately, in the middle of the season of her junior year, she tore the ACL in her left knee, which kept Clara out for the remainder of the season. After surgery to repair her knee, Clara had fought through an intense six-month rehabilitation from which she returned to the courts, ready to win back the starting spot for her senior year. But in the second week of pre-season, Clara's volleyball career ended suddenly when she heard the popping sound of the ACL in her right knee.

Ivy had never had the chance to see her mother play, but had read several old Harvard newspaper articles online, that spoke of the tremendous agility and athleticism Clara had shown on the court, even at just over 6'1" in height.

At just over 6'2", Ivy had been told by her doctors that she was now fully grown. Like her mother, athleticism was also what separated her from most other tall female volleyball players. She had the height, as well as being a gifted athlete. Ivy was powerful, quick, agile, and had a vertical jump as high as any other high school player in the country. She also had the perfect attitude for volleyball; she never got too emotional on the court. Ivy didn't celebrate excessively after a big kill, either, nor did she ever get down on herself on the rare occasion that she made a mistake, or even rarer still, if she got blocked by an opponent. She loved the game for the game, not for the glory or recognition. Ivy was very well liked by the other teammates; when the star of the team is well-liked and respected, it leads to good chemistry for the entire team. This healthy team chemistry is more important in women's volleyball than perhaps any other team sport. Ivy was a volleyball coach's dream, and that was why she was one of the top recruits in the entire country.

– 15 –

When Lisa woke up, her first thought was that she only had two more pills—and that was unthinkable. Lisa could sense the panic and fear rising up in her chest. She knew it was time to reach out for help and that if she couldn't do that, she should at least make the decision to end her empty life once and for all. Lisa reached over to the coffee table next to her bed, and saw that it was only 3:30 a.m. She knew she had hit bottom, that there was nowhere left to turn, and that somehow, she was ready to make a change. Lisa sat up, grabbed the crutches she used to get around with when not wearing her artificial leg, and went to her computer desk.

She went online to search for facilities in New England, and it wasn't long before she found a rehab facility that dealt with addiction to Xanax, as well as anxiety, since the drug and the feeling often went hand in hand. After making herself a cup of tea, Lisa sat down at the kitchen table and dialed the number to the Care Today Rehab facility located in southern New Hampshire. As the phone rang, Lisa thought to herself that if she could survive the monster that was bone cancer, then so too could she survive the addiction that had been hunting her for too long. The moment she heard a voice on the other end of the line, Lisa felt less afraid than she had in a very long time.

– 16 –

Sophie had not been herself all day, and though Ivy had asked her several times if there was anything bothering her, she had simply answered that she wasn't feeling well. When Sophie missed volleyball practice after school, Ivy sent several text messages asking if there was anything that Sophie needed. Ivy noticed that oddly, Sophie had read the messages but hadn't answered. Finally, on Saturday morning, Ivy got a text from Sophie asking if she could come over to Ivy's place. Ivy quickly answered, saying that of course, her friend was always welcome.

Within thirty minutes, the doorbell rang. Ivy opened the door and was surprised to see Sophie with a baseball cap pulled down low over her eyes. She had never known her friend to wear a baseball cap before. Sophie also had a scarf wrapped around her neck and mouth, and Ivy assumed that perhaps Sophie was sick with a cold. That would explain Sophie missing volleyball practice, but it still didn't explain why she hadn't responded to any of Ivy's texts.

Sophie stood outside the door with her head down, until slowly her shoulders began to shake. She was crying. Ivy reached out and hugged her best friend as tight as she could, knowing that when Sophie was ready to share, she would. Still holding hands, the two best friends walked into the apartment. Sophie took off her hat and scarf, and it was clear by her red and swollen eyes that she had been crying all night long.

Ivy made them both a cup of tea, and then Sophie said the last two words Ivy would ever have expected to hear.

"I'm pregnant!"

Ivy was at a complete loss for words. For one thing, she couldn't imagine how her best friend had been in a relationship serious enough to have had sex for the first time and not told her. Then, anger flooded over Ivy at the thought that someone had possibly forced Sophie into doing something she didn't want to do.

"But Soph, how can that be?" Ivy asked, lamely.

Sophie wiped her already swollen eyes.

"You don't know him, Ivy, it's just...just someone I met...I didn't... but he's really...it's over now."

Ivy could not understand how or where Sophie could have met someone that she herself didn't know. Even more confounding, why would Sophie want to keep secret the identity of the boy who had gotten her pregnant? Quickly, Ivy decided that the answers to those questions were not a priority and instead, she focused on her friend.

"How do you know you're pregnant, Soph? Are you sure about it?" she asked.

"I'm over a month late, and yesterday I bought a pregnancy test at the pharmacy and it was positive," Sophie whispered.

So many emotions welled up inside Ivy's mind. She felt anger at her best friend for having made the decision to have sex for the first time without even discussing it with her. On top of that, she obviously had not taken the necessary precautions in order to be safe from getting pregnant, which of course also meant she hadn't been safe from STDs. Ivy thought she knew Sophie so well and couldn't comprehend how or why she had let it happen. But Ivy also knew how much her best friend needed her, and so she decided that she must first support her through the crisis. Only then would she deal with the anger and disappointment she was feeling from the betrayal of their friendship and sisterhood.

Ivy dreaded her next question but it had to be asked.

"Will you have the baby?"

"I need to get an abortion, Ivy, and my parents can never find out who the father is," Sophie whispered, as if not wanting even herself to hear the words.

Ivy was about to ask if having an abortion was the correct decision, but it seemed there was no reason to ask. She understood that it was a decision with which Sophie had already wrestled and that her mind was made up.

"Okay, I will do anything I can to help you get through this. Do you know where or when you can go to have the procedure?" asked Ivy.

Sophie's tone changed to one of control and calm.

"I called the Planned Parenthood Facility here in Boston and I can schedule the procedure for next Friday, rest for the weekend, and be back in school on Monday. I can tell my parents we're working on a project for school and stay here for the weekend. The cost is around a thousand dollars, but I only have about four hundred saved from babysitting."

"Okay, I can get enough cash to cover the rest, so the money problem is solved," said Ivy. Then she continued. "Let's call and find out what time you need to be at Planned Parenthood on Friday. You should take a day out of school, so we need a way to get you excused without your parents questioning it. I won't be able to skip school with you, so we'll need someone we can trust both to bring you and make sure you get back here safely. You cannot do this alone." Ivy paused. "Does the boy know you've made this decision? Should he be there with you?"

"He doesn't know I'm pregnant, and I cannot tell him. It's best for everyone this way," answered Sophie.

Ivy found it strange that Sophie used the word "everyone" when answering the question Ivy had asked about the father of the baby. But again, she held back any additional questions so as not to add more stress to her friend's already overstressed mind. She took a deep breath and held back a nervous laugh. The girls had, for the most part, been rather boring and drama-free, but this was no laughing matter. This was no movie. This was real and Ivy was determined to help her best friend get through it.

– 17 –

Ivy had arranged with the car service to bring her to school twenty minutes earlier than usual. She was waiting in front of Mr. C.'s office when he came waddling down the hall, with his extra-large iced coffee and what looked to be a new jacket. Ivy wondered how and where someone of his size did his shopping. It was clearly too long as well as too big on his shoulders, and Ivy thought perhaps he planned to grow into it, a particularly startling thought. When he saw Ivy by his office door, it brought a smile to his face.

"Good morning, Ms. Miles," said Mr. C.

"Good morning! Looking pretty fancy this morning, Mr. C. Is that a new jacket?" asked Ivy.

"Yes, thank you for noticing," said Mr. C. as he attempted to unlock his office door, which sent him into a coughing fit.

"That cough sounds pretty bad, Mr. C.," said Ivy in a concerned voice. "Did you have that checked out by a doctor?"

"Yeah, I've had this cough now for over a week. I'm on a very strong antibiotic, so they should be kicking in soon. Thank you for your concern," Mr. C. said. "Now stop worrying about me and tell me, to what do I owe this pleasure, Ms. Miles?" Mr. C. tried to catch his breath and get settled into the chair that strained under his weight.

"I have a problem and need to ask for your help. The thing is, I can't tell you exactly what the problem is. I guess if you are to help me, you will just have to trust me without knowing many details," she said.

"Okay, Ivy, tell me what you can, and I will do my best to help," replied Mr. C.

"Well, a friend has a problem and needs to take this Friday out of school in order to deal with it. But my friend does not want her parents to know she is taking the day off school because she is adamant about not wanting to share this problem with them. She needs an excuse from school and well--"

Ivy paused before continuing. "--is this something you would feel comfortable doing, without having more information?"

Mr. C. had never before been asked by a student to do anything of this nature. He was quite flattered that Ivy would trust him enough to ask, but he also knew that if he were to agree to help, he could lose his job. Mr. C. was never one to break the rules. The few times in his life that he attempted to break the rules, he had always been caught.

The most memorable time was when he was just seventeen years old and he and a friend of his wanted more than anything to go to a strip club. Together, the boys went to a shady storefront in Boston where they had heard they could buy fake IDs. It was in a rundown part of town and looked to be some sort of photography retail business. Nervously, the two friends walked in, paid $150 each, a man quickly took their pictures and told them they would be ready later that night. The boys picked up their new IDs the next day and drove forty-five minutes to Providence, Rhode Island, to go to the famous Pink Fox strip club. Confidently, they handed the bouncer the fake IDs that had them each at twenty-two years old. They were sure that the quality of the forgery would fool any doorman, but the problem was that the bouncer was an off-duty Massachusetts State Trooper and he was not fooled by the fake IDs. He called the police and had the boys arrested.

Of course, this was a double whammy of a disappointment. First, there was getting arrested and having Mr. C.'s mother and father drive all the way to the Providence police station to pick him up. Even worse was the fact that Mr. C. was within just a few feet of the stage at the Pink Fox strip club only to have his dreams dashed. Luckily, neither his father nor his mother were bothered much that their son made the mistake of buying a bad fake ID, nor that he was trying to get into a strip club. He had never been in trouble in his life and they saw it simply as a comical lesson learned.

If it were any other student in the entire school other than Ivy S. Miles, Mr. C. would have no problem saying no. But this wasn't any other student, and he knew as soon as Ivy confided in him that he'd help her in any way he could.

"Ivy, I have known you long enough to be confident you are looking to do the right thing for your friend. Perhaps I could set up some sort of a day trip for your friend to tour a college campus on that particular day?" Mr. C. continued. "But Ivy, if I am going to do this, I will have to know who I am writing an excuse for. Are you sure you and your friend can handle this problem on your own? Is there anything else I can do to help?"

Though she was relieved that Mr. C. would help, Ivy thought to herself that no, she wasn't sure she and Sophie could handle this on their own. She wished Sophie would go to her parents and tell them the truth so that as a family, they could make the right decision together. But she also knew that there must be more to the story than Sophie was telling her, and for now Ivy just had to trust that supporting her best friend was the only option she had. For a split second, Ivy thought of asking Mr. C. if he could possibly accompany Sophie to the clinic the day of the procedure but she realized that asking him to bend the rules and write an excuse from school was one thing—asking Mr. C. to get actively involved was quite another.

"The friend I'm talking about is Sophie Pham," Ivy said in a low voice. "Thank you so much for the offer, but I think it's best if you don't get involved any more than you have to. But it's nice to know I can look to you for support if I need it."

Although Ivy had solved one of the many issues in order for this plan to work, she couldn't help but worry about Sophie. She felt that the father of the baby should be involved with the decision, or at the very least be there for emotional support. But most of all, Ivy kept asking herself the question, why was Sophie being so secretive?

– 18 –

Hey Lil' Sis,

I'm just realizing how hard this entire ordeal has been on our mother. The chemotherapy treatments were obviously a nightmare, along with all the surgeries I have gone through. To make it even more stressful for Mama, during the times we were home between chemo treatments we were constantly on edge hoping that my blood counts, specifically my platelet counts, didn't get too low. The thing with chemotherapy is, while the chemicals are attacking the cancer cells, that themselves have gone rogue and are dividing and growing at a speed they aren't supposed to, these chemicals are also attacking all the other "normal" dividing cells. It's like everything else in this world, every good thing has its negative side. In fact, a handful of times, I was rushed to the emergency room because my nose started bleeding and simply could not stop without the healthy platelet counts in my blood to clot properly. So off to the emergency room we'd go, so the doctor could stick this metal wire what seemed to me to be about 3 feet up into my nose. To top it all off, he had a foot pedal that activated the wire instantly heating the tip to cauterize (which is another word for burn) the bleeding blood vessel.

Ives, I know what you are thinking, the smell of burning flesh coming from inside your brain, while experiencing searing pain deep within the space behind your eyes, causing that space to be melted with a red-hot wire, sounds like a great time for all! But it really is not as pleasant an experience as it sounds. If that wasn't uncomfortable enough, they then packed my right nostril with enough gauze to wrap the mummified body of King Tut.

Anyway, you are basically now living full time with Nancy and Jimmy and their baby Sophie, so Mama can focus all of her energy and attention on me. I feel so damn guilty, both for making Mama look so worn down, and being the reason that is keeping her from spending time with you. I feel like I should either get better or not be here. I don't want to be such a burden, but I don't really have much of a say in it anymore! There is nothing I can do about it. I try and believe that though the chemo didn't work, maybe my body's own normal defenses are still at least trying to wage a war inside my body. Maybe my good cells and antibodies are winning one tiny battle after another. I guess I haven't completely given up hope just yet.

Changing topics, I have been playing guitar since I was ten years old. I had been taking classical acoustic guitar lessons twice a week for the last five years as well as attending a four-week music camp in Burlington, Vermont, for the last three summers. Of course, since I became a full-time cancer patient, I don't take lessons anymore, but I still play whenever I have the energy and strength. In the last several months, I have been hearing (I know that sounds weird, but I have never actually sat down and attempted to write a song, they just kind of appear) lyrics and melodies which have turned out to be songs. I have not shared these songs with anyone, but thought I would make a recording for you. Last year for my birthday, I got an amazing (and quite expensive, I must say) microphone and the newest and really powerful desk-top computer, along with some basic home studio recording software. I have certainly had enough time in the last year when I was home, to spend literally hundreds of hours reading and learning how to use the program. Now am ready to actually start recording with it! The song I am going to perform for you is called Empty Prayers. I will also share the lyrics with you. It is indeed a sad song. I am speaking directly to the monster inside me, which is how I always think of my cancer. This will be the first song on the CD that I am making just for you, Ives! Hope you like it!

Empty Prayers

No one else can see you, but I know you're there
I can feel your need to come up for air
No one here to save me, you're my cross to bear
Empty prayers, empty prayers
No one here to save me

Empty prayers, left with empty prayers
Well now you're the hunter, and I'm your prey

Lurking in the shadows, to strike again
Far away laughter, as you slip away
Empty prayers, empty prayers
Far away laughter
Empty prayers, left with empty prayers

Now it's time to make my stand
Now you're the hunted
There's nowhere left for you to turn
Is that what you wanted?

No there ain't no savior, or almighty powers that be
No one sacrificed their mortal life for me
My cries go unanswered, as I beg for clemency
Empty prayers, empty prayers
My cries go unanswered

Empty prayers, left with empty prayers

– 19 –

While holding a paper cup of hot black coffee in each hand, Lisa walked back to her chair in the circle. It had been forty-six days since she checked herself in at the facility, and never before had she felt such a sense of control and empowerment. Lisa was aware enough to know that her battle with her addiction to Xanax and her struggles with depression would never be easy, but she also felt that she was ready to face her problems and never fall back into using drugs not prescribed by her doctor—ever again. A big factor in her newfound happiness was the reason she was carrying not one but two coffees back to her seat in the circle.

Dennis had come to the facility several months before Lisa, after years of addiction that started with Oxycodone and led to injecting heroin. Today he was seventy-two days clean. He had been arrested for dealing heroin, which he only did in order to finance his addiction. Being that it was the first time he had ever been arrested, the judge presiding over the case gave Dennis one opportunity to attend an in-patient rehabilitation program and prove that he could get his life together, rather than go to prison. Dennis was proud to be clean after so many years of using, and he knew that this was his chance to start over. With the opportunity, he was determined to live a good, honest, and productive life.

Of course, neither Dennis nor Lisa expected to fall in love, but in love is exactly where they found themselves. When they first met, they were amazed at how much they had in common. Their first conversation lasted into the early hours of the morning. Dennis and Lisa learned that they had both grown up in South Boston, were both raised by alcoholic mothers, and both had been fighting anxiety and depression since their late teens. That wasn't all they had in common: both were also able to maintain a façade of having normal lives throughout their addiction and both recognized the toll that it took to live a lie for so many years. Dennis had been a construction worker in the union before he was arrested, and even while using, he had been taking night classes, working toward getting his Bachelor's degree in mechanical engineering at a community college in Boston. Dennis valued his construction work and his fellow union members in the way most people value their families. He was, however, determined to sign up for the last two college classes and finally finish the degree he had been dreaming of since graduating high school. Dennis believed with all his heart that once he had that diploma, he would get a high-paying mechanical engineering job at one of the big exclusive firms in downtown Boston. He looked forward to getting rid of his old pickup truck and buying his first BMW 5 series. He couldn't wait to trade his stained and dirty work pants, sweatshirts, t-shirts, and steel-toed boots, for suits, dress pants, button downs, sports jackets, golf shirts, and dress shoes—the work attire of an engineer.

Dennis blamed the physical labor of his daily work life as a construction worker for getting him first hooked on Oxycodone. He had begun taking the synthetic pain medicine only on occasion, to deal with back pain caused by long workdays spent on his feet at construction sites. He felt strongly that had his parents been more supportive and not been so "screwed up," he would already be living the life he thought he deserved. It was his father's fault, he thought, for having given up on the family and leaving when he was only six years old, causing his mother to turn to alcohol and essentially having been drunk for the rest of his childhood. Unexpectedly, Dennis now believed Lisa was going to be a part of that new and better life. He did not share these thoughts with any of the counselors, nor with Lisa. They would just tell him that only he, himself, was to blame for where he was, and a new job or new degree would not change anything. Dennis knew they were wrong and he couldn't wait to show them all how successful he would become.

Both saw the other as their savior. Dennis saw Lisa as someone who could love him the way he always wanted, needed, and deserved to be loved. Lisa knew Dennis's flaws and had seen him at his rock bottom. Regardless, she seemed to truly care for him.

After having had a hard life, a dysfunctional family, surviving cancer, and losing her leg, Lisa too was excited to be a part of the successful life that Dennis spoke of so passionately. She saw him as someone she could love, take care of, and support in his new life, without the need for any drugs. Lisa believed with all her heart that Dennis would succeed and achieve all his goals. In fact, she'd be the strong woman every man needed behind him, allowing him to focus on creating a successful professional career. The couple saw themselves as the perfect match, and together they would become the happy people they always dreamed of being.

– 20 –

As a minor, having a procedure to terminate an unwanted pregnancy turned out to be much more complicated than either Sophie or Ivy had expected. The two girls walked into a clinic in Boston, hoping to make an appointment, only to find out that to have an abortion as a minor in Massachusetts, at least one parent needed to give permission. The two friends fervently explained to the nurse that that was simply not an option. The nurse, who seemed to expect that response, informed them that there were two other possibilities. The first option was to get a lawyer and ask a judge to grant something called a "judicial bypass," which would allow the minor to get an abortion without parental consent. The second and more practical option was to drive to a facility located just over the state line in Maine, which was about a two-hour drive, to have the procedure. In Maine, the nurse explained, a minor is not required to have any parental consent to have an abortion.

The girls opted to call the number of a clinic in Maine and made an appointment to have the procedure done the following Friday. Ivy had spoken with Mr. Bugs and asked if he or his wife would be willing to spend the day with Sophie to help her with a problem the following Friday. She told Mr. Bugs that she had arranged with the car service to drive them to a clinic in Maine, wait two or three hours, and drive Sophie back to the Omni, where Sophie would rest for the weekend.

Without asking one question, Mr. Bugs assured Ivy that either he or his wife would be sure to make the trip.

As to getting excused from school, Mr. C. did indeed write a permission letter for Sophie to visit the Yale campus in New Haven, Connecticut on the following Friday. He had even covered his tracks by actually setting up a campus tour with his contact at Yale. He also gave Ivy a name and number for her to call early Friday morning to inform the Yale office that Sophie wasn't feeling well and would not be able to make the appointment.

Ivy took fifteen hundred dollars from a cash box that she kept in case of an emergency. At just over five hundred, the cash covered the cost of the car service, which Ivy planned to pay with cash to ensure the trip to Maine would not get back to her father. The planned cost of the procedure was expected to be less than a thousand dollars, so together with the four hundred of babysitting money Sophie had, they had it covered.

Although Ivy had worked together with Sophie to plan and prepare for Friday, there was no denying the divide she felt between herself and her life-long best friend. She continued to struggle with the fact that somehow, somewhere, Sophie had met and started a relationship with someone and chosen not to share that fact with Ivy—her best friend. Even more difficult for Ivy to understand was the fact that Sophie had made the decision to have sex for the first time and not discuss it with her at all. Just as confusing was the thought that had she not gotten pregnant, would she have decided to tell Ivy at all?

Ivy badly wanted to ask Sophie all these questions, and sensed that Sophie also wanted and needed to share all the emotions that were going through her head as well. But something kept Ivy from saying anything and so she continued to put all of the questions and issues aside, and be as supportive as she could be.

– 21 –

Mr. C. had always made it known that he very much wanted to buy his sisters' shares of the family's small ranch home. His sisters never showed any interest in moving back to the East Coast, so he felt confident that when the time came, he'd be able to buy the home for himself. Though his mother had never spoken about the family finances, he was fairly certain from comments she had made over the years that the house was fully paid off. With his secure teaching job, he knew getting a bank loan and paying his sisters their fair share was not going to be a problem.

What Mr. C. and his sisters didn't know was that their grandfather, Bobby Connor, Sr., had owned a chain of eight hardware stores in the Boston area in the 1950s, 60s and 70s. He had sold or closed all of the stores by the mid-70s, but had held on to the real estate. As the real estate market boomed in and around Boston, the shopping plazas had all dramatically increased in value. Upon Bobby Sr.'s death, Mr. C.'s father wanted nothing to do with the real estate business and decided to sell all of the properties. As luck would have it, his father sold the buildings at the very peak of the real estate boom in the early 80s. Although it made the couple extremely wealthy, other than buying a new pickup truck and paying off their house loan, they never mentioned the inheritance to anyone, nor did they change the way they lived.

Just days after their mother's death, Mr. C. and his sisters were contacted by a lawyer to meet in his office to discuss the split of the inheritance. The siblings had no idea there was anything more than the house and the four-year-old Volvo as far as inheritance was concerned. It came as a shock to all of them when they were each handed their checks and instantly became multi-millionaires. Once a year, without her children's knowledge, their mother had met with financial advisors, who managed the large sum of money, as well as with a lawyer, in order to ensure her will stay current. As a result, she had left everything in order, including inheritance taxes all paid in full. She had even left the house to her son and made sure her daughters were paid their share of the value of the house. Mr. C. received a check for approximately $4,400,000 and each of the sisters $4,550,000.

Mr. C. bought himself the most powerful computer and two of the biggest and best monitors available on the market. He also bought the most expensive desk and chair he could find on the internet. Aside from those purchases, which in total was just short of $35,000, he told no one of his newfound wealth and changed nothing in his routine. Recently, he had been debating whether or not he would purchase a new and bigger car. With his ever-increasing weight, it was becoming more difficult for him to get in and out of his mother's old Volvo.

– 22 –

Hello Ives,

So I kind of had my first girlfriend, who I met in the hospital. Her name is Lisa, and we were both diagnosed with bone cancer at the same time, almost fifteen months ago now. The doctors found Lisa's tumor near her left ankle, which meant the doctors only needed to amputate the lower part of her left leg, just below her knee. My tumor was near the top of my left thigh and as a result I needed to have my entire left leg amputated just below my hip. We joke that we would be the world's worst three-legged race team at family picnics.

I was just remembering the first time both of us got treatment of adriamycin and cisplatin, which is the most potent of the different chemicals in our protocol. For three or four days after they put the chemicals in our bodies, it was absolute hell. Basically, it is seventy-two hours of not being able to sleep because you have to puke every five minutes! After a few days, the side effects begin to subside. We normally stayed in the hospital for another three days, recovering, which basically meant sleeping. The day we both were hoping to be discharged, we had our first real kiss. It was kind of scary to tell you the truth, the part where you don't really know what exactly to do with the whole tongue thing! After a few very awkward tries, it got better and was actually really nice.

Lisa is a sweet girl. She doesn't have a father, so we kind of have that in common. Okay, okay, just kidding, I love Alan! Maybe he has changed with you, or at least I hope he has anyway, but it does kind of feel like I don't have a father most of the time. Anyway, Lisa's mother does not even visit when she is in the hospital getting chemo treatments. Lisa says her mother is, and has been, an alcoholic all her life. Of course, this means she has never been much of a mother. From the stories I've heard, it sounds like Lisa has had to take care of and worry about her mother all her life.

Lisa has been fitted with a prosthesis, which is just another word for fake leg, and I am amazed at how good she can get around already. As you can probably imagine, it's much less complicated when you still have your knee. It's not something you really think about, but the motion of the foot is actually not very complicated or difficult to mimic as far the prosthesis is concerned. I saw how easy it was for her to learn to walk and how quickly she was up and around. The socket part of the prosthesis, the part that fits what is left of her leg, takes some time to get used to. Eventually, Lisa will be able to use the artificial leg for long periods of time, but for now she can only use it for about four hours at a time, and then her skin gets too sore. It is amazing how she walks almost perfectly already. It makes me want to give it a try. Unfortunately, between the chemo treatments and the two surgeries on my lungs, I have not been able to do much walking on the temporary leg they made me. After the surgery, I was left with only about 12cm of my femur bone, which makes fitting the prosthesis very difficult. Plus, I keep losing weight. The socket they made me has a system to be able to adjust to deal with the changes in volume as a result of the swelling and weight loss, but I just don't have the energy or strength it takes to learn to walk. I have seen other kids here in the hospital that can walk almost normally, even without their knee, so I know it can be done. Unfortunately, it doesn't look like I will get the chance to find out.

What I have had a chance to experience and know all about is something called phantom pain. You probably have never heard of it, but I must say it is quite interesting. When you lose a limb, a leg, arm, or even a finger or toe, your brain senses something is not normal and sends signals of pain to the area that is no longer physically there. For me, I get a feeling like a needle is going into the bottom of my left foot, the same foot the doctors cut off over fifteen months ago... strange, right?

A few months ago, I met an 81-year-old man named Erwin at the prosthetic shop. He had lost his leg in a motorcycle accident when he was a teenager. I mentioned to him my struggles with phantom pains and he said he still gets phantom pains about twice a month and always on the same spot—on the top of the foot that was cut off over 60 years ago! I told Erwin that I found it rather ridiculous, that after so many years, the human brain isn't able to learn that the limb is gone. His response was really interesting: Erwin said that the human mind has a hard time forgetting emotions, especially when it comes to hurt and pain. I wasn't sure what he meant until he explained how he and his brother had started some sort of a business together when they were in their twenties. For twenty years, he and his brother worked together every day and were best friends. Together with their wives and children, they spent weekends, holidays, and vacations together and they were all one big happy family. Until the brothers had a falling out about money, who worked more hours, and who should be the boss. Since the day Erwin left their office, he never again spoke with his brother or any of his nieces and nephews. He said that even though over 40 years had gone by, every time he thinks about his brother, he feels pain in his heart. He said it still hurts him to think that their lives have passed and neither of them could ever find a way to forgive the other.

His point was that pain, whether it's from an amputated leg, a broken heart, or a family grudge, stays with us all our lives. I had never equated phantom pains with emotional pain, but after hearing Erwin explain it, I understood exactly what he was saying.

This is a song that was born from that conversation, and I recorded it for you last night. It's called Phantom Pain.

Love you Ives!

Phantom Pain

You're gone for good and I know that now
But you still haunt me and I don't know how
To end these games
That you still play
Inside my brain
You're only phantom pain
I close my eyes see you so clear

Reach out to touch you knowing well you're not there
How to end these games
That you still play
Inside my brain
You're only phantom pain
The past is an illusion
Now is all there'll ever be
Future is more mind confusion
Of the now that is yet to be
You were killing me that's what I had to face
Now you linger here like a memory trace.
How to end these games
That you still play
Inside my
Brain

You're only phantom pain

– 23 –

Mr. Bugs found a co-worker to take his Friday morning shift in order to accompany Sophie on her trip to Maine. He met her in front of the hotel at 7:30 a.m., where the Lincoln Town Car was already waiting. The driver informed them they should be at their destination in approximately two hours, and off they went.

"Looks like you girls have a chance to once again go deep into the state championships with the team you have this year?" asked Mr. Bugs.

Mr. Bugs thought it important to engage Sophie in conversation to get her mind off the fact that she was heading to an appointment to terminate her pregnancy, but she had been in such deep thought that she was caught off-guard. It took her a few seconds to remember that it was only last month that volleyball had been the most important thing in her life. Until then, Sophie had been focused on the prospect of fighting for a state championship with her best friend leading the way. Now, it seemed almost ridiculous to think that she could have cared so much about some dumb game. Sophie understood what it was like to face real-life problems and couldn't imagine ever wanting to play any sport ever again. Finally, she registered that Mr. Bugs had spoken to her and responded, "Yeah, we have a pretty good team this year. Ivy is unstoppable. We basically just have to put the ball up in the air anywhere on the court and she can crush the ball down."

Mr. Bugs smiled encouragingly. He wanted to keep Sophie talking, to help with her nervousness and anxiety.

"Do you plan on playing volleyball in college, Sophie?" he asked. Sophie was encouraged. It was helping.

"Well, I have reached out and sent my highlight video to a handful of coaches, hoping to at least get a try-out," she replied. "I'm not athletic enough to make a Division I team, but with my grade point average, I could possibly get a partial academic scholarship to a D2 or D3 program." Sophie surprised herself; talking about the future felt good.

"Any idea what you want to study?" asked Mr. Bugs.

"Well, Ivy and I had always dreamed of both studying medicine and going into pediatric oncology. I still plan to study medicine, but I am not so sure oncology is right for me. The good news is, if I study medicine, I don't have to decide what type of doctor I want to be until well after I finish my undergraduate degree." For the first time in several weeks, Sophie actually smiled at the thought of the endless possibilities in the future.

Seeing Sophie's spirits lift the way they did, even if for only a few moments, let Mr. Bugs know that she would survive her ordeal and be just fine.

"Well, I think you will make a great doctor no matter which you choose to be!" he said with a smile.

They rode without speaking for several minutes until Sophie broke the silence. "Mr. Bugs, thank you for coming with me today. This is by far the scariest thing I have ever had to do in my life and it's really nice to not have to do it alone."

"Sophie, there is no need to thank me. I know how much Ivy loves you and that she considers you a sister. I care for Ivy like she is my own daughter, so in a way you could say you are like a daughter to me as well," Mr. Bugs said, tenderly.

Sophie became introspective.

"To tell you the truth, as difficult as it is having to deal with this procedure today, and the thought of my parents finding out about any of this, what hurts the most has been lying to Ivy. In all our sixteen years, we have never kept anything from each other. I put myself into such a bad situation and made such ridiculously bad decisions, I'm embarrassed even to admit them to Ivy." Tears began to stream down Sophie's face.

Mr. Bugs took her hand in his.

"Sophie, you're just sixteen years old, you're supposed to make ridiculously bad decisions! In fact, making bad decisions is a pre-requisite for a teenager!"

Sophie laughed while wiping the tears from her eyes and Mr. Bugs continued.

"I don't share this story with many people, but when I was seventeen, there was a girl from my neighborhood named Ruth. She was so beautiful and smart, and for some odd reason, when I asked her to go on a date, she actually agreed. At that time, I had no car nor did I yet have a license, but I made the ridiculously bad decision to borrow my father's Buick, since he and my mother were out of town for the weekend. Then, in order to calm my nerves before breaking the rules and taking my father's beloved car to go on a date with the girl of my dreams, I made the bad decision to drink a few beers. Being just seventeen, I couldn't handle my liquor, and after the second beer I was pretty much drunk. I grabbed the keys to the Buick, put the car in reverse, and slowly began backing out of our driveway."

Sophie's eyes widened. She dreaded the ending of this story. Mr. Bugs continued.

"As I approached the bottom of our driveway and applied the brakes, I mixed up my left foot with my right and pressed the accelerator pedal instead! I slammed the Buick, trunk first, into the side our neighbor's shiny new white Cadillac."

"That sounds like a scene out of a movie," Sophie said, gasping. "So, what did your parents say?"

"Well, my father was an old tough Russian with only a seventh-grade education. However, he was wise. He told me just what I am telling you now. Of course, he said it all in Russian, but the basic translation was clear. He told me I had made a ridiculously bad decision and now I needed to make it right. That summer, I got two jobs and worked 60 hours a week in order to cover the cost for all the damage I caused to my father's and the neighbor's cars. Both my father and the neighbor forgave me, but I learned a lesson I will never forget."

Sophie smiled.

"I should add," continued Mr. Bugs, "that I never got to see my dream girl Ruth that night. But I did eventually go on a date with her, and we have now been married for almost thirty years, we have three children, and five grandchildren. I guess even ridiculously bad decisions can lead to happy endings!"

Still smiling at Mr. Bug's story, Sophie turned her head and looked at the passing New England foliage. She too hoped to one day look back on all of it as simply a learning experience, but she had her doubts.

– 24 –

To Ivy, it felt like the school day would never end. When the final bell rang, she ran out to the parking lot and called Mr. Bugs on his cell phone.

"Hello, Ivy," answered Mr. Bugs on the third ring.

"How is Sophie? Is the procedure done? How is she doing?" asked Ivy, breathlessly.

"Everything went perfectly and took less time than expected," said Mr. Bugs, reassuringly. "In fact, we're already on our way back to Boston and Sophie is resting comfortably here in the car. We should arrive back at the Omni in less than an hour."

Ivy took a deep breath and felt relief wash over her.

"Thank you, thank you so much," said Ivy, holding back tears of relief.

– 25 –

As Ivy walked toward the athletic building for volleyball practice, she reflected on what she had read in Jake's journal, just the night before. Ivy tried to imagine what it must have been like for her brother to have been a perfectly healthy young man, to then having to deal with his leg being amputated. She stopped walking, put her bags down, and with both hands felt her left thigh over her jeans. She tried to imagine how brutal the surgery must be, what it's like for surgeons to cut through all the muscle and bone in the human thigh. How must it be to wake up from surgery, look down, and see only one foot at the end of the bed, or to actually see, for the first time, the wound where a leg was supposed to be. How could a teenager possibly be expected to deal with something so traumatic, Ivy wondered?

Lately, Ivy was experiencing a new appreciation of her healthy body and her athletic skills. During the last week of practice, she was playing with an even greater level of intensity than before. She was working harder and was even more focused than was her norm, and both the coaches and her teammates noticed. Jake's journals were making a difference in her outlook.

"Ivy!" Someone shouting her name awakened Ivy from her thoughts about the brother she had never known, the way he had suffered so bravely and the gift he had given her in his journals.

Ivy turned and sure enough, it was Stevie Smith, the boy she'd had a crush on since the ninth grade. Actually, Stevie was anything but a boy. Just having turned eighteen years old, he stood 6'5" and weighed 215 pounds, and had the all-American looks of a young Hollywood movie star. He also happened to have hit the IQ lottery by inheriting his intelligence from his mother, who was a leading research scientist in her field of space weather and its effects on Earth. Stevie was as proud of having carried a perfect 4.0 grade point average through all four years of high school and ending his senior year as valedictorian, as he was of any of his baseball accomplishments, of which he had plenty.

Stevie was often compared to two of the best baseball players ever and with good reason. Stevie's father had molded his game by copying the mechanics of Alex Rodrigues's swing, while building his pitching mechanics around the motion of Roger Clemens.

Stevie's father, Steve Smith, Sr., had been a professional baseball player himself, bouncing from one minor league ball club to the other from the ages of eighteen to thirty. He finally gave up on his dream when he turned 30. With no regrets, he married his longtime girlfriend and they started a family. Steve Sr. had rented an old warehouse and opened a baseball training center, working with baseball players and coaches from all over New England. From the time his son Stevie could hold a bat, Steve Sr. focused all his energy into molding his son to be a professional baseball player.

As Stevie came running toward her from the field, Ivy felt butterflies in her belly. She and Stevie often said hello to each other in the hallway, and she had talked with him last year at the end of the baseball season. But that was a conversation Ivy tried to forget. She and Sophie had been standing in front of the school waiting for their ride home, after having watched the final home baseball game of the season. Ivy remembered clearly how Stevie had pitched a two-hit shutout and went four for four at the plate, with three doubles and a homerun over the centerfield fence. He walked around the corner, wearing his baseball pants and spiked shoes. Ivy still remembered the very distinct sound the metal spikes on his shoes made with every step he took. Wearing only a white tank top with a black Nike logo on the front, he saw the girls and jogged over to speak with them.

"Hey, Ivy S. Miles, I was hoping to catch you before you left," he had said, with a grin. "I saw you sitting in the stands and wanted to thank you for coming to see us play. I guess that means I'm required to come and watch at least one home volleyball match next season, right?" He spoke directly to Ivy with a smile that nearly made her knees buckle.

Ivy was totally caught off guard by the question and she answered in a strange monotone.

"Yes…uhhhh…I'm required to come and watch at least one home volleyball match next season."

Ivy could remember so vividly the look of confusion on Stevie's face. He tilted his head to one side, reminding her of a dog. Luckily, at that very moment, the rest of the team came around the corner, yelling for their star player to come and join them in the celebration.

But that was then and this is now. Ivy was now a year older, and much more mature and better prepared to have a normal adult conversation with Stevie. At least that was what she told herself as he came running across the field calling her name.

"Hey, Ivy S. Miles," he said, panting slightly, from the run over to where she was. "You guys don't have a game tonight?"

Ivy tried to play it cool and smiled.

"No. We play in New Hampshire tomorrow afternoon. Right now, we have a light practice to prepare for the match." Ivy surprised herself at how relaxed and normal she sounded!

"Man, are you *beautiful*, Ivy!" Stevie said, catching them both off-guard. Ivy blushed deep red.

"You used to be so hideous and grotesque, almost ogre-like!" Stevie continued. "But you really have grown into your looks!"

At that, Ivy had to laugh.

"Oh, well you are quite the charmer. Thank you for that incredibly offensive yet sweet compliment!" They both laughed and immediately felt the chemistry.

"Obviously I'm kidding, you've always been beautiful!" Stevie said affectionately.

"Thank you!" Ivy tilted her head down and did her best curtsy. "And you're not horrible to look at either, Mr. Smith," she replied, not having to lie.

"I've been following your season and you are killing it this year! You must be overwhelmed with offers from college programs, no?" Stevie asked. But before Ivy a chance to respond, Stevie looked her up and down and added, "I cannot believe how tall you are. What are you, like 6'2" or 3?"

"Just over 6'2"." Ivy smiled. "And I suspect I'm pretty much done growing. I was kind of hoping to get to 6'3", but it doesn't look like that's going to happen. And yeah, I have gotten a bunch of offers from colleges, but I've narrowed it down to a few programs in Florida and California." She was doing everything in her power to stay calm and keep from embarrassing herself in any way. "What about you, Stevie? You must also have offers as well, no?" she asked.

"Well, yeah, I have plenty of options for college scholarships, but I also have the option to pass on college altogether and sign a contract with one of the major league clubs. It's a great position to be in, but I'm really struggling to decide what's best for me," Stevie said.

Ivy smiled. "I'm sure you'll make the right decision, Stevie. I remember someone telling me or reading somewhere, that your father played professional baseball as well. What does he think about the situation?" she asked.

"Yeah, my dad played in the minor leagues for almost twelve years, but never got a shot at the big time. He was close a few times, had a few really good seasons in triple A out in Texas, but he just never got called up." Stevie continued, "So now he's piled all his hopes and dreams on me. As you can imagine, it is not exactly an easy position to be in."

Ivy dreaded having to end the conversation. She was surprised to feel so comfortable talking with Stevie, but she had no choice, she had to go.

"I always like to be the first one on the court at practice, so I have to get changed and help set up the net."

Stevie looked crestfallen so Ivy continued. "Maybe we can continue this conversation another time? What was it that you came running over here for? Or were you just doing your best impression of David Hasselhoff's *Baywatch* character?"

Stevie laughed in appreciation. They had the same taste and sense of humor, it seemed.

"I was wondering if maybe we could..."

At that moment, a boy walked up, extended his hand to Ivy and said, "*Guten tag, ich heisse Gunther, Gunther Yaüch.*" Ivy laughed with surprise.

The young man was even taller than Stevie; he must have been close to seven feet tall, Ivy thought. Yet he was so thin, she suspected a strong breeze could easily blow him off his feet. Stevie hoisted his friend over his head playfully.

"I'll deal with you later, Gunther!"

Laughing, he put his friend down again and watched as Gunther ran, laughing, toward the field. Stevie turned back toward Ivy, a little embarrassed.

"That insane guy is not named Gunter Yaüch, nor does he speak German. His name is Tony, he's my catcher, and he is *insane*!"

Ivy was still laughing as Stevie continued with his explanation.

"Now, as a general rule, all catchers are a little crazy, but Tony seems to be completely out of his mind. Last summer he and his family took a vacation to Germany, and since then he insists his ancestors were from Southern Germany and his real name is Gunther Yaüch. I mentioned to Tony that the story seems rather unlikely, as his full name is Anthony Rizzotti, but he insists he somehow has German roots!"

"Well, Tony or Gunther or whatever his name, seems like an interesting guy," Ivy said, laughing.

"Interesting could be one way to describe Tony, but I'm not sure that's the adjective I would choose." Stevie continued. "I was about to ask you if we could hang out sometime, like maybe this weekend? There's a big chess meet Sunday here in Boston, and I thought you and I could go watch a few matches. It's supposed to be a really exciting tournament!" he said in a serious tone.

Ivy was in total shock that Stevie Smith had just asked her on a date, or at least to "hang out." She was also completely baffled that he would invite her to go watch a live chess match.

"Well, I don't know much about chess, but I'd be up for something new!" she said.

Stevie grinned that winning grin of his again.

"I'm just kidding about the chess, Ivy. I'm a baseball player, lord knows I can barely play checkers, let alone chess! But I like that you were willing to try!"

Ivy laughed, hard. "I'm going to get you back for that one, Stevie!" She reached into her backpack, grabbed a pen and paper, and wrote down her name and cell phone number.

"Here's my number. Call or write me later tonight or tomorrow morning and we can make plans. Maybe we can do a pros and cons list about you turning professional versus going to college. I did that when I was deciding if I should stay in state for college, and it really helped."

Stevie's friends were shouting to him in the background, but he didn't take his eyes off Ivy.

She looked at him shyly.

"I am really, really happy you came over to talk, it was really sweet."

Suddenly, Ivy realized that she was moving towards Stevie for a hug. Just as he too realized it and awkwardly began moving towards her, Ivy tried to stop herself and reached out as if to shake hands. With his body still in motion, her hand ended up flat against his stomach. As if having a mind of its own, her hand began to feel his washboard abs over his t-shirt. This all happened in a matter of seconds, but felt like it was happening in slow motion. Embarrassed, Ivy pulled her hand back and with her shoulders slouching down, and her eyes on the ground, she said, "Oh, I was so *close* to making it through an entire conversation without making a total fool of myself in front of you, Stevie!"

Both of them burst out in laughter.

"Let's try this again," Stevie said.

He drew Ivy into a warm hug, wrapping both his arms around her, and giving her an electric feeling like she had never experienced in her life. Ivy hadn't realized how much she had needed affection; without thinking, she put her head on Stevie's shoulder and wrapped her arms around him right back. They held each other there for several seconds, then, suddenly self-conscious, Ivy picked up her bags and walked through the gym doors, quickly, disappearing into the locker room.

A moment later, as she rushed to change into her volleyball clothes, she couldn't keep from smiling. She had just had the most perfect conversation with the boy that she'd had a crush on forever. Ivy was amazed at how comfortable it was to talk with Stevie, and even more amazed that he had asked her on a date. And the hug, where did *that* come from? Ivy could not wait to tell Sophie. She was not going to believe it.

– 26 –

During their early years, Miles & Begosian had represented many of Silicon Valley's first and most successful technology companies. In return for legal expertise and service, they had insisted that a percentage of payment be made in the form of stocks. As a result, the partners now owned stock in Apple, Google, Microsoft, Dell, Amazon, and several other tech companies. This meant, of course, that they had more money than they could ever spend in a lifetime. Not that that was saying much for Alan; virtually every dime he spent was a business expense anyway. He had never even owned his own car because he had never taken the time to learn to drive. Instead, he chose to use a car service to get him around. His wife Clara had purchased a handful of cars during their marriage, but she had been gone for more than fifteen years now.

Alan had always known how little his wife Clara had expected of him during their marriage. This was especially true during the eighteen months that Jake was in and out of the hospital, which also happened to coincide with when Clara had been pregnant with and given birth to Ivy. Alan never could understand why so many people at the law firm—junior partners, secretaries, paralegals, assistants and others—could need so many days off. The reasons the employees gave for the time off were always the same, too—weddings, honeymoons, births, birthday parties, school plays, family vacations, or funerals. Alan couldn't remember Clara *ever* asking or even expecting him to help in any way with either of their two children, and had certainly never expected him to be at a birthday party or participate in family vacations.

There had only been one time that Clara had asked Alan to take time off work and that was when she asked him to come with her to pick out a new car. Alan remembered being rather baffled at this request but the next day, she picked him up from his office and together they drove to a car dealership. Alan knew virtually nothing about automobiles but did his best to show interest in the fact that Clara wanted a certain color, leather interior, and a sunroof. After Clara had made her decision to buy a white SUV that was on the lot, she told Alan that the paperwork would take several hours, and she drove him back to his office. Alan recalled how, as he opened the passenger side door, Clara had grabbed his hand and, looking him in the eyes, told him how much she appreciated him taking the time out of his day for her. He never thought to ask why Clara had asked him to go with her that day.

Alan recalled how after Clara's death, the SUV had sat parked in the Omni parking garage for over two years. Because it was clearly not being used, it was considered a fire hazard and the building management contacted his secretary, Cathy, several times, requesting that the car be moved. Each time, Cathy had passed the request to Alan, but he never responded. One day, Cathy took it upon herself to go to the apartment and try to find the keys. She found them still hanging in the kitchen where she imagined Clara had hung them the last time she came home, two years earlier. With the keys in hand, Cathy went down to the parking garage. She planned to drive the SUV to the dealership. What she hadn't considered was that after so long sitting in the parking garage, the car now had several inches of soot and brake dust covering the windshield, as well as a dead battery.

Cathy called the dealership and explained the situation to the manager, who instructed her to simply leave the keys at the front desk in the lobby of the Omni; he would send one of his mechanics to get it started and have it towed back to the dealership. After that, he would give the SUV a thorough inspection and before the end of the week, call to let her know what the dealership would be willing to pay for the truck.

After Cathy hung up, she walked into Alan's office a bit nervously and brought him up to speed on the events of the morning. He sat silently for a time, which made Cathy think that perhaps he was upset with her for what she had done, without his permission.

Alan had taken a deep breath.

"Cathy, I read the requests from Omni management that you forwarded to me with regards to the Clara's car." He paused. "I suppose I never got around to making a decision about what to do with it. I appreciate you taking care of it. The dealership can pick it up and have it inspected, but there's no need to sell it. If you're interested, I'd like you to have it."

In all the years she had been working for Alan, this was the first time that Cathy had seen him show any sign of human feelings and she was honored by his act of kindness. It wasn't so much the value of the truck; Cathy was, after all, one of the higher paid personal assistants in the entire country, and she could certainly afford to buy a car on her own. It was the fact that Alan would want her to drive Clara's car, and Cathy knew that it meant something to him.

Sitting in his office this morning, Alan remembered how Cathy had simply thanked him for the car; she knew him well enough to know for sure that he wouldn't want an unduly emotional moment. Then, something occurred to Alan. His daughter would most likely want to get her license, and may even need a car the following year when she turned seventeen. Perhaps he too would take driving lessons, he thought, together with Ivy, so that he could drive too. Alan flashed a look of puzzlement that such a ridiculous thought had entered his mind and returned his attention to the file on his desk.

– 27 –

It was time for Dennis to leave the safety and protection of the rehab facility and go back to the real world. He had been there for ninety days and naturally, he was worried that it would be difficult to stay sober with the many temptations around every corner out in "the real world." He planned to attend support meetings three or four nights a week, and he had Lisa to lean on for support as well. Lisa knew that she too would need the support from her new love, and decided to leave the program early to allow him to move into her apartment. They both agreed it was best if they started their new sober lives together.

From the day they left the facility, Lisa and Dennis were both completely focused on creating a healthy and productive life together. Dennis was welcomed back with open arms to his union job and with his new sobriety, he was more responsible and productive than ever before. Management took notice, and he was offered a foreman position. His new job didn't pay much more, but gave him a sense of pride and felt like a step in the right direction. He also signed up for the classes he needed to finish his mechanical engineering degree, and was excited to receive his diploma in the spring.

Lisa also marveled at the way her boss and co-workers welcomed her back and how supportive they were upon hearing of her struggles with depression and addiction. For the first time in her life, she found comfort in talking honestly and openly about her past. Not just her past dealings with depression and addictions, but her experience as a cancer survivor and living with an artificial leg. She began meeting co-workers for coffee after work, and created connections she never thought possible. She was fascinated to learn how many of her co-workers were also taking prescription medication for anxiety and depression.

The relationship between Lisa and Dennis blossomed. They attended support meetings together, and agreed that the meetings were a crucial part of their newfound sobriety. They found solace in nature and the outdoors. They bought new mountain bikes and nearly every weekend loaded them in the back of Dennis's old pickup truck to find a new destination to explore. Riding the trails of New Hampshire, Vermont, and western Massachusetts, Lisa was especially proud of how much physically stronger she had become. Dennis and Lisa agreed that these were the happiest days of their lives.

The two also found a new hobby in cooking healthy and elaborate meals together. They chose and printed recipes from the internet, usually from one of the many cooking shows they enjoyed watching together. The couple would explore the many organic farmer's markets throughout Boston, searching for fresh ingredients. They tried their best to reproduce the meals. The journey of finding all the ingredients and preparing and cooking the food became as enjoyable as actually sitting down to eat the meal. The couple became coffee and espresso aficionados and traveled to many different family-owned coffee micro-breweries in New England, to try and find the best possible coffee or espresso to drink throughout the day.

But perhaps the most exciting hobby they shared happened in the bedroom. Dennis was an experienced lover, and was well aware that Lisa was not. It was a slow and beautiful process for them both to have new experiences together. For the first time in either of their lives, they were both living in the moment and it felt wonderful.

But one evening, Dennis didn't come home after work, nor did he call or respond to any of Lisa's texts. Of course, Lisa wanted to believe that Dennis was simply running late at work and perhaps his cell phone had run out of batteries. Finally, at 9:30 p.m. the phone rang.

"Lisa, it's me. There's no need to worry, I'm fine," said a voice that Lisa did not recognize at first.

Standing in the kitchen, Lisa got goosebumps. Dennis went on.

"I got pulled over by some young rookie fucking cop on a power trip, and when he ran my name there was some bullshit warrant out for my arrest. It was all bullshit, but this *pig* couldn't wait to bust my balls and cuff me and throw me in the back of his squad car. That son of a bitch better hope I never run in to him when he's off duty. It would be a lot different if he wasn't hiding behind that badge and gun."

Lisa heard someone agreeing and laughing in the background.

"So, when I got to the station and talked to the captain on duty," Dennis continued, "we got it all sorted out. Turns out it was just an error in the system and somehow the original warrant from before I did my time in rehab never got officially cleared in the system. It's all set now and I'll be home in an hour or two. That *pig* had my truck towed and the lot that it's sitting in is already closed. I ran into a buddy of mine down here at the station and he'll give me a lift home. Just don't wait up, I'll be home later." Before Lisa could respond, Dennis hung up the phone.

– 28 –

After volleyball practice, Ivy took a short shower and jogged out to the black town car in the school parking lot waiting to bring her back to the Omni. She wanted to get back to the apartment as quickly as possible to check on Sophie. As the car pulled up to the Omni's front entrance, Ivy grabbed her bags and walked as fast as she could to the elevator. Just as she was getting in she heard her phone buzz. Mr. Bugs had sent her a text message.

Ivy,

I let Sophie into the apartment and left her bag inside the door. She seemed to be doing fine. Let me know if there is anything else I can help with.

My wife and I can't make it to your game tomorrow in New Hampshire, but good luck and have fun!

Bugs

Ivy smiled. She was relieved that Sophie was okay and was touched by the fact that Mr. Bugs would even think to drive more than an hour to New Hampshire just to watch one of her games. When the elevator doors opened, Ivy rushed to unlock the door to check in on her best friend. Unsurprisingly, she found Sophie was fast asleep in her room. Gently, Ivy sat down on the bed and lovingly placed the back of her hand on her friend's forehead to check for a fever. The gesture woke Sophie, and she slowly opened her eyes.

"It's done, Ivy, I won't be a mother just yet!"

"It *is* a bit too soon to be pushing a baby carriage around at this point in our lives. You would look awfully funny handing off a newborn baby to Coach Purry every time you went in to play," Ivy said, hoping it wasn't too soon to make light of the situation.

"You want to talk or rest?" she added.

"I slept the entire car ride back and for the last hour here. I am all sleeped out," Sophie answered, in little more than a whisper.

"What was it like? Did it hurt, Soph?" Ivy asked her friend.

Sophie sat up a little and spoke in a monotone. "Well, we walked into this medical office and two nurses took me right into a private room. Mr. Bugs was in the waiting room the entire time. The nurses took all my vitals to make sure I could survive the procedure, I guess. One of them went over a million options for painkillers or local anesthesia and gave me a pill to help calm me down a bit."

Sophie paused at the memory. Ivy touched her hand.

"One of the nurses laid a heating pad over my belly," Sophie continued, "just before the doctor came in to start the procedure. It didn't really hurt that bad, just kind of like bad cramps and weird pressure. Then I went into another room to rest, and that was pretty much it."

There was a long silence, then Sophie began to cry.

Ivy knew that nothing she could say would make Sophie feel better, so she just held her best friend in her arms while rubbing her back the way she imagined her mother had when Jake was in the hospital.

Ivy's emotionally exhausted best friend quickly fell back asleep. Just then, Ivy heard her phone buzz from the other room, announcing another text message. Carefully, she slid her arm out from under Sophie's head then pulled the blankets up to her chin, and tucked her in. After looking down at her friend with concern, Ivy quietly closed her bedroom door behind her and walked to the kitchen to check her phone. The message was from a number that Ivy didn't recognize, and her heart began to pound. Maybe it was from Stevie!

Hey Ivy,

I have spent the last hour of my life reading the rules of chess. I figured I could surprise you if it ever happened that we actually tried to play. Let me just say that chess may be the most bizarre game ever invented by man! The pawns, rook, castle, king, and queen I'm okay with. But then you have this horse dude that randomly moves in an "L" shape...REALLY!

Anyway, I just got invited to work out with the Red Sox triple A team in Pawtucket, Rhode Island. We leave in about an hour to have dinner in Providence with a few of the coaches. We'll stay both tonight and tomorrow night in a hotel somewhere in that area and are hoping to be back here in Boston sometime early Sunday evening.

If you have time and if you still want to, maybe we can try and make plans for Sunday night.

It was really nice speaking with you today.

Stevie

Ivy had heard the saying, "walking on clouds" before but had never really understood the meaning until she read his message. It suddenly seemed to her that the entire day was like something that only happened in the movies. For the entire last two years, every time Ivy caught a glimpse of Stevie in the hallway or anywhere on the high school campus for that matter, she imagined speaking with him and flipping her hair like the hairdresser in a Reese Witherspoon movie that she had seen several times. But this was no movie, this was the real thing, and it was so much better than she could have ever imagined! Ivy wanted to wake Sophie and tell her all about the conversation with and the message from Stevie, but knowing that her friend needed rest, instead, Ivy slid open a drawer, grabbed Jake's journal, and sat down on the couch to spend a few minutes with her big brother.

– 29 –

Hey Ives,

I seem to think so much about God and religion and how it all fits into the world and my life. Everybody is always telling me or writing me that they are praying for me or that I am in their prayers. Don't get me wrong, Ives, I appreciate when people say, but instead of simply being thankful, I cannot help but wonder what value there is or what it even means to be in someone's prayers.

I have reasoned out that God exists, as it seems fairly logical that there is something bigger than what we can comprehend. The question that I keep coming back to is why would a God that is all-knowing, all-powerful, and perfectly good, allow for all the evils in this world? Why would God create cancer and then give it to a child and let them suffer and die? It seems illogical. So here is what I have reasoned out, Ives.

As with any and all religions, it is to be accepted on blind faith that God is perfectly good, which means God didn't actually create all that is good in this world, he ***IS*** *all that is good in this world. All the beauty and happiness that we know* ***IS*** *God. God actually* ***IS*** *perfectly good. Now here is where it gets strange for me. If we agree that God* ***IS*** *all that is good, then it would stand to reason that he must have* *actually chosen to create all that is bad, pain, hurt, evil, in order for all of us to be able to experience him, the good, to its fullest potential.*

Even more fascinating and difficult for me to get my head around is the fact that as a result of having cancer and experiencing all the pain and suffering I have had to endure over the last sixteen months, I now have a better appreciation and understanding of all the good I have in my life. The time I spend with Mama, Lisa, the nurses, you, or even alone, I now appreciate those precious moments more than I ever did before. Even my sick and battered body I look at differently, and I have a greater appreciation for, as a result of the cancer that is killing me. As a result of God creating evil, it has given me a better understanding and appreciation for the good that God is.

Okay, so now there is smoke billowing out of my ears. Bottom line is this, I don't blame or hate God for me getting sick. Instead, I try and thank him for giving me all that I have. That being said, my mind sometimes disagrees. I know that because these lyrics appeared to me last week. I myself am not even sure of the meaning of some of them, but this is how they showed themselves.

I haven't yet put these lyrics into song, so I guess for now it is just a poem.

Why Me

Sometimes I think, such rotten luck to have won this lottery,

So many souls to choose from in this big world but you had to pick me
Was this even by choice or was this all part of some destiny?
Why Oh, Why Oh, Why, did you pick me?

I tried to run I tried to hide but didn't get nowhere

It seemed the harder I try the more I felt the loneliness and despair
Will I find peace of mind or will I ever have a heart that feels free
Why Oh, Why Oh, Why, did you pick me

May I be paroled early, by your faithless jury's Judging and piercing eyes?
Or will you commit perjury, while your sacred clergy's Truth becomes your lies?

I always played it safe, never expecting much to come to me

Watched others reach for the stars while I sat home and watched the stars on TV
Does this path lead to nowhere, do you even know where my dark path will lead?
Why Oh, Why Oh, Why, did you pick me?

As always, Ivy read Jake's words several times to make sure she didn't miss a single thing. Though she had not spent much time thinking about God and his existence, she felt like she could comprehend the essence of what Jake was explaining. Regardless, it all was quite overwhelming to try and take in. Ivy decided she would need some time to let Jake's words sink in a bit.

As she always did after spending time with the journal, Ivy wished that Jake was with her to discuss the things he wrote about, not to mention the excitement that she was feeling about Stevie, or her feelings of betrayal that her very best friend in the world wasn't being honest with her. Ivy so badly wanted Jake and her mother to be able to come to her volleyball game tomorrow to cheer her on. Those thoughts were not new to Ivy, but she couldn't help but feel sad.

– 30 –

Over the past five years since Mr. C. had last seen a doctor, he had needed antibiotics several times due to chest colds and recurring skin infections. The skin infections were a result of what he had diagnosed as a sort of bedsore that he often got on and around his tailbone. He had had no trouble researching the correct medicine for those issues and then simply ordered it from the internet. However, a particular chest cold had made its way deep into his chest and lungs. Though he had taken seven days of the strongest antibiotics he could find on the internet, he was having trouble catching his breath after even the slightest movement of any kind. Mr. C. had not gone into work on Wednesday, Thursday, or Friday. By late Friday evening, he was more and more concerned about how shallow his breathing was. He told himself that if the antibiotics didn't start to kick in by the morning, he would drive himself to the emergency room in the neighboring town.

Mr. C. downed half a bottle of Nyquil, and, because lying down made it almost impossible for him to breathe, tried his best to sleep while sitting up in his father's old La-Z-Boy reclining chair, next to his computer desk. By 8:30 p.m., he knew that he had made a mistake by not going to the emergency room earlier in the day. There was no chance to sleep; he had been coughing nonstop. He felt extremely dizzy, as if he was not getting enough oxygen. He panicked and called 911. He gave the emergency operator his address and pleaded with her to send an ambulance as soon as possible. Within minutes, he heard the sirens of the approaching ambulance followed by a knock on the door. Without thinking, Mr. C. attempted to get up to unlock the front door, but he made it only one step before he lost consciousness and all 500-plus pounds of his massive body fell forward. His momentum propelled him forward like a cruise ship in the harbor, the bulk of his torso landing on his computer desk, causing it to flip over. The desk, along with the two 42" flat-screen TV monitors, ended up on top of Mr. C.'s limp body.

The frantic paramedic had checked the doors and windows and found them all locked. Fire trucks arrived and three firemen joined the paramedics in the rescue effort. One of them used the back of an ax to break the small glass pane above the doorknob of a side garage door, and cleared the remaining glass away with his glove. He reached in to unlock the door. The door swung open and the firemen entered the house with the paramedics following behind, carrying cases filled with medical supplies and equipment. They spread out to search for the man who had made the 911 call.

First year firefighter James Willbarger, nicknamed Rook, walked into the last bedroom down the hall and was the first to see Mr. C.'s body lying on the floor. The lights were off, so he flipped the light switch and saw just the lower half of Mr. C.'s torso sticking out from under the desk and monitors. At first glance, Rook wasn't sure what it was he was looking at; under the desk and computer monitors was something that resembled human feet and legs, but none quite like he had ever seen before. Rook was startled when Mr. C's leg moved.

"The last bedroom down the hall, I found something!" Rook shouted.

He knew he should be pulling the desk and monitors off the body, but instead he stood in shock waiting for the others to come and take over for him.

The firemen came running into the room, only to see the rookie fireman standing and staring. The more senior of the two took immediately action.

"What the hell are you waiting for, Rook?" asked the senior fireman.

Before Rook had a chance to respond, the paramedics arrived with their equipment, saw Mr. C's gargantuan feet, legs, and thighs, and gasped at the sight. All five men stood in awe of what they were seeing.

Finally, the senior firefighter barked out his commands in a sharp staccato. "Guys! Let's carefully get the desk off the body and let the paramedics do their jobs!"

As gently as possible, the men moved the video monitors that were lying on Mr. C.'s torso, and picked up the desk that had fallen directly on the middle of his back, pinning him under it. After the desk was picked up and moved out of the way, the paramedics looked at each other and with that glance, and without words, communicated to each other *just when we thought we had seen it all!* By that time, Mr. C. had begun to regain consciousness, but he still had a very difficult time breathing deeply enough to give his brain and his oversized heart the proper amount of oxygen it needed to function. One of the paramedics attempted to take Mr. C.'s blood pressure, but, frustrated, realized that the arm cuff he had wouldn't fit around the man's wrist, let alone his upper arm.

"We're going to do everything we can to get you feeling better." said the paramedic.

The men all exchanged glances again. The question that everyone was thinking but not saying was, *how on earth would they get this man out of this house and transport him to the hospital?*

– 31 –

Sitting in the front passenger seat of his friend's VW camper bus, Dennis grabbed the tape lying on the dashboard and popped it into the tape deck. Soundgarden was the music that he had listened to when he first began using heroin. Chris Cornell's lyrics had always struck a chord with him, and often it seemed to Dennis that the lead singer understood him better than anyone else in the world. He had never told anyone, but he sometimes believed the lead singer was speaking directly to him.

The front seats in the VW swiveled around and Dennis was facing the back of the van, in which sat a very attractive but very young girl, who, it seemed to him, couldn't have been more than in her early teens. She was lightly slapping her forearm, looking for a good vein. Next to the girl sat the owner of the van, who was cooking up a hit of heroin for her. Dennis already felt the incredibly peaceful and calming feeling that only his drug could deliver, and he couldn't stop smiling. All the worry, fear, pain, stress, and shame that had been stalking him since entering the rehab facility over six months ago were simply washed away. He didn't have to worry about Lisa, or work, or finishing his degree, or those ridiculous meetings where everybody was fooling themselves about how much happier they all were without drugs in their lives. How could he have been lying to himself all that time? Dennis knew in his heart that only heroin could bring him real happiness.

He closed his eyes and focused on the sounds of his friend cooking the next hit, more aware than ever before how peaceful the ritual of using heroin was to him. He loved the sounds and smells of the process. The smell reminded him of the incense from the Catholic church he was forced to attend every Sunday, during the darkest times of his life. When for nearly twelve months, after his mother had been arrested for drunk driving and possession of cocaine, Dennis had lived with a foster family. The couple who took him into their home were well respected, attended church every weekend, and were revered by the community for opening their home and taking in troubled teens. But what the community didn't know was that in the evenings, the father would join the boys in bed and force them to perform unmentionable acts on him and one another. One day, Dennis built up the courage to tell the priest from the church what the foster father had been doing to him and the other boys at home, and begged the priest to contact the authorities. That evening, he was sure that at any moment, the police would storm into the home to rescue them from evil. He waited, but no help came. Instead, later that night, the priest came to the home and joined the foster father in the sick and humiliating acts. It was not long after that evening that Dennis began experimenting with drugs and alcohol. Within just a few months, he had found the answer to all his troubles, his one and only true love—heroin. Now, after a six-month separation, they were reunited, and Dennis once again felt like he had the answers to all his problems.

When Dennis woke up the next morning and realized what he had done, he didn't cry; he was too numb for that. But he felt an overwhelming emotional pain and deep shame. He felt the emptiness stalking him once again. Just as Dennis had forgotten how peaceful the high from heroin was, so too had he forgotten how much it hurt to come down. Dennis knew he had to go back to the apartment and face Lisa. He could try and pretend, but there was no way of hiding what he had done and how hard it would be to face the disappointment on her face. He also knew that if he was high, it would make that conversation much easier.

Dennis began to wonder if it was all worth it. Maybe it was time to just end it once and for all. One of his heroes, Kurt Cobain, had used a shot-gun, but that struck him as too messy. Hanging always seemed clean and quick, but he would never want to be found hanging from a belt or rope. He knew that his buddy had a handgun hidden just behind his front seat, and thought about grabbing it, going outside into the woods, and with just a pull of the trigger, just one shot to the head, ending it. But in the end, Dennis realized suicide was not an option, because that would mean leaving behind his heroin, the one thing that had always been there for him. It was the one and only thing in Dennis's life that had never disappointed him, and he wouldn't do that to his drug. Instead, he decided to get high one more time and later in the morning, deal with everything else.

– 32 –

As Ivy checked in on Sophie, she thought that if her friend was awake, she'd ask if she wanted to go downstairs to the restaurant. Quietly, Ivy opened the door to her bedroom and was surprised by what she saw. Sophie was standing at the window, talking on her cell phone. When she noticed Ivy, she hung up quickly. Ivy frowned.

"Sophie, what's going on? Whatever it is, why would you keep it from me? We have never, ever kept secrets from each other. Let me help, please!" Ivy did everything in her power not to show any sign of the anger and disappointment she was feeling inside.

Sophie stood perfectly still and continued to stare out the window. Finally, she spoke.

"I will tell you when I can, Ivy. I am so, so sorry, but I just can't right now, okay?" Sophie turned toward her best friend, tearfully. "I'm so, so, sorry!" Once again, she began to cry.

Ivy pulled her best friend to her and held her, knowing that was all she could do in that moment. It was clear to her now that Sophie wanted and likely needed to tell whatever secret she was keeping, but for some reason couldn't. Knowing this somehow changed everything for Ivy. She knew that Sophie must have her reasons and that one day, she would share them with her.

"Sophie, any chance you're hungry?" asked Ivy. "I thought maybe we could go down and have an early dinner at the restaurant downstairs."

"I haven't eaten anything all day so yes, I'm starving!" said Sophie, with the first bit of enthusiasm in her voice that Ivy had heard that day.

It was still quite early and the dinner rush had not started, so the girls were virtually alone in the beautiful, modern restaurant which had been redone just a year earlier. Nobody on staff had yet realized whose daughter Ivy was, but when they did, she would be treated awkwardly and differently, and she desperately wanted to take advantage of her time with Sophie.

Ivy was reminded of an article she had recently read in a magazine, about the fact that humans are the only species on the earth that have an awareness of the concept of time and consequently are constantly aware of the date, the day, month, and year. As a result of this awareness, humans fear their time running out and are the only living species that fears death. Ivy had been trying her best not to focus too much energy on the future nor dwell on the past. She did all that was in her power not to worry about what would come tomorrow or next month or next year. Of course, there were times when Ivy knew that she must think and plan for the future, such as when it involved which college she would attend and what she would study to have the career that she dreamed of. But she did her best to not use any more energy on the planning of these types of things than absolutely necessary. Instead, Ivy began focusing more on the moment she was in, here and now. Right now, she and her best friend Sophie were seated by the window, in one of the lavish restaurants at the Omni, waiting for their food.

Ivy smiled to herself as she remembered the hug Stevie Smith had given her at school. Sophie noticed and grinned.

"What's going on in that head of yours, Ivy? Something, or was it someone, you are thinking about just made you smile."

"Oh, yeah, I guess I was just remembering how..." Ivy's voice was deliberately nonchalant, "...Stevie Smith stopped to talk to me after school today and asked me on a date!"

The waiter arrived with two plates laden with a delicious dinner. Seeing the bubbling excitement between the two young ladies, the waiter grinned as he walked away.

"What?! Stevie Smith asked you on a date?" said Sophie.

Eagerly, Ivy replayed every detail of her conversation with Stevie and showed Sophie the text message that he had sent her earlier in the evening. Ivy was so happy to have the Sophie who had been her best friend for the last sixteen years back. Sophie had been acting so distant for the past few weeks and now both realized how much they had missed each other's company. They spent the next several hours talking about Stevie, volleyball, college, and their futures.

"Should we even attempt to order dessert?" asked Ivy.

"Oh god no, Ivy, I cannot eat one more bite!" Sophie said as she held her stomach and slid down the chair as if she had fainted. They had enjoyed their time together so much that both had almost forgotten what Sophie had gone through earlier in the day.

"Okay, Sophie," Ivy said. "But be honest. How is your body feeling? Do you have any pain at all?"

Sophie told Ivy that she was feeling much better than she had expected after the procedure. She said that she had read online that some women experience more pain and cramping than others, and she was relieved that she had virtually no discomfort. "I feel really good, considering," answered Sophie.

"Okay, then let's go back upstairs, I want to show you the journal Jake left me and you can listen to the songs he wrote and recorded, they are amazing!" said Ivy.

They went back up to the apartment and while Sophie was reading through Jake's journal, Ivy wrote a text message back to Stevie.

Hey Stevie,

It sounds pretty exciting to get to play with a professional baseball team like the Pawtucket Red Sox. I gather from a few comments you made that you're feeling pressure and expectations from your father and everyone else involved in your sport. In the end it's you that's making it happen and you should be proud of yourself!

I'm available all evening Sunday, so when you find out when you expect to be back in town, let me know. You're welcome to visit here at the apartment where I live. I just checked and saw the Boston Red Sox are playing Sunday night, so maybe we order food up here to the apartment while watching the game.

I can't wait to spend time with you, Stevie!

Ivy

– 33 –

Over the years, Alan and Harry had fought legal battles against some of the best and brightest legal minds in the world. Alan knew that everyone reacted differently to important moments in their lives, and it fascinated him to notice the way that, before a big case, some lawyers were nervous, others boisterous and loud, while still others got more focused and intense as the time came to walk into the courtroom. After all the years of studying how people responded to big moments in life, it seemed to Alan that people were simply either born with the instinct of a fighter or not.

Today, Alan, his partner Harry, and Cathy were sitting on one side of a long, modern conference room table, across from a man they hadn't seen eye-to-eye for more than twenty years. Cavanaugh Law was one of the largest and most successful law firms in Washington, D.C., and James Cavanaugh was a bulldog and a legend in the world of law. Now in his late 70s, if anything, James had become better and sharper with age.

This was the first meeting of a case that Alan had been preparing exclusively for, for the past three months. Harry was quite focused and had already fired multiple questions to each of the three partners of the law firm representing their client, who was running a few minutes late.

Alan had been watching his partner take control of rooms such as this for as long as he could remember; Harry had a way of creating conflict through conversation and throwing people off their game by pushing them out of their comfort zones. By simply observing their reactions, Harry gathered important bits of information and was able to almost instantly gauge their strengths and weaknesses. He had been doing it for so long, he wasn't even aware he was doing it. Alan fully enjoyed watching the show unfold in situations just like this.

Harry was just warming up. He gestured at the impressive, gleaming conference room table. "Who chose this table? Was it one of the partners or did you bring in an interior decorator to set this conference room up the way you have it? There does seem to be a certain feng shui here in the office. Perhaps it was an Asian firm you used."

The Cavanaugh partners looked at the table, then each other, slightly confused. But Harry wasn't done. "Now I *want* to say this could be some sort of Brazilian rosewood, but that wouldn't make sense because anything crafted with Brazilian rosewood is highly illegal." Harry turned to a disgruntled looking James Cavanaugh.

"Jimmy, what do you think, could this possibly be Brazilian wood?"

James hesitated slightly before he replied, acid dripping from his voice. "Harry, I'll be honest with you, I haven't the faintest idea of what wood this table is made of, nor do I care. We're not here today to discuss the manufacturing materials of furniture."

Harry turned his attention to Cathy. "Cathy, do you think this table would fit in our main conference room? Do me a favor before we leave today, make sure you ask the receptionist where they bought this table and see if you can take some length and width measurements of the table as well as the room." Without missing a beat, Harry turned to the youngest lawyer in the room and asked, "Son, do you think you have a measuring tape here in the office?"

The perplexed young lawyer looked at James Cavanaugh for help and after what seemed like an eternity, replied, "I know where you can buy a tape measure."

"Well, of *course* you know where you buy a measuring tape, but that wasn't what I was asking," answered Harry. He turned back to James Cavanaugh. "Jimmy, how do you expect this young man to represent your company in these complex legal matters? He can't answer a simple question about a measuring tape, for Christ's sake!"

At that moment, to the great relief of the young lawyer, the doors opened and the receptionist ushered Cavanaugh's clients into the tense room.

Alan smiled surreptitiously at his partner. *It's showtime*, he thought to himself, and suddenly it seemed that the back pain that had been plaguing him for weeks had disappeared.

– 34 –

It is often in moments of crisis that we face the truth of who we really are and reflect honestly about our lives. On the floor, surrounded by medics and firemen, with an oxygen mask over his nose and mouth, struggling to catch his breath, this, it seemed, was Mr. C.'s moment to realize that his life was completely out of control.

Although he had never been one to go out partying every weekend, up until five years ago, he always had a group of friends with whom he had participated in activities like going to the movies, celebrating birthday parties, and going to gaming gatherings. Of course, up until five years ago, his true best friend had always been his mother. Since the day she had died unexpectedly, Mr. C. now realized, from his prone position on the floor, he had shut everyone out of his life and had been hiding in a world of junk food, online gaming, and little else.

A voice interrupted Mr. C.'s train of thought.

"Sir, we are making arrangements to transport you to the hospital. Is there anyone you would like us to contact?" One of the paramedics looked at Mr. C. with kind concern. "Any friends, family, or loved ones we should get in touch with?" he added.

Mr. C. realized, at that moment, that no one would care if he lived or died. He thought, perhaps he could tell the paramedics to get in touch with his sisters, but they were both a six-hour flight away and he hadn't spoken with either of them in years. For a moment, he really began to question if he even wanted to live anymore. Shaking his head, he closed his eyes and wondered if there was a way for him to just fade away. It would be best, it seemed to him, if he could just simply let go and perhaps meet up with his mother and father in a better place than this one. But even with these thoughts going on inside his head, and with the paramedics all staring at him, his waterlogged lungs kept drawing enough oxygen to keep his swollen and overworked heart pumping blood to his body. All the while, more and more emergency workers were arriving at his residence to try and make sense of how to get him out of the house and then transported to the hospital.

The younger of the paramedics kneeled down, close to Mr. C's ear, and spoke softly. "Sir, if we get you in a specially sized wheelchair, do you think you could walk a few steps through the doorway? Otherwise, the firemen are preparing to cut the frame of the doorway to try to carry you out."

The reality of the humiliating situation crashed down on him once more. He reached to slide his oxygen mask aside in order to speak. "Yes, if you help me get up, I am sure I will be able to walk a few steps."

The paramedic nodded encouragingly. "Then let's make it happen." Mr. C. nodded back, touched by the young man's friendly manner.

"Okay, I will let the guys know before they start doing major renovations to your home. One thing I know about firemen, if you give them any opportunity to use their toys, they will. In fact, they would like nothing better than to saw half your house down just to have a story to tell," said the young paramedic. "Sit tight and we will try and get a hold of an oversized wheelchair from one of the hospitals."

Mr. C. turned his head in embarrassment and shame at the thought of being the source of the firemen's talk and laughter. At least the young man who had helped him had been nice enough not to laugh in his face.

Within fifteen minutes, the wheelchair was delivered to the house. With the help of two paramedics, three firemen, and two police officers, Mr. C. was slowly raised off the ground and placed in the wheelchair. Slowly and methodically, he was rolled to the doorway of the bedroom, helped to his feet, and, amazingly, able to take the four steps out to the hallway. The medics folded the special, oversized wheelchair to move it through the doorway after him and once again assisted him to sit back down. The same procedure was repeated to get Mr. C. through the front door and finally out of the house.

The next challenge was how to get him into the ambulance. He was simply too heavy to lie on a gurney and be carried by medics as they normally would. Again, the young paramedic asked Mr. C. if he thought he had enough strength to climb the three steps to get into the ambulance. He agreed to try, and with all six of the men helping, he slowly, carefully, one step at a time, climbed up into the ambulance and sat down on the gurney. Nearly two hours after having arrived, the paramedics had their patient in the ambulance. With lights and sirens blaring, Mr. C. was finally en route to the hospital.

By now, Mr. C.'s blood pressure was dangerously low and he was burning up with a fever of 102 degrees. His eyes were closed in a semi-conscious, dreaming state, far away from all that was happening in the real world. In his dream, he was walking along the beautiful white beaches of Southern California, the hot sun beating down on his back and a cool wind against his face. He was handsome and thin, muscular even. Everyone, especially all the women, looked at him with envy. He walked toward some friends who had gathered to play a beach volleyball game. They saw him coming and called him over in hopes that he would want to join. He was, after all, the best player around—the undisputed king of the beach! The men slapped his shoulders and handed him the ball and Mr. C. hit it between both his hands a few times to knock the sand off as best he could. Then he tossed the ball up in the air several times to judge the wind and sun and how it would affect his vision when he served. Finally, he raised the ball up, looked to the other team and saw the nod of their heads to signal that they were ready for the game to begin. He tossed the ball a bit to his left, taking into consideration the strong cross wind blowing that day, took two long steps, and jumped, blasting the ball down the right side, just barely clipping the line, for an ace, and the crowd roared!

"Mr. Connor, Mr. Connor, sir, we are at the hospital and we need to get you out of the ambulance and back into the wheelchair," said the paramedic, hoping he could get his patient's help one last time. "Mr. Connor! Sir, can you hear me?"

Mr. C. frowned. Why wasn't the other team giving the ball back to him for another serve? Why was the sound of the waves suddenly replaced by the sound of a siren? Why was he so cold?

"Sir. Mr. Connor! Listen to my voice. We need your help to get you out of the ambulance. Can you do that for me, Mr. Connor?" asked the paramedic.

Slowly, painfully, Mr. C. realized where he was. Opening his eyes, he nodded at the paramedic, and with the same two paramedics and several orderlies from the emergency room that were called on to assist, he was helped to a sitting position on the floor of the ambulance and lowered one step at a time until they had him safely in the wheelchair.

Moments later, Mr. C. was in an emergency room area where a curtain was pulled around him for privacy. For the next three hours, he was given fluids through an IV; he had become severely dehydrated. He was starting to feel better when he was wheeled into a room equipped with a sturdy bed for morbidly obese patients. The nurses positioned him under a contraption that looked similar to a child's swing set seat. It was, in essence, a small crane to help move patients weighing up to 1,000 pounds, while simultaneously measuring their weight. Once secured in the seat, the crane began to slowly lift him up, out of the wheelchair, and into the bed. One of the nurses picked up a clipboard and began to jot notes.

Mr. C. was quite lucid after having been given the IV fluids and medicine to bring the fever down. Lucid enough to see the display of his weight on the screen. 527 pounds. He didn't want to believe it. He *couldn't* have let himself get to over 500 pounds. As the nurses busied themselves, he turned and stared out the window, totally humiliated. Tears rolled down his cheeks.

Mr. C. closed his eyes and very quickly, sleep overcame him. Off he went back to the service line, this time with the volleyball back in his hands!

– 35 –

Ivy woke up earlier than usual for a Saturday, excited for the volleyball match in New Hampshire later that afternoon. Sophie was still sound sleep and Ivy thought it best to let her rest for as long as possible. Quietly, Ivy closed her bedroom door. Then she got dressed and headed downstairs to eat at the Omni restaurant. She walked out of the elevator and into the restaurant, where the buffet was already fully prepared for hotel guests. Only a handful of those guests were awake this early, so Ivy sat her usual table and a server greeted her with a warm smile.

The server, Sunny, was in her late 30s and a single mother. Like many of the employees of the Omni, Sunny cared very much for Ivy and was always happy to see her.

"Good morning, Ivy, how are you, honey?" Sunny asked in a very motherly and pleasant tone. "You have a game in New Hampshire today, don't you?"

Ivy beamed up at her.

"Good morning, Sunny! Yeah, we have a game this afternoon at twelve-thirty, that's why I'm up so early. I figured I'd start the day with a solid breakfast before the bus leaves at ten." As she often did, Ivy directed the subject away from herself. "How is your son doing since changing high schools? I hope it went better than what he was expecting."

Sunny couldn't help but smile before answering as she thought to herself once more how mature and thoughtful Ivy was for her age.

"Mark was so nervous about the change, but in the end, he is happier at his new high school than he ever was before. Not only did he hit it off with several of the boys from his ninth-grade class, he even met a really sweet girl from the tenth- grade class, and now has his first girlfriend!"

"That's great news!" said Ivy, with a grin.

Sunny nodded. "Yup, all the fighting we did over moving to this side of the city, it was all for nothing! He loves his new school."

"Wow, that must be a weight off your shoulders, Sunny. I am so happy for Mark and for you, too! So how much shorter is the commute in the mornings now? You said it used to take you around forty-five minutes on the train every morning, right?"

"You have a good memory, young lady! Yes, now the commute is down to under twenty minutes or so," said Sunny. "I even joined a gym for the first time since Mark was born and have been getting up early and working out in the mornings before work. It's so nice to focus on me again after all these years of putting Mark first."

"I thought you looked in better shape this morning. Okay, so next step is to find a cute boy for you to fall in love with, right Sunny?" Ivy said in an overly serious tone and wiggling her eyebrows.

They both were laughing when Sunny spotted several guests looking to be seated. "Good luck with your match today, honey," she said, as she headed toward the guests to greet them.

– 36 –

Hey Sis,

So, I was thinking today, that I hope for your sake, that you inherit more of Mama's traits than I did. Mama, as I am sure you are well aware of by now, is the happiest person I have ever known, and pretty much everyone who meets her agrees and tells me so. I know all the nurses and the other patients on the oncology floor all love when I check into the hospital because that means Mama will also be around for the week.

My primary nurse, Amanda, is 24 years old, very pretty, and very cool. Last week, she was telling me how all the nurses were talking and all agreed that, when Mama walks into the room, she brings with her a special energy. It's as if, and I quote, "the shades are opened to let the sunshine in."

Seems I am much more like our father when it comes to the way I interact with the world, so no sunshine for me. I have never had many friends and I certainly have shown none of the athleticism Mama has. The closest thing I get to having ever played a sport is bouncing an old tennis ball off the wall of my bedroom, which I do pretty much every day. I lay on my back, turn the opposite way on my bed and throw the ball against the wall and try to catch it with both my left and right hands. Now if this were only an Olympic event, I could win a gold medal. Maybe you will be a volleyball player, too. Mama doesn't play much anymore because her knees are worn out, but I have gotten to see her play, and she was awesome! It was two years ago when she played in an alumni volleyball game on the Harvard campus. Even with her bad knees, Mama could still hit the ball as hard as any of the other women. I remember how much fun she and her old teammates had on the court. All the other women were so nice, and many told me how much they loved having our mother as a teammate.

Like Dad, I have always been happiest when I am alone and lost in a good book, listening to music, or practicing guitar. I've read hundreds of books, no specific genre really, just anything I come across. In fact, I pretty much love any and all genres except fantasy. I tried reading some fantasy books like The Lord of the Rings *but found that it was just a bit too abstract for my brain to get into! I do of course love all the classics, and even enjoy the writings from modern authors such as John Updike, Tom Clancy, or even John Grisham.*

That being said, I do have, without question, a favorite book of all time and it is called Lonesome Dove *written by Larry McMurtry. It is a monster of a book at over 365,000 words and yet I have read it four times. In case you aren't aware, Lonesome Dove is more than three times longer than the average book! It's not easy to explain why I love the book so much, nor is it easy to really explain what the book is about, but I'll try. It is a fictional story about two men who had spent their lives together fighting in the wars of early America in the 1800s, but who had both long since retired. Captain Call and Captain McCrae, or Call and Gus as they refer to each other, after having spent twenty years fighting Indians and Mexicans bandits, then spend fifteen years hanging around a little town called Lonesome Dove. Call lives to work and nothing else, so of course he reminds me so much of our father. Call also has a son named Newt. Newt is being raised by Call, Gus, and their gang, but Call will not admit to being his father. It's not until near the end of the book when Newt is seventeen, that his father even calls him by his real name, otherwise referring to him as "the boy." Now Gus on the other hand, is the complete opposite of Call, never working unless absolutely necessary and always contemplating the meaning of life. Yet these two men have spent their entire lives together and make up the perfect and seemingly unequaled partnership. I think it's the way in which the two men complement each other that fascinates me, because I am envious of what they have. The relationship between Call and Gus is the most beautiful friendship or partnership possible.*

The book basically follows the men as they decide to put together a group of young boys and men and drive 3,000 head of cattle from Texas to the then unsettled land of Montana. I can imagine you are already rolling your girly eyes, thinking that it's some dumb book about cowboys and Indians, which in some ways it is! But it is also about so much more. All that takes place throughout this trip across the early lands of America, all the different characters that come together by chance or fate, the experiences, the death, the fighting, the adventure, the friendships made, it all seems so real, and at times, too painful to endure. Yet in the end, it is all these amazing experiences that have created the lives that Call and Gus have lived together. The same holds true for all of us, right? Of course, many of the experiences that we have and must endure are painful, but it seems that these are the times that make us who we are and truly define us.

Call and Gus often recall stories from their past. The way they, and the other men that were with them during those times, all remember the names and details of the endless stories they shared together, makes me think that life is not only about having experiences, but sharing them with other humans and then speaking about them to agree that they did indeed happen.

To be honest, other than Mama, I haven't really had anyone to share what few life experiences I have had up until this point in my life. Of course, I am super close with Mama, but I'm guessing it is still quite different to share life with friends than it is with your mom. I fear the monster will take me before I get the chance to drive my 3,000 cattle across the country and experience all that comes with it. I mean that metaphorically as I do not aspire to be a cowboy, but I'm guessing you're following what I am saying!

So that's my explanation as to why the book means so much to me, because it gives me a glimpse into what I imagine it is like to be a real man and living a full life. This may be as close as I can get to experience the adventure of life without actually experiencing it myself... just in case I don't.

I captured and recorded a song this past week. Sometimes these songs and lyrics that show themselves and are quite abstract, but to me, this one explains how scared and disappointed my mind truly is about not getting the chance to experience life. The thing is, without experiencing life, how can I possibly be expected to make sense of facing death at my age? I listened to the recording a few times and was rather startled at how sad and dark it seems to be.

I hope the song doesn't bring you down too much, but these are pretty dark times for me, as I am sure you can imagine!

Ill Prepared is the second song on the CD. Love you, Ives!

Ill Prepared

I'm ill prepared, for this particular hard day's life lesson

I had never feared, the great unknown and what tomorrow brings
I'm finding it hard, to make my way with no sense of direction
Seems to me odd, it wasn't supposed to be this way

I give and I give I give my all and keep on giving
I give and I give but the world takes it all for free
I give and I give can't give no more and keep on living
And now, I've given up on me

I never dared, say what I want or what it is I needed
I always tried to look ahead but I was left behind
But now I've lost, with nothing left I know I've been defeated
But at what cost, when no one really even cares?

– 37 –

Ivy loved everything about the game of volleyball. She was always happiest when she was on the court, completely focused on her game, actively working to keep all other thoughts clear from her mind. She found joy in practicing her passing and hitting technique, both during practice on the court as well as off the court. At home, Ivy would often close her eyes and visualize all the movements that she was working to improve and perfect. As an outside hitter, it was natural to be the most offensive player on the court. Ivy dreamed of getting the perfect set, which for her was right at the antenna, high and tight to the net, so that, when timed correctly, she could hit the ball at its highest point over the block and crush it straight down.

Ivy's appreciation and respect for all aspects of the game was one of the attributes that set her apart from most other talented players. She worked equally hard on her offensive attack as she did her footwork and the technique required to receive a serve perfectly to the setter. She worked tirelessly on her footwork and timing associated with blocking, both her solo blocking, as well as when working with her middle blocker to defend against the opponent's offensive attack. What she was most proud of was her defense and her ability to read and pick up a hard-hit ball when she was in the back row. She had the goal to not only be the best offensive player she could be, which she thought was to be expected, but also be as good a defensive player as the best libero or defensive specialist on the court at all times. Of course, at 6'2", it wasn't easy to have the body control and quickness that a much shorter and smaller defensive specialist has, but Ivy worked hard each and every practice to reach her goal.

Sitting in the bus surrounded by her eleven teammates and two coaches, Ivy realized how much she enjoyed the comradery of the team. She thought about the last journal entry of Jake's that she had read and agreed with her brother completely—the sharing of experiences with others is what makes life special and fun. Ivy's team was like a family, and as with all families, it takes work for everyone to get along. On this year's team, there were happy times and moments of dysfunction and chaos. She would make sure to read the *Lonesome Dove* book that Jake had written so passionately about, and Ivy smiled at the thought that she was the captain of this group of cowgirls that looked to her to bring them together as they began their long cattle drive to Montana. Of course, this was just a metaphor, but Jake would know that.

Ivy had come to embrace the role of team leader. Clearly, she was the best player on the team, and she thought it an honor to be given that responsibility. In the sport of volleyball, perhaps more than any other sport, a team could not function, much less enjoy success, without all six players on the court doing their jobs to the best of their abilities. Ivy was always quick to give the most credit to her teammates with the least amount of natural athleticism, knowing how much harder they had to work in order to do what was asked of them. She was particularly proud of one girl this season, a senior she had watched work harder than anyone to earn a spot as a "starter." Jenny Bradford was very tall, but had been far from fit and was very slow. Coach had given her a spot on the team as a freshman based solely on her height, which at that time was 5'11". He hoped with that height, Jenny could find enough athleticism to become at very least a solid middle blocker. In the last three seasons, she had yet to play in a game, but had never missed a practice, and more impressively, never once complained. Every year, Jenny had improved, working especially hard on her footwork and continuously improving her fitness. During her junior year summer, Jenny had joined a gym and performed a variety of specific exercises, aiming to increase her vertical jump and agility. At least twice a week after practice was officially over, she asked Coach to help her work on her footwork at the net. Jenny was still the least naturally athletic girl on the team. The difference, of course, was she had worked tirelessly to get absolutely all she could out of what little natural talent she had. Ivy had such respect for Jenny and would always help her in any way possible to improve her volleyball skills. Ivy always joined Jenny after those practices when she worked with Coach to work on their timing on the double block.

At the start of the season, when Coach announced that Jenny would be given the starting middle blocker spot, Ivy asked if she wanted to be her partner in the pre-game warm-up routine. The "warming up" was done before each practice and game, when two players threw a ball back and forth and then proceeded to hitting, bumping, and setting with each other. Normally, the two best players partnered for the warm-up routine, but Ivy felt through her hard work and determination, Jenny had earned being her warm-up partner.

Ivy realized that they were similar height and weight and both worked tirelessly to be the best volleyball players they could be. The difference, of course, was that Ivy was given the gift of natural athleticism and Jenny was not. Ivy had learned early in her life that it is an unfair world that we live in. We are all given a life that has its positives and negatives, and that's all we have to work with. Jenny could practice all day and night, but the reality was that she would never be a great athlete. Regardless, Ivy respected Jenny for working as hard as she did, and was proud to watch her squeeze every last bit of athleticism and ability out of what she was given.

Ivy's approach to her role as leader of the team brought a wonderful energy and excitement, and the bus rides to away games was where this feeling shone brightest. Though never the center of attention during these bus rides, Ivy very much enjoyed watching and participating in singing to whatever pop song was popular at the time, or whatever else the other girls would come up with.

As the bus pulled up to the school in New Hampshire, Ivy asked that the music be turned off and for her teammate's attention. She had come to enjoy these mini speeches or pep talks more than she ever imagined, and had even begun to loosely plan what she was going to say. With all eyes on her, while standing in the aisle in the front of the bus, Ivy began her speech.

"Okay girls, the team we're playing may not be strongest team in our league, but as we have experienced in past games, it's often the less talented teams that we have the most difficulty with. This phenomenon is nothing new in sports. It often happens that the better team will play down to the level of their opponents. So today, let's all do our jobs to the very best of our abilities. Let's all stay one-hundred-per-cent focused until the last point of the game. Let's all respect one another by playing as hard and intense in the game as we do every day in practice. Most of all, let's go out there and have fun!" Ivy's intensity and spirit gave everyone listening, including the bus driver, goosebumps. The girls burst out in cheers and exited the bus.

Coach watched in amazement at the level of maturity and emotional intelligence Ivy possessed at such a young age. He was continuously amazed by her as a volleyball player, but even more so as a person.

Less than two hours later, Ivy's team won the match in three straight sets of flawless and focused volleyball.

– 38 –

Since being admitted to the hospital, Mr. C. had undergone extensive testing. It was determined that he was severely dehydrated and suffering from an infection in both lungs. He was treated with fluids, antibiotics, and an inhaler every hour, and finally was showing signs of improvement.

The attending doctor was quickly able to link the death of Mr. C's mother to his dramatic weight gain. The doctor explained that food addiction is as real as alcohol or drug addiction, and referred him to an eating disorder specialist. The doctor assured Mr. C. that, with a combination of psychotherapy and an extreme lifestyle change, he could make a full recovery.

Alone in his hospital room, Mr. C. thought about his mother's sudden death and realized that in the five years she'd been gone, he had never once cried. Had his mother not died on the surgery table, none of this would have ever happened. For the first time, he faced the fact that he was as addicted to food as a heroin addict is to his drug.

– 39 –

It was Saturday morning, and Stevie was standing on the Pawtucket Red Sox field behind the batting cage. He had three bats in his hand and was taking very slow and controlled swings, which was his normal warm-up routine before taking his turn in the batting cage. Standing next to him was John "Moose" Barrett, who looked more like a football player than a baseball player. Now in his second season playing for the Triple A Red Sox organization, the 5'9" and nearly-250-pound catcher was one of those rare breeds of professional athletes who never stopped working to improve his game, and never stopped believing that he would one day play in the big leagues. Over a decade ago, when Moose had graduated high school, although he was a solid catcher and hitter at the high school level, no professional scouts or college coaches took any notice of him. But all he ever wanted to do was play baseball, so he packed a suitcase and headed to Florida, the baseball hub of the world. In Florida, there were several semi-pro leagues where Moose hoped he could find a team that would give him a shot. He worked harder than any coach had ever seen, pushing himself to his physical limits every single practice, day in and day out. It took him over a decade, but now in his second season in Pawtucket, Moose believed more than ever that he would get the call from a major league team, sign a contract, and reach his goal of being a professional baseball player in the major league.

Moose had spent the last eleven years watching kids like Stevie question their decision to give up a college scholarship and chase the dream to play in the major league. The vast majority of these kids ended up disillusioned and with regrets, since no matter how much talent any young player started with, no one was guaranteed success in the game of baseball. Moose had seen so many kids like Stevie, who were big, strong, fast, and powerful, with all the talent and physical tools needed to succeed, all start their journey with tremendous confidence and without any doubt in their minds that they were destined for greatness. The reality, he knew, was that most would fail to realize their dreams. Moose had decided long ago that there was simply no way of making sense of who would and would not have a successful baseball career. Some young men looked as if they had never seen the inside of a gym and lived on nothing more than fast food and beer, yet often they were the ones who had the ability to see and hit a curveball. While Moose worked hard to simply keep his spot on the dozens of Single A and Double AA teams on which he played, he had especially resented these kids. Even with the hundreds of hours he spent watching videos to analyze his swing and even more hours in the batting cage, and with dozens of coaches all giving him different advice and tips, it wasn't until three seasons ago that something clicked, and from one day to the next, Moose was suddenly able to hit the elusive curve ball.

Moose had realized in his mid-twenties that resentment, jealousy, and envy were doing him harm. As he got older, and perhaps wiser, he began taking the younger kids under his wing and to those that would take his advice, began enjoying the role of mentor. He felt it was a start to his back-up plan, that if he didn't make it to the big leagues by the time he turned 30, he would make the transition to coaching, scouting, or some sort of back office job in baseball.

"You have a beautiful swing, kid," Moose said to Stevie. "What are you, 6'4" or 6'5"? It's not easy to keep your swing short with such a long body."

"Yeah, that's been my challenge since I shot up over the years. I think I'm done growing now and I've been working hard to keep my swing compact and try to drive the ball more. But I know driving the ball against high school pitchers or in a cage taking batting practice is a lot different than doing it against guys pitching at this level or in the big leagues!" said Stevie.

Moose already liked him. Stevie's answer showed he was aware that it was not going to be easy to make the transition to professional baseball.

"Did you watch any videos of your swing with Coach and the boys this morning? What did they have to say?" asked Moose.

"Yeah, we were in there for a while this morning. You know, my old man spent a bunch of years in the minors and he built my swing around A-Rod's mechanics. We've been using video for years, constantly trying to tweak my swing. The coaches had some suggestions, mostly based around how to get my legs and hips engaged earlier to try and create more power. The thing is, my dad is really sensitive about making even minor changes. So, until I either head off to college or sign on with a minor league team, I'm guessing he won't allow any changes to be made," Stevie replied, looking away, a bit embarrassed.

"Are you leaning one way or the other as far as playing college ball or turning pro?"

"It's such a tough decision I'm faced with," said Stevie, reflectively. "Both options are a dream come true. Every young athlete in this country dreams of getting a full-ride scholarship to play the sport they love in college. But every Little Leaguer in the country also dreams of signing a professional contract for a shot at the big leagues. It looks like the sign-on bonus I'm going to be offered will be pretty significant and easily cover the cost of a college education. My thinking is that I could turn pro and if things don't pan out, I can always go back to college. Plus, I imagine turning pro immediately would give me the best chance at making it to the big leagues. But I've seen how many guys in the last decade or so that have gone the college route, have had success in the majors after their college careers were over."

Moose nodded in agreement and responded, "Stevie, sounds like you've done a lot of thinking about this decision, and all I can tell you is to listen to yourself and not to the scouts or your teachers or coaches or even your father. There is no right or wrong decision; either way gives you a chance to succeed and follow your dreams. Just follow your heart and everything else will work itself out. Most of all, don't do it for the money. If you think going to college and getting a degree is best for you and your future, do it. I've seen enough to know that a million bucks isn't going to make you happy. I don't profess to know much, but this I know for a fact, money doesn't buy happiness!"

"Stevie!" One of the coaches called Stevie's name. He was up. Quickly, he threw down two of the three bats he had been swinging, and put the other under his left armpit. He adjusted the Velcro straps of both black leather batting gloves and looked up at Moose with a grin. "Thanks, Moose, I really appreciate you speaking with me."

As Moose watched Stevie walk into the cage, he thought to himself how much he loved the sport.

"Swing away, kid!"

– 40 –

Lisa hadn't heard from Dennis since he had phoned her the previous night. Lisa hadn't slept all night, hoping that her worries were for naught, and that at any minute, Dennis would walk in and explain to her that it was all just a misunderstanding and he was still clean. But she knew in her heart that Dennis had started using again and decided that the best thing she could do for herself was go to a meeting. It meant attending the meeting alone for the first time, and also meant admitting to the others that she suspected the love of her life had fallen off the wagon. She also knew the support from those who had gone through the experience before was exactly what she needed. Lisa had been through enough therapy at the rehab facility to know that she would have to work harder than ever to maintain control of her emotions and not give in to the temptation of turning to Xanax as the answer to her problems.

Slowly, Lisa got dressed and decided to ride her bike to the meeting. She realized that not only was this to be the first time attending a meeting without Dennis, it was also going to be the first time she would ride her bike in Boston alone. While unlocking her bike and carrying it out from the space where she and the other tenants of the building stored their bikes, Lisa realized how much physical strength she had gained in the last six months. Before starting her new life with Dennis, she had never even attempted to ride a bike since losing her leg over sixteen years before, let alone pick up and actually carry a bike. It gave Lisa a sense of pride, even in the face of her dream man and dream life crumbling in front of her, knowing that she could now easily bike the five miles to a meeting where she was confident enough to talk about her problems with a group of strangers. All of this was a huge accomplishment for her. Just as she was getting on her bike, she saw Dennis crossing the street and walking towards the apartment.

Lisa thought he looked as if he had aged ten years in just the past few days. Since meeting Lisa in the rehab, Dennis had shaved twice daily, so she he had never seen him with more than a shadow of a beard. But now, after having not shaved nor slept in nearly 36 hours, Dennis was disheveled and had a faraway look in his eyes. He was almost unrecognizable to Lisa and instantly, something deep down in her bones told her that the man she loved and adored was a danger to her, and she should, at all cost, get away from him. But Lisa still felt so much pain and regret that she wasn't able to save her mother and had ultimately abandoned her, leaving her to die alone. She vowed to herself that she would not give up on Dennis.

Slowly, she leaned her bike next to the entrance of the apartment and waited for Dennis to come to her. She was shocked when he walked right past her, without even making eye contact, wordlessly unlocking the front door and going inside. Lisa looked after Dennis for a moment and took a deep, slow, shaky breath. Then, calmly, she brought her bike back to the storage garage, locked it next to where Dennis's bike was standing, and went back up to the apartment. She may have given up on her mother, Lisa thought, but she was determined not to give up on this man. No matter what.

– 41 –

"Hello, Ivy! What are you doing home on a Saturday night? You should be out celebrating the big win with your teammates!"

Ivy's smile lit up her face. "Hey, Stevie!"

She had waited and hoped for his call and now, here he was.

"You think we should be out clubbing with the Euro-hipsters down on Lansdowne Street?" Ivy said, trying to stay calm, despite how excited she was that he'd called her. "To be honest, I was kind of hoping you would call. How did everything go for you today in Rhode Island?"

"Well, the coaches are amazing and most of the players are very cool, but it's stressful to have my dad here with me. He's so sensitive and takes everything so personally."

Ivy listened carefully as Stevie spoke. He continued. "I mean, God forbid these professional coaches give me any suggestions about my swing mechanics or pitching motion. Sometimes I feel like he thinks I'm his Mona Lisa and he is Da Vinci. Hopefully he doesn't cut off his ear…wait, it wasn't Da Vinci who cut his ear off. That was Van Morrison or Van Halen or one of the "Vans," wasn't it?"

Ivy was not sure if Stevie was joking, and not wanting to embarrass him, said, "I think you mean Vincent Van Gogh. I get those painters mixed up, too!"

"Are you sure, Ivy? I could have sworn it was Vinny Van Halen that painted 'The Starry Night,' or my personal favorite 'Wheat Field with Cypresses' in 1889. Damn, baseball players should never make jokes having anything to do with art or history!" Stevie said, laughing.

"Stevie, you're a little shit, do you know that?" Ivy responded, feigning anger, realizing that she had once again fallen for one of Stevie's jokes for the second time in as many days.

"I'm sorry, Ivy, I promise it will never happen again!" Stevie said, still laughing.

"I have a feeling that's a promise you cannot keep!" Ivy laughed. "So you were saying that your father sees you as his work of art?"

"Yeah, he thinks he's built my technique to perfection and it should in no way be tinkered with, discussed, or questioned, much less changed," Stevie said. "The thing is, at this point, I'd like to hear the opinions of other professional coaches and maybe even let them try to make a few changes just to see what the results would be. I get the sense that the coaches would rather my father not be here this weekend so they could speak directly with me, but for now, he is still the boss."

"I guess your dad just wants what's best for you and your future, right?" asked Ivy. "It must be hard for him to let you go."

"Yup, I keep telling myself the same thing. In fact, it seems like I've been telling myself that same thing forever. Yet here I am, all these years later and nothing has changed. Sometimes I even worry what he'll do when I leave home."

Ivy nodded, listening intently, and Stevie continued.

"It feels to me like he's dedicated his entire life to me and my baseball career for as long as I can remember, and it scares me that he'll be completely lost when I'm no longer there to shape, mold, coach, and generally boss around."

Ivy thought how different her life was from Stevie's. Ever since she decided to move into the Omni, she was completely on her own. She had coaches, teachers, Bugs, and the Pham family, all of whom she could look to for support, but the reality was she had been her own boss for more than three years now. All of her life, Ivy had dreamed of having her mother, or even her father to some extent, to come home to. She longed to have a parent in her life to give her advice and love, and to be there by her side as she was making the difficult transition from childhood to adulthood. But in listening to Stevie and the issues he was facing with his father, Ivy realized that everyone has their challenges, and that clearly there was no perfect situation in life.

"I lost my mother when I was a baby," Ivy said. "And my dad has never even seen me play volleyball, so it's hard for me to put myself in your shoes. But in the end, your dad will have no choice but to let you go. For both of your sakes, maybe you could sit down with him and tell him how you really feel. Maybe being honest with him and telling him your fears and your dreams would create a better relationship."

"You're probably right," said Stevie. "I've been thinking along those same lines. But the thing is, it's so hard to talk to him man to man because I get the sense he still sees me as a kid. I may be 6'5" and can throw a 92-mile-per-hour fastball, but when he talks to me, I feel like he still sees a twelve-year-old. Weird, right?"

Ivy smiled with understanding.

"As I said before, it's hard for me to imagine, but I would definitely not call your situation weird."

"The thing is, I see how much my mother loves her work doing research at Boston College. I haven't had the chance to tell you about my mom yet, but she studied at Stanford and MIT here in Boston, so that's where I get my book smarts from, I guess. Not that my dad isn't intelligent, he just never had any interest in school. My mom did her doctoral thesis on the weather and storms in outer space and their effects on satellite communications here on earth. Because her thesis drew attention from the space community, she continued to work in that field and is as passionate about the weather in space as my father is about baseball."

"Wow, that's cool!" said Ivy, truly interested to learn about Stevie's mom.

"I grew up reading all the space books and magazines that were hanging around our house," Stevie continued, "and now I'm really curious about space and physics, too."

There was a long pause. "I really do love the game and I would never say this to my father, but in some ways, I fear having success in baseball.

I have this strange feeling, if I were to have a long career in the major leagues, when my playing days came to an end, I wouldn't be content having only been a professional athlete my entire life."

Once again there was a long pause before Ivy said, "Maybe you can ask your German catcher Gunther to speak with your dad for you? He could shed some light on your complex father-son relationship."

"Oh god, please, anyone but Tony." Stevie laughed, happy to be changing topics.

"So, what are your plans for tonight, Stevie?" asked Ivy.

"There's a game tonight at McCoy Stadium in Pawtucket, so my dad and I will be hanging in the bullpen, which is where all the pitchers warm up if they're needed."

"Sounds fun!" said Ivy.

"What about you, got any hot dates?" asked Stevie.

"Well, there is this one really super-hot guy that I have had a crush on forever, but he's busy tonight. I'm hoping he has time to hang out with me tomorrow night, though. I guess I'll just sit home alone, watch girly movies, and eat a half-gallon of ice cream!" answered Ivy jokingly but in a flirtatious tone.

"Well, I'm sure the guy knows how lucky he is to have the chance to spend time with you, and he will do his best to get back as early as possible," said Stevie.

Ivy blushed furiously.

"Talk to you tomorrow?" she said.

"You bet," said Stevie, who was also grinning, ear to ear. "And Ivy?"

"Yes?"

"Thanks for listening."

– 42 –

To Lisa, it seemed like time had slowed to a crawl since Dennis had leaned over to her side of the bed to kiss her forehead before leaving for work Friday morning. It was as if the last forty-eight hours had brought her into some alternate universe where nothing was as it was supposed to be. Since returning to their apartment the previous afternoon without as much as a hello and without even bothering to take his work boots off, Dennis had lain down on the couch and slept. Lisa kept thinking to herself that she should have gotten on her bike the previous day and gone to the meeting and focused on herself, her own sobriety and emotional health. Instead, she stayed in the apartment, hoping somehow Dennis would wake up and tell her he was going to find a way to make everything right again. She had tried to sleep but every few hours she woke up and checked to see if Dennis was still asleep on the couch, and if he was still breathing. Finally, she got out of bed, got dressed, and made a pot of coffee. As she was pouring her first cup, she heard Dennis get up and walk to the bathroom.

Dennis closed the door behind him and Lisa heard the shower running. She couldn't shake the feeling that Dennis had somehow forgotten she existed. She didn't feel like eating but decided to make a vegetable omelet, thinking that Dennis had most likely not eaten much in the last several days. She set the table, made the omelet and toast, and waited for Dennis to come out of the bathroom. Moments later, when he walked out of the bathroom carrying his work boots in his hands, he looked like a new man. He had showered and shaved and seemed to have normal color back in his face. For a split second, a feeling of hope overcame Lisa. Maybe she had been wrong and Dennis had not started using heroin again. Dennis put his work boots by the door and turned toward her.

"Morning, baby. Unless my nose deceives me, I smell one of your famous vegetable omelets. I don't suppose you happen to have a hot cup of coffee to go with it, do you?"

"Not only do I have coffee for you, but it just happens to be the last of the Ethiopian beans we got from that little roastery in Maine last month," said Lisa, in as normal a tone as she could muster.

Dennis hugged Lisa from behind and kissed her on the side of her neck as if nothing out of the ordinary had happened in the days before.

"Oh, from the place up in Kennebunkport? Did we use all of that already? I love that coffee!" To Lisa, Dennis sounded like he was trying his hardest to sound "normal" while ignoring the fact that he hadn't come home or called for more than two days.

Dennis poured himself a cup while Lisa brought their omelets over to the set table. Dennis took his first sip of the coffee and said, "Oh man, is that deeelish! It just doesn't get any better than that. If that's the last of it, let's plan a trip back up to Maine so we can stock up again, okay?"

"Sure," Lisa said, and then trailed off, unsure.

Dennis had sat down and eaten as if he hadn't eaten in days. Lisa watched him intently and realized he hadn't yet looked her in the eyes. She couldn't help but feel an overwhelming sense of sadness as it hit her that the love affair they had together for the last six months was over. The feeling was crushing; she had convinced herself that she had found her soulmate and life was going to be easy. She had finally found a man to love who loved her back equally and unconditionally. Now the trust they had built over the last several months was gone. Reality had come crashing back down with all its weight and complications.

After furiously eating every last bite of eggs on his plate and gulping down the last sip of his coffee, Dennis got up and walked to the door and put on his work boots, seeming to ignore the strange silence between them. Then he looked up.

"I have to go out and do some errands. I should be back in a few hours."

He opened the door and disappeared outside before Lisa had a chance to respond.

"I'll be here waiting, Dennis," Lisa whispered as she stood in the kitchen, alone.

Chapter 43

The assignment for literature class, *The Bluest Eye*, was like no other book Ivy had ever read. She gazed out the window and reflected on society's standards of beauty as it related to girls and young women. She had never before focused on her looks, makeup, or fashion. In fact, since she began playing volleyball at the age of twelve, she didn't even own a dress or skirt, and for the most part lived in sweatpants and a t-shirt. She was very aware of her height and often people told her that she was pretty, or more recently, which she still wasn't exactly comfortable hearing, hot. But she had never put much thought into how differently people treated her solely based on her looks. The book changed Ivy's perspective forever, and she was grateful to her teacher for assigning it.

When Ivy was in her early teens, she was already six feet tall and extremely thin. She had long legs but had yet to develop any feminine curves, and like most teenagers, was painfully self-conscious. As she got older, her body filled out and she developed more muscle in her legs, shoulders, and biceps than most girls her age. Ivy had the body of a voluptuous young woman and that sometimes made her feel awkward, too.

Being tall meant that some people would stare and make ridiculous comments like "it's going to be hard find a husband" or "you must hate being so tall."

Ivy felt like retorting, "Are you saying that because of my height I should be unhappy?"

But she never did respond in such a manner. Instead, she chose to explain that she was a volleyball player and in her world it was the norm to be tall. She certainly didn't share the fact that she was still hoping to grow another inch or two, always having had 6'3" or 6'4" as her ideal height.

After having read *The Bluest Eye*, Ivy realized that she had been naïve for not having recognized the world treated her differently, both because of her father's wealth and her looks. The idea that society treated her better because she was an attractive, white, blue-eyed girl weighed heavily on her.

Ivy changed into her sports outfit, and took the elevator down to the fitness room. Like always, she was the only person in the small but well-appointed gym.

She did her normal forty-five-minute strength training routine, a forty-five-minute ride on the spinning bike, and finished with fifteen minutes of abdominal work. Lying on a mat, still catching her breath, she could not take her mind off Stevie, nor keep the smile off her face.

– 44 –

Hello Ives,

Earlier today I was thinking of this bizarrely intense moment I experienced about three or four days after the surgery to amputate my leg. I can imagine that this detailed story could seem totally gruesome, so if you are the squeamish type just skip this one, I will totally understand!

I woke up after the surgery with the sixteen centimeters of my left thigh that I still had left, wrapped in a cast just like you would get if you broke any bone. They do this to prevent the swelling that occurs as a result of severe trauma to the body such as having a limb cut off. It was the day that my doctor cut the cast off for the big unveiling. Needless to say, actually seeing what was left of my leg for the first time was emotional, but this is where the story gets interesting.

It was actually kind of funny. I looked down to see all these staples which were keeping together the skin that the surgeons had pulled over the bone, and a tube that was coming out of the wound to allow the blood and fluid to drain. Dr. Gebhardt was poking and prodding the swollen mess of my once beautiful leg (okay, maybe not that beautiful, really more bony than anything) and without looking up at me he actually said, "Everything looks great, Jake!"

"Doc, I believe we will have to agree to disagree on this particular subject!" I said.

Even my doctor smiled at that joke, which is saying a lot! Maybe you had to be there to see the humor in it, but to me it was funny because the truth was it looked really quite unattractive. After applying more iodine and reapplying the bandages to keep the wound clean, my doctor told me to lie back down because he would re-wrap my thigh very tightly to prevent any further swelling. Like a good sheep, I did as I was told and let him get to work. He turned his back to me as if to block me from seeing what he was doing, and rolled something called a compression sock on what was left of my leg. Ives, I had never experienced anything like it before that moment. The shockwaves of pain shot through my body, mind, and spirit, and without even thinking about it, I clenched my hands into fists and began punching Dr. Gebhardt over and over on his back and shoulders. Once the compression sock was rolled all the way up, the worst of it was over and the pain began to subside. The doctor finished by lightly wrapping over the compression sock with several layers of elastic bandages. Then he turned around and apologized for not warning me about the pain, explaining that in all his years of practice he had found there was no good way to prepare someone for the pain of re-applying the compression sock. He was probably right, but man, the pain was intense.

It is sometimes hard to believe that my leg is actually gone. I mean, I know it won't grow back or anything, although sometimes I dream that scientists will come up with some sort of new technology where they will be able to perform a leg transplant and some little old grandma will have died and donated her body and organs and I would end up with a little old lady leg, all shriveled up with varicose veins. But I can tell you this, little sis, I would take it in a second. It is not easy to learn to get around with one leg. I have to use crutches for every little thing I do, and it is exhausting. Of course, everything is exhausting as my body seems to be getting weaker by the day. It sure would be easier if I still had my two normal legs to get around with, but I don't and all the wishing in the world won't change that fact, right? So, I march on and I put one foot in front of the... well you know what I mean.

I hope this entry doesn't bum you out too much, Ives. That certainly was not my intent. I am just writing what comes to me, and today it was this story.

This song is called Born a New Man and is #3 on the CD. I find the lyrics to be very interesting. If I had to guess, I am talking to the cancer inside me. I know it is typical that people turn to religion when they are facing illness or death, and the reality that I will soon be gone makes me want to believe there is something else after this life. It's just too frightening to believe when our lives here end, we just die and there's nothing more.

In fact, I have begun to look at my impending death as not just an end to this life, but also a sort of second birth into some new life. I know it sounds cheesy or impossible, but what can I say, Ives, I'm only human.

Love you, Ives!

Born A New Man

I got some things I got to say

Clear some thoughts out of my mind
I know you just can't stay
You won't never be satisfied
You've turned me against my friends
All my loved one too
Can't go on like this no more
My time here is through

Now I'll take foot after foot
Yeah hand after hand
Got my finger on it now
I'll be born a new Man!

Won't someone come and help me
Can't you see I need relief
You've taken everything from me
You aint nothing but a thief
It sure has been so long
Just trying to survive
So cold and dark and grey
I just want to feel alive!

– 45 –

It was already 7:00 p.m. on Sunday night and Ivy couldn't help but feel disappointed that Stevie hadn't called to make plans. After years of attending volleyball camps and tournaments, she knew that these things always took longer than expected and she wanted to believe that if Stevie could be back in Boston and had time to spend with her, he would call.

Ivy and Sophie were talking on the phone about how exciting it was for Ivy to learn more about both her mother and brother's lives from reading Jake's journal, and Sophie was in the middle of asking if she thought Alan had ever read any parts of Jake's journal when Ivy's cell phone rang and Stevie's name appeared on the caller ID. Breathlessly, she told Sophie it was Stevie, and they disconnected so Ivy could take his call.

"Hi, Stevie, it's been a long weekend for you, huh?" Ivy said in the most understanding and non-judgmental voice possible.

"Hey Ivy, yeah, we haven't even left yet. Turns out a few agents heard we were in town this weekend and drove in from New York. We got the chance to meet with two of them that represent a bunch of young prospects like me. They all seem nice but in kind of a creepy way."

"Oh, creepy is not a very positive way to describe someone. What are they doing to set off your creep-o-meter?" asked Ivy with a laugh.

"Creep-o-meter, I've never heard of that before, but I like it," Stevie said laughing. "Well my creep-o-meter was indeed in full effect tonight! It's not that they were creepy like they were wearing evil clown masks or anything like that, it's more like they're working too hard to make me feel like I was somehow different than all the other young prospects out there. They were saying all the right things, you know, but it sounded almost as if it was all just a bit too rehearsed, and they kept harping on the idea that they only want what is best for me and my career. It seems so obvious to me that this is only about money to them, and I can't help but believe those guys have made the exact sales pitch to hundreds of guys before me."

"Well, at least you have your dad there to protect you from those creepy old men," Ivy said, half-jokingly.

"Yeah, these definitely are the times I am most appreciative of my dad being here with me. He has the experience and knowledge of how all this stuff works because he's already seen the business side of the game. So basically, I just sit there next to him looking pretty and let him do all the talking," said Stevie.

Ivy loved Stevie's sense of humor. "Well luckily for you, it's very easy to look pretty. At least you don't have to work too hard at that, right?"

"That is very true! I've always maintained I am particularly the prettiest right after a shower when my hair is still wet." Stevie laughed, then grew serious. "In the end, those guys wanted to make me feel like they were looking out for my best interest, and we're somehow friends. But it's just part of the game. It's big business and they're doing their jobs," Stevie said, as he realized Ivy was the only person in his life that seemed to take the time to understand what he was going through.

"Did you have a chance to talk more with your dad about your decision to go to college or turn pro?" Ivy asked.

"Whoa, now that's the big one! Well, I definitely didn't talk to my dad about it, he already assumes I'll be turning pro. As far as making up my mind, I'm not sure if this weekend helped or made it harder for me to decide. The thing is, the Pawtucket Red Sox is a Triple A ball club, which is the last stop before the big leagues, so life here is pretty lush. If I were to sign a contract, the reality for anyone coming out of high school like me, is that I would start my career playing in what they call the rookie league. Rookie league life is closer to that of a high school ball player than it is to the Triple A world I'm seeing this weekend," said Stevie.

"You had mentioned before that you expect some sort of sign-on bonus that you could put away and use to pay for college if for some reason baseball didn't work out, right?" asked Ivy.

"Yeah, that's the plan anyway. If I were to go as high in the draft as some of the prospect reports have me now, I could expect somewhere between one and three million, which to be honest just sounds like Monopoly money at this point. Whatever the final amount, it certainly looks like it will be more than enough to have as a fallback if things don't go as planned."

Ivy waited for Stevie to continue.

"Ivy, seems like we only talk about my soap opera drama of a life. Tell me about your family. Everybody knows your dad is like the Sandy Koufax of lawyers." Stevie paused. "It occurred to me as I was making the Sandy Koufax reference that you have no idea who in the hell he is." Stevie laughed. "He was one of the best pitchers that ever lived, so what I meant was that everybody knows your dad is some sort of high-powered lawyer. What about you mother? What is she like?"

Ivy spent the next several minutes telling Stevie all about her family history. She was excited to share with him all the new information she had learned over the last week since she had received Jake's journal. It was interesting to her that it had only been a week since she began reading the journal one entry at a time, and yet she already felt as if she had learned more about her brother and her mother than she ever thought possible. Jake had even given her insight into the fact that Alan had not been affected by anything Ivy had done or as a result of losing his son and wife in the same week, as Ivy had always suspected. It was now clearer than ever that her father was simply focused on his work and little else, and had always been that way.

Stevie was fascinated by Ivy's story and asked if she would share Jake's songs with him. Of course, Ivy was happy to share and appreciated how intently Stevie had listened and the questions he asked. Stevie said that he and his father were just about to leave and make the hour-long drive back to Boston. He and Ivy agreed to try and get together the following night if possible.

"It was really nice talking with you, Ivy," Stevie said before hanging up. "It's funny how much we must trust each other in order to share all this stuff we have going on in our lives."

"I totally agree," said Ivy, with a warm smile. "It's been an amazing week for me. I'm so happy you let me into this exciting time and I'm looking forward to watching your story unfold. I have total faith that you'll make all the right decisions and you'll reach all your goals, Stevie Smith. See you tomorrow at school?"

"You are a good egg, Ivy S. Miles! Definitely see you tomorrow at school," Stevie said before hanging up.

After a few minutes of sitting on the couch in a glow and reliving the conversation she had just had, Ivy dialed Sophie, who, upon hearing about the phone call was genuinely happy for Ivy. After the emotional roller coaster Sophie had been on over the last several weeks—lying to her parents, skipping school, the aborted pregnancy, and having to lie to Ivy—the fact that Stevie was pursuing her best friend was the most welcome news possible. Sophie could hear in Ivy's voice just how excited and happy she was and that fact alone warmed Sophie's heart. Of course, that it was Stevie Smith, the boy that Ivy had dreamed about for the last two years made it even more amazing.

"Ivy, you deserve this, you know. Stevie is lucky to have you in his life."

– 46 –

It had been a very demanding week and Alan planned to spend the entire day in his hotel suite in Washington, D.C., preparing for yet another tough week ahead. He needed to catch up on reading and making notes on the nearly two dozen legal papers, documents, briefs, and reports given to him by his colleague at the U.S. Department of Justice. In the week upcoming, Alan would be working with the chief of the Computer Crime and Intellectual Property Section or CCIPS, the department of the government responsible for implementing the national strategies in combating computer and intellectual property crimes worldwide.

Because of his chronic and increasingly uncomfortable back pain, Alan was lying flat on the floor as he read a pending litigation case the government had against a foreign government, involving telecommunications technologies.

After hours of reading in every possible position, attempting in vain, it turned out, to relieve his back pain, and the severe acid reflux he had developed in the last few months, Alan finally wrote to Cathy, instructing her to make an appointment at a doctor's office back in Boston for the following Friday afternoon. Alan realized how lucky he had been that never before in his life had he had any sort of health trouble other than the occasional cold. But the thought triggered a flood of memories about all the suffering and pain his son Jake had gone through during the last eighteen months of his life. Though the Dana Farber Cancer Institute and Boston Children's Hospital, where Jake had received his treatments, was within walking distance from his law office at that time, Alan had only managed one visit to the hospital during those months. He knew he should have been more supportive of both Jake and Clara during those years, but at that time in his career, he and Harry were in their highest demand. In fact, Harry often told him that he should take time off from work to be more a part of his wife and child's fight against cancer. However, very early on in his life, long before his marriage to Clara, Alan had decided that his work would always come first, and he simply could not allow himself to share his finite time and energy with his family.

Alan had never truly understood why Clara had chosen him to begin with. He had never been able to make sense of what it was that she had seen in him to make her pursue the relationship with such certainty. He knew Clara could have had virtually any man she wanted, but for some mysterious reason, she had chosen him. It seemed to Alan that choosing him was the biggest and perhaps only mistake Clara had made in her short life. Had she found someone else to marry and father her children, Jake would never have been born and would not have had to suffer those months of treatments and surgeries. Maybe Clara would still be alive; Alan had always assumed it was the stress of Jake's illness that was the cause of the aneurysm that took her life. Now he was alone, with a daughter whose life, as Harry often pointed out, he had absolutely nothing to do with other than to financially support her. It seemed obvious that it would have been best for everyone had he never met Clara to begin with.

Painfully, slowly, Alan got up from the floor. He realized that it was late afternoon and he had yet to eat anything. He had only had one cup of tea earlier in the morning. He had no appetite but he knew he had to try, so he called down to the hotel restaurant and ordered a soup, salad, and coffee to be sent up to the room.

Alan decided to lie down on the sofa while he waited for room service. He closed his eyes and fell asleep almost instantly. He dreamt of

Clara. In the dream, she was disappointed in his inability to show any fatherly emotions to Ivy. Suddenly, he was in a courtroom and called to the stand to be cross-examined by Jake with Clara acting as the presiding judge. Jake began firing questions about his "emotional fitness" to be a proper father. Alan was vigorously agreeing and began explaining that it was never his idea to marry and have children. He blamed Clara and she slammed her gavel down again and again, shouting for order in the court. Alan woke up, startled, and stood up quickly, only to feel a terrible, shooting pain down his back and through his stomach. Gasping, he doubled over until the pain began to subside. Just then, he heard a knock on the door. Gingerly, he walked to the door and let in the young man wheeling a silver cart with the food that he had ordered.

Moments later, Alan, still shaken from both the dream and the severe pain, sat down and took a few sips of the steaming hot coffee but immediately felt the familiar discomfort of acid reflux.

It was late evening and Alan had only finished half of the readings he needed to be familiar with for the meetings that began at 8:00 a.m. the following day. He was simply too exhausted to go on, and decided that it was best for him to sleep and finish his preparations before the meeting in the morning. He set his alarm clock for 4:00 a.m., and was asleep within seconds of lying down in his bed.

– 47 –

It was past 9:00 p.m. on Sunday evening, and although Stevie had expected to have left Rhode Island several hours earlier, he and his father were still sitting at a restaurant with two agents from New York. The agents had explained that they could essentially guarantee Stevie a minimum $1,500,000 sign-on bonus, and if he went in the draft where they expected, the number could get as high as $3,000,000. These numbers had been thrown around in the past, but it just hadn't felt real when Stevie and his father had talked about it.

While the agent was speaking with his father, Stevie again thought about how important continuing his education was to him. Yet tonight, more so than ever, he realized that it was going to be difficult to walk away from the opportunity to turn pro and collect the early sign-on bonus. If nothing else, the financial opportunity was almost too great to pass up. As he had this thought, the words spoken to him from Moose the day before, "Money don't buy happiness kid," ran through his mind.

The meeting wrapped up after 11:00 p.m., and on their way home Stevie found himself wondering what was going on in his father's mind. As a general rule, they only spoke about Stevie and baseball.

Stevie asked, "Hey Dad, when would you say were the best times in your life? Like, when were you the happiest? And don't give me any of that 'it was the day I met your mother' crap!" he added, laughing.

"Son, with all that you have going on right now, why in the hell would you ask me a question like that? You should be thinking about which sports car you're going to buy first! With all the money that'll be coming to you, you can pretty much have whatever you want!" he said.

"I would look like a total idiot driving around town in a sports car. Maybe I would buy myself a diesel pickup truck, but certainly not a sports car." Stevie paused and added, "Do you think we could buy you and Mama a Porsche or Corvette for you two to cruise around in on the weekends?"

"Now let's think about this. You're asking if *we* can buy a car for your mother and me, with your money. Once you sign this contract, I will no longer be making decisions for you. You're eighteen years old and you'll be on your own."

Stevie realized that what his father was saying was true. Soon he would be on his own, as a legal adult.

"Wait, you never answered my question. Seriously, in your sixty-plus years on this earth, when were you the happiest?" Stevie asked with a devilish grin, knowing full well his father was only forty-nine.

"I'll give you sixty, you little punk! You know I'm not a day over thirty-nine!" Stevie's father joked. Then he thought for a long moment.

"So, you want to know when the happiest days of my life were? Well, here's the thing, I've had a pretty amazing life. I always had a great relationship with my parents. They were supportive of my needs, especially when it came to my decision to pursue a career in baseball. And of course, with your mother, I really did hit the jackpot when I met her. After almost twenty years together, we're happier now than we have ever been. But as far as when I was the happiest, that's a no-brainer, Son. It's right now!" his father said.

Stevie assumed he was joking and laughed. "But seriously, Dad, was it when you were playing ball?"

He glanced over at his son once more, smiling, then returned his focus to the road.

"Son, it's now, this is it. It doesn't get any better than this weekend for me. I have had the honor to watch and be a part of this incredible journey with you for the last ten years. I saw a gangly, goofy boy who would literally and quite often, I might add, trip over his own feet. I watched that boy develop into one of the best baseball players for his age in the entire country. I asked more of you than any father should dare ask of his child, and never, not even one time, did you give anything less than one-hundred-per-cent effort. There were days when I could see in your eyes that you were tired, when you wanted to just go to the movies or a buddy's birthday party like a normal kid."

Stevie looked at his father's dimly lit profile, remembering those times too.

"Instead of allowing you to go, I insisted that you continue working on your game. What I found was that it was on those days, when you were the most tired, that you worked your hardest and made your biggest gains. I don't know where you got the drive and ability to stay so focused and motivated, but you always had it."

Stevie shook his head and smiled.

"If all of that wasn't enough, everyone who meets you makes sure to let me know what a genuinely nice young man you are. I hope someday you'll be lucky enough to have kids that make you as proud as I am of you. I wouldn't trade the last decade of my life for anything in the world, Son, nothing!"

Stevie was silent for a moment, stunned by the show of emotion from his normally stoic father.

"So, let me get this straight. If God himself offered you a deal, to trade my being born in exchange for a guarantee that you end up in the Baseball Hall of Fame, you're telling me that you would turn down that offer?"

His father laughed.

"Son, you know what a weakness I have for Cooperstown, so of course I would make that trade, in a heartbeat. But let's be reasonable here, God ain't making that offer!" Father and son laughed harder in that moment than they ever had together.

Stevie's father reached over, and as he had so many times before, pulled the bill of Stevie's cap down over his son's eyes and gave him a playful swat.

– 48 –

Dennis had tried to pretend that he could spend a "normal" day with Lisa as he had every day since leaving rehab. But reality had come crashing down on him by early Sunday afternoon, when he ran out of the apartment in need of a fix. He went to his old dealer, bought two fifty-dollar bags of heroin, shot up on his dealer's couch, and less than an hour later, was back in the apartment with Lisa.

After over twenty years of using, Dennis would have to make the decision to check himself back into rehab or a methadone program, but he wasn't ready just yet. He had tried to fall asleep next to Lisa, but that didn't happen. Dennis got up, got dressed, and walked out of the bedroom, closing the door behind him as quietly as he could.

Lying in bed, pretending to be asleep, Lisa's heart ached. She wanted to get up and plead with Dennis to go back to rehab, but after all the years of watching her mother be a slave to her addiction, Lisa knew it would do no good. She would be patient and wait for him, and would help in any way he asked, but to get clean again he would have to want it himself. Lisa knew this was the heartbreaking truth and there was nothing she could do about it. As she heard the apartment door close, she was once alone again and cried herself back to sleep.

Dennis found himself back in the old VW van of his friend who everyone called "Olive Oyl." Tall, thin, with long and straight black hair, he had a striking resemblance to the girlfriend of the cartoon character Popeye, thus the nickname. The same young girl as before, Tina, was lying back on the sofa bed of the VW van, drowsy, high and contented after Olive had just injected a hit of heroin into a vein in her hand. Dennis felt a hint of jealousy as he watched how little of the drug Tina needed to get high.

Olive Oyl told Dennis that he needed a pack of cigarettes and asked him to keep an eye on Tina because she had nearly OD'd just two weeks before. Dennis took a five-dollar bill out of his wallet and asked Olive to grab him a six-pack of Budweiser.

Olive slid the old van's side door open, which made the dome light come on.

"Shut the door!" Dennis and Tina said, in unison.

Immediately, Dennis slid over from the front passenger seat and sat down on the floor next to where Tina was lying on the sofa. Slowly, he began unbuttoning her shirt to expose her pale, undeveloped chest. Gently, he began massaging her breasts, causing her to moan with pleasure. Tina reached up with both hands and grabbed Dennis's head, steering his mouth to her breast, causing her to arch her back and let out a slight squeal. Clumsily, Tina began taking her clothes off, mumbling "take your pants off" to Dennis.

Dennis knew from experience that while on heroin, he would have no problem performing sexually, but he had no chance of reaching completion. Of course, that fact did not deter him and thirty minutes later, when Olive came peeking through the fogged-up window, he saw that neither had any clothes on and that both bodies were glistening with sweat. He opened the driver's side door and the dome light switched on, getting the attention of both Dennis and Tina once more.

"How did I know this is what I'd come back to, Dennis?" Olive said. "She's jail-bait that you're messing with!" He cracked open a cold Budweiser. "But I won't tell if you don't."

Dennis looked at his friend in mocking disbelief. "Don't tell me you haven't had her yet, bro. You're way too much of a dog to have kept your hands off this beauty, regardless of how old she is or isn't!" Dennis reached for a beer and drank half of the can in one pull. Then he offered the can to Tina, who drank the other half.

Olive just laughed. “Well, you crazy kids don't mind me. Please continue where you left off while I relax here and enjoy my beer. But I will need to turn the light back on so I can enjoy the show!”

“I have a better idea,” said Tina in her girlish voice. “Come back here and join us, just please keep that goddamn light off!”

– 49 –

When Alan's alarm clock woke him at 4:00 a.m. Monday, he knew there was no way he could attend the meetings he had scheduled for that day. His back and abdominal pain had intensified significantly overnight and he noticed that his eyes had taken on a strange yellow color. He needed medical attention, quickly.

He emailed Cathy, instructed her to cancel all meetings for that day, and to find a doctor that would see him right away. Alan lay back down on his bed, hoping to find some relief from the pain, and again fell asleep. For the past twenty years, even when working until the early hours of the morning, Alan's internal clock had never allowed him to sleep past 7:00 a.m.

Still groggy, he woke up and realized it was after ten in the morning. Reaching for his phone, he saw a message from Cathy, saying that she had arranged for Alan to see a doctor at a private practice at 10:30. If he hurried, he could still make the appointment on time, but every movement he made sent shooting pains down his back and through his stomach.

Two nurses from the practice were waiting anxiously outside with a wheelchair when the car arrived. With their assistance, Alan got out and put up no fight as he flopped down into the wheelchair, and they rolled him into the office.

Dr. Rosenberg, one of the most prominent and well-respected physicians in the country, walked into the exam room. Before introducing himself, he immediately noticed both Alan's eyes and skin had taken on a yellow tone, a symptom that his patient was suffering from jaundice. By the manner in which Alan held his hands over his stomach, it was obvious the patient was experiencing abdominal pain as well. Without asking one question, he suspected that Alan was suffering from stage four cancer of the pancreas. After a short exam, Dr. Rosenberg recommended he immediately be admitted to a hospital for a full body CAT scan and diagnostic testing.

In his long career, he had seen many patients receive a pancreatic cancer diagnosis similar to what he suspected Alan was facing. Regardless, Dr. Rosenberg still felt a kind of heartbreak for people who would likely be given a death sentence in the next forty-eight hours.

– 50 –

Ivy stepped out of the shower to read a message from Stevie that he was just pulling into the Omni parking lot. She quickly dressed and went down to meet him in the lobby. Stevie watched as Ivy stepped out of the elevator, and thought to himself that he had never seen a more beautiful girl in all his life. They both quickened their steps and without thinking, she fell into his arms. He held her tight against his body. Because both were so tall and strikingly attractive, it seemed the entire lobby had stopped to watch the beautiful young couple embrace. At that moment, neither seemed concerned about the attention they were receiving; they were simply too focused on one another.

Stevie, standing nearly three inches taller than Ivy, rested the side of his cheek on the top of her head. He breathed in the wonderful aroma of freshly washed hair that smelled of either vanilla or coconut, he wasn't sure. Finally, the two released each other from the long and emotionally charged hug when Ivy noticed that her hair, still wet from the shower, had left a wet spot on Stevie's grey sweatshirt.

"Hello Stevie, I imagine it's a bit strange that I live in a hotel, but welcome to my home!" Ivy said. "Oh, I got your shirt wet, sorry about that."

"I happen to be very sensitive both physically and emotionally, so if I catch a cold as a result of my shirt being wet, I'm blaming you!" Stevie joked before continuing. "And yes, it is a bit strange and intimidating to meet the girl I have a crush on at her family's penthouse apartment in the most exclusive hotel in Boston, but somehow it makes sense! After all, you aren't like any other girl I've ever met!"

Ivy flushed with pleasure. Suddenly, she became aware of all the eyes on her and Stevie.

"Well, let's go up to the apartment so I can make you a hot chocolate before you catch a cold. I don't want your father thinking I'm a bad influence on you!" The two laughed and Ivy took Stevie's hand. As soon as the elevator doors closed, Stevie pulled Ivy into his arms, looked her in the eyes and asked, "Ivy S. Miles, may I kiss you?"

Ivy had definitely not been expecting that question.

"May…you…kiss me?" she stammered.

"Yes, I kind of think having our first kiss in an elevator would be romantic and unforgettable. So, do you grant me permission to kiss you?" asked Stevie again.

Without answering, she first licked her lips to wet them and then softly and slowly took his top lip between hers, and with just the tip of her tongue ever so slightly licked his lip before he responded and opened his mouth, allowing their tongues to meet. It was a kiss so filled with emotion that neither would ever forget it. Just as she opened her eyes again, the doors opened and Ivy quickly and nervously turned to exit the elevator. When she turned back, she saw that Stevie had not followed her. She stepped back, only to see him still standing in the elevator with his eyes closed.

"What are doing, Stevie? Aren't you coming?" asked Ivy.

"Oh yeah, just give me a minute. I want to make sure I place the memory of that kiss in the correct compartment of my brain so I never, ever, ever, forget it. Not there…uhhh, no, not there either. No, that's for my memories of unicorns. No, that's how to bake cupcakes. Okay, got it!" he said and then stepped out of the elevator.

Ivy laughed and said, "So is this what you do every time you kiss a girl for the first time?"

"Ivy, I will not lie and pretend that I haven't kissed other girls." Stevie paused. "But I can say with one-hundred-per-cent certainty that I have never felt a kiss like that."

"Well, I've kissed dozens of boys, so for me it was just average," Ivy responded.

"Did not see that coming!" said Stevie and they both burst out in laughter.

They entered the apartment and Stevie was struck by the views of the Boston landscape. He knew that Ivy lived in a hotel, but he wasn't prepared for how luxurious the penthouse was. Despite the fact that she came from one of the wealthiest families in Boston and just happened to be one of the best volleyball players in the country for her age, she somehow managed to remain as down to earth as any girl he had ever met. Even at 18 years old, Stevie was aware of how truly special Ivy was.

Stevie stood silently for a moment while taking in the cityscape. "Wow, this view really is amazing, Ivy!"

Ivy walked up beside him. "I've been living here for four years now, but I still get a feeling that we're looking over a city of nearly 700,000 people and it always has a way of putting my life in perspective."

"What exactly do you mean by that?" asked Stevie as he stepped behind her, pulled her into his body and wrapped his arms around her.

Ivy was flustered, not expecting Stevie to hug her, but gathered her thoughts and responded, "I get this feeling, in the mornings when I wake up and look out at the city, that I'm not alone, like there are all these people waking up and getting their day started just like me. Then I think that many of those people have challenges that I can't even fathom, and it makes me appreciate what I do have."

"I need to start looking at my life that way instead of stressing so much about my pitching mechanics or batting technique or whether I should or shouldn't go to college," Stevie said lightheartedly but also sincerely.

"Yeah, appreciating what I have has become even clearer to me over just this past week, since I've been reading the journal from my brother," Ivy said. Stevie took Ivy's chin in his hand.

"I heard every word you said when you were telling me about your brother and the journal, but can you explain it again because it was a little confusing."

Ivy once again explained the story of her brother and the journal.

"First off, that's such an intense story. But before you continue, are you saying I missed your sixteenth birthday by less than a week?" asked Stevie.

"Yup, if you had flirted with me just a few days earlier, we could have celebrated together!" said Ivy in a nonchalant, playful tone.

"Well, I would like to give you your late birthday present," he said, in a low voice.

Stevie kissed Ivy again, this time longer and more passionately than in the elevator. After several minutes of kissing, while still holding Ivy close and looking directly into her eyes, Stevie continued.

"First off, I can't believe that 'late birthday present' line actually worked, that was totally epic! But it is seriously kind of scary, how it somehow feels like we've known each other forever." Stevie paused and continued. "And I don't mean that in like a cheesy movie kind of way."

Ivy smiled dreamily.

"Is this not how it feels when you meet someone you like? I've never had a boyfriend before, so this is all new to me, Stevie," she said.

"Well, I've dated a few girls and it's never felt anything like this," Stevie said.

Ivy blushed.

"Ivy, would you allow me to hear one of the songs you mentioned your brother recorded for you?"

Touched by the request, Ivy walked over to the CD player and put on the last song Jake wrote in his life, "Smile." Stevie sat on the couch and Ivy returned and sat on the floor between Stevie's legs. As the music played, she laid her head on his knee and in complete silence the two listened to her brother singing lyrics that were far beyond the emotional intelligence and sophistication of what any teenager should have to face.

The song ended, leaving them in a comfortable, if sad silence for some time.

Reluctantly, Stevie spoke. "Thank you for sharing that with me, Ivy."

With Ivy's head still on Stevie's knee, Stevie began running his hands through her hair, giving her goosebumps.

"I wish we had gotten to know each other sooner. I'll be moving away in less than six months," Stevie said, after a time.

Not sure of what to say or how to respond, Ivy stood up and as she had seen in the movies, straddled Stevie's lap. The feelings, both physical and emotional, that she was experiencing were all new to her. Even as nervous as she was, it felt so natural for her to experience such feelings with Stevie.

After spending several hours together, the two teenagers walked out to the parking lot to his old pickup truck, which looked out of place, surrounded by mostly luxury and sports cars.

Before getting into his truck, Stevie asked Ivy, "Would you grant me one last kiss before bid I ye farewell, my lady?"

"Oh, I do love it when you talk so formally with me!" Ivy smiled.

She grabbed both his hands and leaned back on the truck. With their fingers interlocked and their hands by their sides he leaned his weight on her body and they shared a short but passionate kiss. Ivy's body was experiencing feelings that she had never felt, and she wished he could stay longer so they could explore the new feelings further.

Finally, Stevie got in his truck, rolled down the window, and said, "I couldn't have asked for a better first date Ivy, thank you."

"It was definitely special!" Ivy leaned in and kissed him one last time.

"See you in the morning!" Stevie said before turning the key, relieved that the old engine started on the first try.

He drove away, watching Ivy waving in his rearview mirror.

In the past, Ivy would call Sophie to share with her all the details when something this exciting happened in her life. However, this time everything seemed different. Ivy felt more alive than she ever had before. In fact, it had been so special that she didn't need or want to share her experience with anyone. Ivy wondered, "Is this what it feels like to fall in love?"

– 51 –

It was 3:00 a.m. and Mr. C. had been awake since midnight. He had slept all day and night Saturday and most of Sunday day. Now, having been in the hospital for more than forty-eight hours, the IV antibiotics had quickly and effectively done their job, and he felt as if his breathing was improving by the hour. The medications did not, however, free him of the overwhelming sense of shame of why he was in the hospital. No matter how hard he tried, he couldn't stop seeing the red numbers on the screen of the machine that had lifted him into the hospital bed. Over five hundred pounds. He didn't want to believe his body had gotten that big but the numbers did not lie, and the crane used to get him into his oversized bed was not in his imagination.

The nutrition specialist had come by earlier in the evening but Mr. C. had been sleeping. Rather than wake him, she had left behind a packet of information on obesity and food addictions as well as brochures to several rehabilitation facilities specializing in obesity. When Mr. C. awoke, he read through a brochure from a long-term inpatient facility in Colorado called The Boulder Eating Recovery Center, and in that very instant, he experienced a moment of clarity and, surprisingly, liberation. Mr. C. decided that as soon as he was released from the hospital he would quit his job at the school, close up his house, and move into one of the recommended centers. He would focus on the health of both his body and mind and focus on nothing else but his health.

With these goals set, Mr. C felt his mind begin to clear and he experienced something that he hadn't felt in many years—hope. A peaceful calm washed over him and he knew, for sure, that he was ready to start a new chapter in his life.

– 52 –

Ivy woke up early Tuesday morning thinking of the wonderful time she had with Stevie the night before, and she couldn't keep the smile off her face. With an extra bounce in her step, she sat and read the next entry from Jake's journal.

Ives,

It's so hard to think about anything but cancer and dying when you in fact have cancer and are actually dying. Okay, I know that sounds like a BAD line from a BAD movie, but it just came out that way so I am going with it. Last week, I read an article about a young mother of two children who had an inoperable tumor in her brain. Although this woman was given only six months to a year to live, her motto was:

"I am not dying of *cancer, but rather* living with *cancer!"*

It made me laugh when I read this because it reminded me of the type of thing I would say to Mama to try and make her feel better. I just can't believe this woman really wakes up in the morning happy to be "living with" a tumor in her brain that will take her life in a matter of only months. If I am wrong, then she is clearly a bigger man (or woman in this case) than I can ever hope to be.

It seems everything I hear or read these days leads my stubborn mind back to my own mortality which in turn leads me think about religion which in turn leads me to think about what happens after our lives end on this earth. What I struggle with most is, the more I try and make sense of death, the less Christianity makes any sense whatsoever. Here is the core problem I have with Christianity.

I have read dozens of self-help and spirituality type books that all have one basic theme in common. Of course, they each have their own way of leading up to this theme, but in the end they all end up at this common thread of thought which is:

Life is found in the present, in the here and now!

Essentially what they all mean to say is, worrying about all that has happened in the past and all that will happen in the future is fruitless and this manner of thinking is what creates all of our problems. So, in other words, to find true happiness and peace within ourselves, one must only live in the moment and not dwell on the past or worry about the future. This concept goes against the natural impulses of the way our minds work. We humans tend to overthink experiences and replay them almost like movie scenes over and over on a repeat loop in our minds. What makes this even more dangerous and hurtful to ourselves is that within this movie, we create our own realities of events that happened in the past and they become our personal versions of how we interpreted these experiences. The thing is, most often these versions do not accurately depict what actually happened, and in doing so, we fuel our anger, jealousy, shame, or whatever other emotions that cause us pain.

If that isn't bad enough, humans also love to dream of the future, of what we must do, must have, or must achieve, in order to be happy. In the human mind, tomorrow will hold all the answers, when our dreams finally come true. Only then will we finally find peace and feel fulfilled. The reality as you may or may not already know is, tomorrow will come and nothing changes. Achieving goals, buying things, starting relationships, or anything else that we think we need to make us happy, all come and go and tomorrow we simply need more to find happiness.

In fact, when you really think about it, all that happened in the past, when it actually occurred was in fact in the past "now." Any and all things that will occur in the future will of course happen in the future "now." Anything other than the here and now is simply not real and will ultimately cause us pain and sorrow when dwelled upon.

Yet with virtually all religions, everything they teach and ask us to believe with blind faith has all supposedly happened thousands of years ago. All the stories, all the lessons, all the alleged sacrifices that were made for us all happened long ago. Regardless, we are expected to worship words from books that were written thousands of years ago and are told to take the information learned and live our lives according to those rules. If we live in accordance with these rules, when we die, we will be ensured a VIP entry to the pearly gates of heaven.

So in my case, Christianity is asking me to live every minute of my life worrying, stressing, and dwelling on lessons that all happened thousands of years ago, in order to hopefully receive an invitation into the promised land where I will find peace and happiness far in the future.

In all likelihood I am not going to live to see my sixteenth birthday. No, I don't feel any more comfortable writing that last sentence than you probably feel reading it. However, I now know that my chances of surviving are down to just about nil. *I certainly don't want to die; more than anything I want to stick around for another sixty or seventy years, but the chemo didn't work and the tumors are now in both my lungs, my hip, as well as in my spine. Anything in the area of the spine is inoperable.*

So yes indeed, I am jumping around a bunch in this particular entry, but I am quite hopeful that I will be able to bring it all around in the end and make some sort of a coherent point, maybe... hopefully. Just come along for the ride with me, Sis!

I just read that scientists had recently calculated how many humans have died on earth since the beginning of human life. The number is somewhere around 100 billion humans. There are currently around 7 billion people alive on the earth today. That means the total of the earth's current population would have to be wiped out over fourteen times to equal the amount of total deaths the earth has seen. Ivy, this fact just absolutely blew my mind. To think that 100 billion times mothers and fathers and sons and daughters and uncles and aunts and cousins and girlfriends and boyfriends and communities (you get the point, right?) have lost someone they love is overwhelmingly difficult to put in perspective. The reality that 100 billion times a human just like me woke up one morning for the last time before their life came to an end is something I have worked hard to try and truly grasp.

When I began to think of my life in those terms, in those sheer numbers, it makes it very difficult to look at my life and believe it to be of much importance. Again, I am not saying I am happy about dying of cancer at fifteen years old, but if 100 billion people have died before me, it seems to me that I will simply be yet another death added to this running tally of humans that have come and gone on this earth. I have a hard time believing there is a God looking down on us to see who abided by the rules of the Bible or Koran or went to Temple or Church or whatever other random rules all these religions have.

Aside from Mama and maybe our father in his own way, if I die tomorrow it is simply of no consequence to the rest of the 7 billion people on this earth. I hate to sound so cynical, but I am just writing my true feelings as I had set out to do when I started keeping this journal for you. I do not want to die, Ivy, but I also don't feel like I can pretend there is some kingdom just waiting for me to take my last breath until they invite me in to join the VIP party for all of eternity.

Okay, this entry has to come to an end as it is just too heavy. I promise to tell some simple happy story next time, okay?

These lyrics and the melody came to me this past week. It's quite a dark song called, "Life Has Slipped Out of Line," which is a quote taken directly from my favorite book that I wrote about before, Lonesome Dove. *One of the characters, a friend of Gus and Call who are the two main characters, makes some bad decisions and he finds himself on the wrong side of the law. This character is standing on his horse with his hands tied behind his back with a noose around his neck which is tied to a tree. The character is waiting to be hanged by Gus and Captain Call, the same men with whom he had ridden side-by-side with for so many years, and trying to find the words to explain what had happened to put him such a situation. Trying to figure out what he could say to perhaps convince his friends to spare his life. Instead he just felt tired and chose to sum up his thoughts by simply stating that "life had slipped out of line" and proceeded to kick the horse out from under himself, thus ending his own life. I kind of get that feeling sometimes, too. I sometimes feel like we look so hard for the answers to why things are the way they are and for deeper meaning to all that happens in our lives, both the good and the bad. In the end it may be easier and more reasonable to simply state that life just slipped out of line.*

So here are the lyrics and the recording I made is #4 on the CD. Sorry to be sounding so dark today, but it's so difficult to always stay positive. If I could only think like the woman with the brain tumor, that I am "living with cancer," maybe I would be better off, but that is just not my reality!

Life Has Slipped Out of Line

Tragic emotions waltzing through my mind
Frantically searching for thoughts and answers I hoped I'd never have to find
I pray each day that I'll feel free

Alone I weep, afraid to face this oh so dark reality.

I dream of falling in love or my child being born

I hope if push comes to shove I can pull out this thorn… from my heart that glows with pain and sadness

Illuminated by grief and madness
How long must I mourn or dwell or bleed?
Life has slipped out of line, or so it would seem!

Ain't nothing bring comfort in this constant state of flight
Darting eyes and senseless motion help suppress the emptiness I feel inside
I scratch and claw, just to feel, what is real, an instant of life, that's free of pain
That may escape every now and again!

– 53 –

Tuesday morning, Ivy went directly to Mr. C's office to thank him for helping with Sophie's situation and to let him know that everything was okay. But once again she found that he was not in his office. As she hurried to her first class of the day, Ivy suspected, with some worry, that Mr. C.'s cough had something to do with his absence.

Ivy was trying to concentrate on what her politics teacher was saying, but her mind kept wandering back to Stevie. It wasn't easy for her to control her excitement; he was planning to visit her at the Omni again later that evening after his baseball practice. Ivy had never felt as alive as she had over the last week since Stevie had first spoken with her; she wouldn't exactly say she was in love, but was there another word for the feeling? If so, Ivy didn't know what it was. The question that kept circling her mind was how far she'd be willing to go with Stevie tonight. It was after all only their second "date," if you could even call it that. Ivy had never gone further than kissing and the "petting" that she and Stevie had done but she felt ready to experiment more with her sexuality. Ivy was also fairly certain that Stevie was experienced and perhaps was expecting more than just kissing. She wasn't quite ready to give Stevie her virginity, but perhaps was ready to share other of her "firsts" with him; after all, she *was* now 16 years old!

"Ms. Miles, judging by that smirk on your face, you are clearly thinking of something other than US Politics. Would you care to share with the class what it is you're thinking about right now?" her teacher asked.

"I'm sorry, Mr. Callahan," Ivy said, doing all she could to keep from laughing at the idea of actually sharing what she was thinking of doing with Stevie.

The day dragged by, but at lunchtime, Ivy overheard some boys talking about going to Fenway Park to watch the Red Sox play the Yankees later in the evening. She had rarely asked her father for any favors in her life but decided to text Cathy a message:

I was wondering if you know of anyone that might be able to get two tickets for the Red Sox game tonight at Fenway Park. I realize it's a very late request and assume the game is already sold out, but I figured it can't hurt to ask.

Not thirty seconds later Cathy replied:

I was just about to write, letting you know your father wasn't feeling well and had to cancel all his meetings this week. He is scheduled to arrive in Boston this evening. When I have more information, I will let you know. As far as the tickets, I should have an answer for you shortly.

Less than five minutes later Cathy wrote,

I was able to get to tickets directly from the owner of the Red Sox. I'll send the details ASAP.

Ivy could not wait to tell Stevie about the tickets, but decided she would keep it a secret until they got to the stadium. Then something struck her—she couldn't remember her father ever being sick enough to cancel meetings. Was something wrong? The worry floated out of Ivy's mind as quickly as it had entered it.

The school day came to an end and Ivy and Sophie were walking across campus to volleyball practice. She immediately felt the butterflies begin to flutter when she saw Stevie coming toward them.

"Hello ladies, would you mind if I walk with you to the gym?" asked Stevie in his charming manner. He then reached for Ivy, pulling her into him for a much-needed hug. Sophie looked on and glowed with happiness as the embrace lasted longer than a simple friendly greeting.

Ivy's words spilled out. "Are you still planning on spending this evening with me? Because what I have planned to do with you tonight is going to rock your world!"

Stevie and Sophie looked at each other and raised their eyebrows. Ivy looked between the two, confused for a moment.

"Uh, you both need to get your minds out of the gutter! I am so not talking about *that*!" Ivy protested. The friends burst into laughter.

Ivy stopped laughing long enough to add, "Although if I *were* talking about that, I'm quite sure I would *indeed* rock your world, Mr. Steven Smith!"

The friends laughed even harder.

"Seriously Stevie, I really do have a very cool surprise for you. Can you meet me at my place by seven?"

"I'll be there," said Stevie. "but can you at least give me a hint?"

"It is so crazy good that I will keep it a surprise!" she said, giving Stevie a mischievous smile.

"I must say, Ivy S. Miles, I do like it when you tease me like that!" answered Stevie while returning Ivy's gaze.

"You can cut the tension between you two love birds with a knife!" Sophie interjected playfully as they all arrived at the gym.

– 54 –

After having spent the last forty-eight hours of being poked, prodded, scanned, blood taken, etc., Alan was released from the hospital and got into the car that waited to bring him to his private plane at a nearby airport. He barely glanced at the driver who was holding the door open, but did notice that the driver was wearing what looked like a cross between a bowler hat and some sort of German alpine hat. Alan decided he would eventually have to inquire about the choice of the hat. But not now. The driver closed the door and got behind the wheel.

"How long to the airport?" Alan asked, still feeling the effects of the pain meds.

"If we hustle, I can get you there in forty-five minutes on the freeway," the driver answered in a deep and friendly voice. "There is another more scenic route we can go, and I guess that would put you at the airport in about an hour and a half. What'll it be, boss?"

Alan hesitated. He wasn't used to being spoken to in this way. Most drivers replied to him with curt answers and never met his eyes. This driver's eyes were peering at Alan kindly in the rearview mirror as he waited for a reply.

"Let's take the scenic route. I'll have my assistant inform the pilot that we'll arrive in approximately ninety minutes."

"Will do," said the driver. Then he turned to take Alan in. "My name is

Toots, Mr. Miles." Alan nodded but the driver wasn't done talking. "What put you in the hospital today, boss? You not feeling well?" asked Toots.

"Mr. Toots? What kind of a name is that?" asked Alan.

"It's just Toots!" the driver said, laughing, "My god given name is Duncan Heets, sir, but I've gone by Toots since I was nineteen years old."

"Is there a story behind this nickname?" asked Alan, surprising himself.

"Well, I made a mistake when I was nineteen, and as a result spent the next thirty-seven years of my life paying for my sins in a prison in Texas." Toots glanced in the rearview mirror. Alan looked stunned. Toots continued. "My first cellmate and I shared an eight-by-twelve-foot cell. His name was Terry, he gave me the nickname Toots after just the first week in the prison on account of my belly's reaction to the Texas prison system's fine cuisine. I can spell it out for you, but I'm guessing you can do the math." Toots chuckled.

Alan was unsure how to react. He was not a defense attorney and had never met someone who had spent time in prison.

"Sorry to lay that information on you like that, boss. But you see that is just how it is. I made a mistake, paid for it for most of my adult life, and now here I am driving you from the hospital to your private airplane."

Alan spoke. "Duncan, if I may ask, what was it that you did to put you in prison for thirty-seven years?"

"Nobody has called me Duncan in a long time, but I sure do like how that sounds!" Toots said, laughing. Then he grew serious. "I killed my younger brother Josh."

Alan's mouth hung open for a moment.

"Now we had just ordered our first beers at a Negro bar, that's what they called 'em back in Texas in those days," Toots continued. "Then me and Josh got into it like we had a thousand times before. It was one of those hot and dry Texas summer days and after working side by side all day, Josh and I both had short fuses. Try as I might, I never could remember what it was that we were arguing about that day."

Toots changed lanes and was silent for a moment.

"Mr. Miles, sir, we never even threw a punch, we just ended up wrestling on the floor. Not but a minute later my little brother was lying there with blood coming out of both his ears and he had stopped breathing. They say he must have hit his head when we fell and that was it, he was gone."

Alan nodded to himself.

"Now, back in those days, the Texas police didn't take kindly to a young and strong Negro like me having killed his own kin. So the judge gave me the maximum sentence of thirty-seven years with no chance of parole. When I went in I was not quite twenty and when I got out four years ago now, I was fifty-seven years old."

Alan shook his head, incredulously. "Did you have a lawyer to represent you when the state charged you with first degree murder? It sounds to me like it most certainly should not have been tried as a murder, but more likely a case of manslaughter."

"Well, that's all in the past, Mr. Miles. Josh has been gone for forty-one years now. I paid my debts and I am a free man. It doesn't matter what happened all those years ago. Not to me it doesn't, anyway," Toots said with a tone that ended that line of questioning.

Alan stared out the window and his thoughts flooded in. He tried to remember where he was in life when he was twenty years years old. He would have been in his freshman year at Harvard, he calculated. Then it dawned on Alan that although he had never spent a night in prison, he had never truly been a free man, either.

All his life Alan had lived in a self-created prison, where his work was his judge and jury. He was a multi-millionaire, had the respect of the legal community all around the world, and a daughter that anyone else would be beyond proud of, and yet had never once taken the time to enjoy any of it, not even for even a split second. In stark contrast, here was a man who had spent thirty-seven of his sixty-one years of life in prison, yet Toots seemed to be happy, appreciative, content, and truly free.

"You got family? Wife or children?" asked Toots.

"My wife has been dead almost fifteen years now. There is a daughter, but I have never been family to her. I have my partner at my law firm and my assistant that has been with me for the last twenty-five years, but I guess that isn't exactly family either," answered Alan.

"Well, maybe it's time you pay your debt and become family with your daughter," said Toots before asking, "What's her name?"

"My wife Clara named her Ivy. She just turned sixteen," answered Alan.

"Well, I am sure she is a fine young lady. I guess Ivy will be off to college before long," said Toots.

"She'll be going in a few years. She takes after her mother, I've been told she is a talented volleyball player. Perhaps she'll play in college the way her mother did," said Alan, which was the first time the thought had occurred to him.

There was a long pause before Alan asked, "Duncan, after thirty-seven years in prison, what did you do the day you got out? What was it that you missed most?"

"For so many years I dreamed of having a root beer float like I had had as a child. I took a bus back to the town where I grew up, thinking I would go to the same little ice cream shop, but it was all gone. The neighborhood, the fields, the shops, they were all gone. In their place were buildings and malls and fast food restaurants. Wouldn't you know it, Mr. Miles, I couldn't find one place in all the city that made a root beer float...not a one. I went to a grocery store that was bigger than anything I could have ever imagined and bought a bottle of root beer and a tub of vanilla ice cream and made myself the one thing I had been dreaming of drinking all those years."

"So, was it as good as you remembered it?" asked Alan.

"Well, the root beer tasted like medicine, and the cold ice cream made my teeth ache from all my cavities. I never got to see a proper dentist in prison," answered Toots, laughing before continuing. "But I found a coffee shop called Starbucks and something called a white chocolate mocha Frappuccino, and I quickly forgot all about the root beer float." Toots paused. "Mr. Miles, the one thing I know about this life we are all living is this, change never stops happening. What was yesterday is long gone. Maybe tomorrow they'll close that Starbucks shop and I'll have to find me a new drink, but that's just how it is. Every day we wake up, it's like we are born all over, not knowing what life has in store for us."

– 55 –

Mr. C's breathing had improved significantly; the injuries from the fall were only bruises and would heal with time. He was relieved to be released from the hospital, and he contacted a taxi service that had vans available for obese patients. Within the hour a mini-van arrived at the hospital with both the middle seats folded into the floor, allowing him to slide in and sit on the back bench. He avoided the glances of the driver; he had made up his mind that his future would be different starting now. Thirty minutes later the taxi pulled into his driveway, and with the help of an oversized walker, he slowly made his way into the garage.

He saw the broken pane of glass on the side door now covered with cardboard and assumed that the firemen had done it in order to unlock the door from the inside. He made a mental note to find out which fire department responded to the call Friday night so he could send them a thank you gift expressing his appreciation. He hadn't had his keys with him when he was rushed to the hospital, but remembered the key his mother had always left hidden under an old glass jar on the bottom shelf in the garage. He had to push around dozens of large clear trash bags filled with plastic frozen dinner trays and empty soda bottles in order to get to the shelf where the jar was standing. Those simple movements left him short of breath and he suddenly felt dizzy. He leaned back against the moldy garage wall until he was able to catch his breath, before reaching down and finding the key. Once inside, he went to his computer room to check how much damage was done from the fall.

The firemen had moved his desk right side up and placed the keyboard as well as the speakers back on the desktop. Both flat screen monitors, cracked and clearly no longer functioning, had been moved to the corner of the room. Mr. C. went into the closet and found an old flat-screen monitor and plugged it into his computer. From his front pocket, he fished out the brochure from The Boulder Eating Recovery Center and went to their website.

Moments later, Mr. C. picked up the phone.

"B.E.R.C., this is Maggie, how can I help you today?" said a woman in a tone that sounded almost too happy.

"Hello, my name is David Connor and I am calling from Boston, Massachusetts," said Mr. C.

"Hello David, what can I do for you today, dear?" replied the woman.

As he explained the events that had unfolded over the past week, he surprised himself at how much information he was sharing.

"Well, David sweetie, making this phone call is a brave thing to do and you should be proud of yourself for taking action and control of your life. We absolutely have room for you here and we will get you started back on a road to a healthy body and a healthy mind just as soon as you can make the trip here to Colorado."

Mr. C. frowned. "I'll have to figure out how to get out to you, I won't fly nor can I drive that far."

"Don't worry, we have patients from all over the US. I can recommend to you several companies that specialize in helping our patients make the trip here to our facility. The companies have specially fitted conversion vans for shorter trips and larger RVs for the longer trips. How does that sound?"

Suddenly, he felt as if all of the events of the last days were in some sort of divine order. He knew it was time for change and felt the community in Colorado was going to be the best place for him.

"That sounds perfect. I will contact them ASAP and when I know more I will let you know."

"I think you're making a great decision by coming here and putting your faith in our program," she said warmly. "I will send you the paperwork we need regarding insurance and payment options along with the transportation information. We will have a room waiting for you when you are ready."

"I can't thank you enough," said Mr. C., tears clouding his eyes.

Chapter 56

"Duncan, how long have you been driving for this car service?"

Alan was fascinated by the clarity with which Toots had been speaking, and found everything he said to ring true. Only yesterday, Alan was solely focused on his preparation for the meetings in Washington, and now those same meetings seemed—*were*—unimportant.

"Well, I guess it's been about a year now. The boss only calls me when he is short a driver, so it's not a full-time job, but it's better than nothing. You know, with my past, Mr. Miles, it aint easy to find work."

Alan nodded. "I will begin chemotherapy treatments at the hospital you just picked me up from. For now, I will stay at a hotel in the city, but perhaps I could find something closer to the hospital. Wherever I am, I'm going to need someone to drive me and help out if or when I need it. If you're interested, I can offer you full-time work for the next six months. After that, we can look to see where I'm at with regards to my health. Perhaps twenty-five hundred per week for the next six months would be in order."

Toots raised his eyebrows in surprise. "What?"

But Alan wasn't done. "The offer includes full health insurance and dental. I will arrange to immediately find a car that you can also use as your personal transportation during the time you're working for me."

There was an awkward silence.

"Now Mr. Miles," said Toots finally, "why would you want to pay someone like me so damn much money? I've never made more than three hundred dollars in a week ever in my life and twenty-five hundred just don't make no kind of sense to me. That's way more than the going rate. And you want to give me health insurance and dental, too? That's just crazy." Toots broke into a reluctant smile. "Well, I guess this is my lucky day."

Alan smiled for the first time in recent memory. He handed Toots his business card.

"Call my assistant and work out the details with her, all right?"

Toots took the business card from Alan and very carefully tucked it into the front breast pocket of his crisp, white button-down shirt. Just then, they pulled up on the tarmac and stopped next to the already open stairs of Alan's Gulfstream G650. Toots hopped out and walked around the back of the Lincoln to open the passenger door for Alan.

Slowly and with some pain, Alan climbed out of the car and for the first time, he looked Toots directly in the eye.

"I very much enjoyed speaking with you today, Duncan." Toots grinned and shook Alan's hand.

Alan tilted his head. "By the way, before I forget. Is there a story behind the hat?"

Toots took his hat off and studied it. "This thing? I saw it in a pawn shop and it reminded me of the hat my father used to wear when I was a kid. If you don't care for it, I do have a black driver's cap that I can wear the next time I pick you up."

Alan grinned. "I like the hat just fine, Duncan. You be sure to wear it whenever you want."

"Well, thank you, Mr. Miles. I really appreciate the offer and I'll be calling Cathy first thing in the morning," said Toots. "And Mr. Miles, I'm looking forward to meeting your baby girl Ivy!"

– 57 –

After volleyball practice, Ivy got home and still had about an hour before Stevie would arrive for their big date. Glancing at her watch to be sure, she grabbed Jake's journal and sat down on the couch to spend some much-needed time with her brother.

Ivy,

As I am writing this entry, you are asleep in Mama's arms next to me on my bed. You are so little and both of you look beautiful and peaceful. I find it sad that I am writing these words with you asleep right next to me and yet you will not read them for nearly fifteen years.

I'm sure Mama already told you this story, but I will tell it again. The day the surgeons informed us that they had scheduled surgery the following week to amputate my leg, Mama and I walked out of the Dana Farber Cancer Institute in a daze. Neither of us knew what to say or how to respond. The doctor explained that it was my best option, along with the chemo treatment, to save my life. I heard what the doctor had said but simply couldn't comprehend the concept of actually having my left leg cut from my body.

Mama and I were walking back in silence to the parking garage when suddenly she stopped and sat down on a bench in the hospital courtyard. I sat down next to her and as we were both quietly looking up at the clear blue sky, a pigeon flew down and landed in front of us. Making that cooing sound that only pigeons can, it began not walking, but sort of hopping closer to us. We noticed that instead of a left foot, it had a gnarled stump. Regardless, the pigeon had no trouble moving. He then stood perfectly balanced on his one normal foot while the left stump hung just centimeters off the ground. For what seemed to be hours, though I am sure it was only seconds, the pigeon stared at us as if to say,

"Look at me, I faced what you are facing and I survived."

We sat in silence, as the bird performed a series of movements that seemed to be showing off its mobility despite its handicap. Probably it was just a dumb pigeon that was looking for some bread, but to us, it seemed it had a message.

When the pigeon finally flew away, we looked at each other and smiled. Without words, we knew what we had just witnessed was something special.

I am not exactly sure about my faith or the existence of a god, but that pigeon sure seemed to be a messenger of hope at a time when we needed hope more than anything in the world.

You are just starting to wake up so I will take you in my arms and see if I can keep you quiet and let Mama get some more sleep. She wouldn't say it, but I could see in her eyes that she was fighting another headache. She can use all the sleep she can get.

I love you, Ives!

– 58 –

The jet landed in Boston, and as Alan got into the waiting limo, for the first time he could ever remember, he had no interest in getting back to work. Suddenly, Alan saw the insanity of his life. Why had he never before had an interaction like the one he had experienced earlier in the day with his driver in Washington. Although he spent less than two hours with Duncan, it felt to Alan as if he had shared more with him than he had even shared with his wife Clara in their nearly twenty-year relationship. It had come so naturally to speak with him.

Alan assumed that it was most likely a result of the pain medicine that he had taken before he had left the hospital—that made sense—and he also thought that surely, the news of his terminal illness had influenced him.

Then, it struck him—if he had been able to connect with a perfect stranger like Duncan, perhaps he could connect with his daughter Ivy as well? Alan knew it wasn't nearly as easy with his daughter, because he was certain that she resented him for being such a failure as a father. It dawned on Alan, uncomfortably and almost comically, that there wasn't a single person in this world that he feared more than his sixteen-year-old daughter.

The realization that he was afraid of his own daughter made Alan close his eyes, shake his head, and make a snorting sound of laughter.

So much so that the driver of the limo service that had picked Alan up at the airport glanced back in the rear-view mirror and asked, "Is everything in order back there, Mr. Miles?"

Alan smiled hesitantly. "Yes," he said, smiling more broadly now. "More than ever."

The driver dropped Alan off at the front entrance of the Boston Ritz-Carlton. Alan had decided that he would spend the next few nights at the hotel before returning to D.C. on Friday in order to start with the chemo treatments on Monday. He wasn't ready to face Ivy and tell her about his health situation, but he realized, with perfect clarity, that he needed to share his diagnosis with Cathy. He would do so via email.

Once in his suite at the Ritz-Carlton, Alan was drawn immediately to the living room area, which was filled with light from floor to ceiling windows. Amazed at the sight of the Boston skyline, as if he had never seen it before, Alan stood mesmerized for several minutes.

He walked to the kitchen and poured himself a glass of water, then swallowed two pills. He wrote an email to Cathy with the general details of his illness. He explained his decision to move to D.C. full-time for the next six months because of his chemotherapy treatments.

Alan knew, deep inside, that he would never work again. He thought of asking Cathy to speak with Ivy for him, but knew that he should face his daughter himself. He owed Ivy at least that much.

– 59 –

The driver dropped Ivy and Stevie as close to Fenway Park as possible. Laughing, Ivy helped a blindfolded Stevie out of the car and turned him so that he was facing the stadium.

"Okay, ready?"

"Ready as I'll ever be!" said Stevie, laughing too.

Ivy removed the blindfold.

Stevie shielded his eyes for a moment, as he took in the sight. It was 6:45 p.m. and the sun was just beginning to set. The crowd gathering around Fenway was excited and moving inside to take their seats.

"Ivy, you did not get seats to the sold-out Yankees game tonight, did you?" Stevie asked incredulously, turning to face Ivy.

"Well, sort of," said Ivy, with a grin.

"What do you mean, 'sort of'?" Stevie laughed.

Ivy smiled mischievously. "We'll be watching the game tonight, but not from just any seats. We're going to watch from the owner's luxury box."

Stevie's eyes widened. "No way! How did you do that?"

Ivy shrugged. "Well, my father's partner is friends with the owner of the Red Sox, so..."

Unable to control his excitement, Stevie picked up Ivy and spun her around the way a father does to a small child. He finally put her down and with a hand on either side of Ivy's face kissed her on the lips.

"I hope this isn't some sort of a ploy to get me into bed, Ivy S. Miles. You should know I'm a gentleman and it's not going to be that easy," said Stevie, causing them both to burst out laughing. "I am so underdressed. If I had known, I would have rented a tuxedo or bought a suit! My father is not going to believe this!"

"You look perfect just the way you are," said Ivy, beaming now.

"I can't believe you did this for me, this is insane!"

"Maybe you'll be playing for the Red Sox someday, so you might as well meet your future boss sooner than later." said Ivy.

"Ha, ha, very funny." Stevie hugged Ivy again.

Moments later, accompanied by a security guard, the two stepped out of the elevator and into the luxury box. They were both amazed at the size and style of what appeared to be more of a restaurant than a luxury box. Stevie stared out through the floor to ceiling glass window and gazed at Fenway Park. The lively crowd was hurrying to their seats and spilling—the mood was absolutely infectious.

Stevie turned and looked at a grinning Ivy again.

"Am I dreaming?"

At that moment, a man in grey dress pants and a white button-down shirt appeared and extended his hand to Ivy.

"You must be Ivy. I'm John Henry. Harry told me that Alan's daughter would be joining us this evening," he said, smiling graciously. "He also said that because of your height and beauty you wouldn't be difficult to notice, and I must say, he was not wrong, young lady!"

Ivy shook his hand. "Thank you so much for having us, Mr. Henry, we really appreciate it."

Stevie held out his hand too. "Mr. Henry, Stevie Smith. I am Ivy's plus one. It really is a thrill to be here in your suite. Thank you so much."

"Stevie, Ivy, I'm happy to have you both here with us tonight. Welcome to Fenway Park."

At that moment, another man joined them. He was significantly younger than Mr. Henry, and had a slightly arrogant manner. Mr. Henry introduced him, "Jim, this is Ivy Miles, daughter of Alan Miles. I believe you've heard that name before."

"Jim Callaway, nice to meet you." The man held out his hand. "Your father is the infamous Alan Miles? I received my law degree at Harvard and I must say, your father and Harry are celebrities at the Harvard Law School."

Ivy raised her eyebrows and smiled. "Celebrities, huh?"

"Yes, in fact," Jim continued, "I wrote a paper on the work your father and Harry did on the case Apple brought against the Chinese government."

Mr. Henry smiled and patted Jim on the back. "Ivy, Stevie, I sincerely hope you've both brought your appetites with you. They should be bringing up the fresh Maine lobster any minute now. Let's get you all a drink before they throw the first pitch."

As they made their way to the bar area, Stevie leaned in close to Ivy and said, "Thank you again for doing this for me tonight. I don't know what else I can say except I wouldn't want to be here with anyone else in the world."

– 60 –

When Harry arrived at the Ritz-Carlton suite, Alan was on his laptop researching and reading all he could find about treatments for pancreatic cancer. Although it had been less than a week since Harry had last seen him, Alan looked as if he had aged ten years. Neither of the men spoke. Harry walked straight to the bar and poured two tumblers of Glenlivet Scotch with ice.

Alan slowly made his way to the bar and sat at one of the stools. Harry slid the glass in front of him.

"I just got a message from John Henry. He wanted me to tell you what a charming young lady you raised your daughter to be," Harry said. After a moment, he continued. "Ivy asked Cathy if she could get her two tickets to the Red Sox game earlier this evening."

Alan sipped his scotch and was silent. Harry continued. "Am I right in assuming that you haven't told Ivy about any of your health issues or your planned move to D.C.?"

"Harry, you'll have to take care of all the finances for Ivy, she's too young to be given the responsibility to manage her inheritance. I'm meeting with my financial advisors tomorrow and will instruct them to sell all the real estate I currently own. Once all my assets are liquid, you will only need to meet with money managers a few times a year. I'll have the team brief you when the work is done," Alan said.

Harry sighed. Discussing Ivy was not on the table, apparently.

"Alan, you do realize Boston has some of the best hospitals in the world, right? Is there any particular reason you've decided to move to D.C. to have the treatments? Or is dying alone your way of punishing yourself for your shortcomings as a father and husband?"

True to form, Alan ignored the question and asked, "Harry, will you continue to work when I'm gone?"

"I would have quit working a long time ago if it wasn't for you still bringing in case after case," Harry replied. "I never lived for law the way you did. Don't get me wrong, some of my greatest memories are the times we were in a courtroom and I would look over and see the other attorneys cringing at the thought of facing two of the greatest minds that have ever practiced law."

Alan chuckled at the memory.

"Of course, mine being the greater mind between the two of us," Harry said with a smirk. "But I've always had my life outside of law. I'm happy just sitting on a beach with a good book and a cigar, or taking friends out for dinner and drinking wine until the early hours of the morning. You see Alan, these are activities that normal humans do. But then that's always been your problem, you have never done anything normal in your entire life."

"I got married, I guess one could call that normal," Alan said in an unconvincing tone.

"Sure, you got married, but that was more because you were afraid to say no to Clara than it was you actually wanted to get married. Clara was the best thing that happened to you, but even she couldn't pry you away from your work." Harry paused. Alan looked down at his hands, silently.

"I don't know why you are the way you are," Harry continued, "and I strongly suspect you know even less than I do, but I wish more than anything you would have your treatments here in Boston and spend the time you have left being a father to Ivy. Unfortunately, I know you probably won't do that because you need to die exactly the way you have lived—alone."

Harry smiled a little. "As for me, I'll be spending more time in

Northern California. I bought a small working vineyard out in Napa Valley and I aim to learn all there is to know about the art of wine making. I tell you what, you beat this cancer, and once you recover, come and join me. We can start our second partnership, Begosian & Miles Winery. Hell, we built the most feared law firm in the world, what's to stop us from creating the finest bottle of wine in the world?"

Alan tried to manage a laugh. "I doubt very much I will be in the 3% that survives pancreatic cancer, but if I do, I'll take you up on that offer, Harry."

There was a convivial silence. "But I do think that Miles & Begosian Winery has a much better ring to it."

Harry looked at Alan with surprise.

"Alan, in all the years I've known you, that may have been the first time I've heard you attempt to make a joke. See, there is hope for you after all," Harry said, smiling. "Wherever Ivy ends up, I will make sure she has anything and everything she needs. That I can promise you."

"Thank you." Alan's voice came out in almost a whisper.

Then Harry looked at him wryly. "Alan, you've never seen Ivy play volleyball before, have you?"

Meekly, Alan shook his head.

"She has a game Saturday here at her school. How about we see if Cathy and her husband are available and the four of us go and watch her play? It would be quite a surprise for her if we all showed up together."

Alan thought about the idea of sitting in a hot high school gym surrounded by parents, students, and faculty, cheering for Ivy and her team. He was reminded of the one and only time he watched his wife play volleyball at a home game during her junior year at Harvard. She explained that it was an important game against one of their biggest rivals and promised that if he came to watch her play that one time, she would never ask him again. He agreed and sat through the game. Having to endure the noise coming from both the crowd and the student brass band that played at every break of action, he vowed never to go to another sporting event in his life. Alan also remembered how appreciative Clara was that he had made the effort and stayed until the end.

"I'm planning to fly back to D.C. Friday morning, so I won't be able to go. But I'm quite sure Ivy would appreciate it more if you and Cathy were there to support her," he said, finally.

"I sometimes forget how detached you truly are," said Harry. "Ivy has no mother, no grandparents, no cousins, aunts, uncles, she only has you. I know you may have absolutely no connection or emotions when it comes to…" Harry paused, "…well anything, really, but Ivy isn't like you. If you are indeed planning on moving to D.C. to die alone, the least you could do is watch your daughter, who happens to be one of the best players in the country for Christ's sake, play the game that she loves." Harry said.

Alan knew that everything Harry had just said was true. He was moving to D.C. so he could die alone. He didn't have any connection to anyone else in the world other than Harry and perhaps in some way, Cathy. But most of all, Harry was right; Ivy needed him to come and show that he cared about her life.

"I'll talk to Cathy and have her change my flight plans to Sunday morning and ask if she's available to join us on Saturday," Alan said as he gingerly walked back over and sat back down on the couch.

"How's the pain?" asked Harry.

"As long as I take pain meds every four hours it's not too bad, but drinking that scotch probably wasn't a very good idea." Alan closed his eyes and within seconds, he was fast asleep.

Harry finished his last sip of scotch, quietly shut off the lights, and closed the door behind him. As he got into the elevator, he felt his eyes fill with tears as he tried to imagine a world without his partner and best friend Alan Miles in it.

– 61 –

As Lisa unlocked the door to her apartment, the sounds of Dennis's favorite Soundgarden CD came drifting out to meet her. She hadn't seen him for days and now, she felt a jolt of anxiety and anticipation spreading throughout her body.

The living room was dim, with the curtains drawn. The music was louder. A man Lisa didn't recognize was plunging a needle into a young girl's arm. The needle glinted in the low light.

Lisa heard the scratch of a lighter and saw a flame. There was Dennis. "Lisa, these are friends of mine," he said, without taking his eyes off the spoon or the flame licking the bottom of it.

Lisa stared at Dennis, at the flame, at the two limp figures on the couch, and then her disbelieving eyes traveled back to Dennis again. "I came back just to take a quick shower," Dennis continued, "but I guess I lost track of time. Sorry to be in your way here. We'll take off." His voice was unrecognizable to Lisa.

The young girl's eyes rolled into the back of her head as her body slowly relaxed and she leaned back on the couch. The man put away the syringe and elastic band into some sort of small carrying case that was lying open on the glass coffee table. "Whoa," said Dennis, interrupting him, and he gestured at the elastic band.

"Dennis—" Lisa managed to say in a whisper that came out as a croak. The air in the apartment was acrid and smoky. "What are you doing?"

"I'm sorry you have to see this, baby." Dennis put the lighter down only to pick up a small syringe and fill it with the liquid leftover in the spoon. He reached for the elastic, tied it around his upper arm, and turned his head to Lisa. "But I need a fix."

Wordlessly, Lisa turned and went to the kitchen. Flicking on the light, she put on a pot of coffee, filled a pot with water for pasta and opened the refrigerator to look for some sauce. Or something. Anything. As she peered into the refrigerator, Lisa felt a wave of cold nausea hit her. In her living room, right now, were two strangers and Dennis. And they were all shooting up heroin. Lisa hung her head in disbelief.

– 62 –

Like pretty much anyone who has ever met our parents, I wondered how Mama ended up with someone like our father. I asked her a few months ago and this was her explanation:

Mama's mother was forty-three and her father fifty-five when she was born, so she said she always assumed that she was not planned. Her father was a brilliant, larger than life character with absolutely no interest in children—his or anyone else's. He worked as a psychiatrist and had a private practice before he switched careers and took a position as professor at Cambridge University. Mama said most of her memories of her mother involved her waiting hand and foot on her husband from the moment he woke up and walked out the door, to the moment he came home. Her mother had no friends, no family, no hobbies, and no life. Her sole reason for existing was to take care of her husband's every want and need, so much so that she was not even particularly concerned with her own daughter's well-being.

When her dad died of a heart attack at the age of seventy-two, Mama was sixteen years old. Just four months later, her mother took her own life by downing a bottle of pills. She didn't bother to leave a note to anyone, which Mama felt was consistent with her behavior. She had not shown any interest in her daughter during the sixteen years she was alive, nor upon her death.

Mama vowed that she would never allow herself to be in a relationship where she was dependent on her partner. She wanted to find happiness from within and looked forward to having children and being a better mother to her own children than her mother was to her. When she met our dad, Alan, she saw in him a brilliant mind, much like her father's, and was immediately drawn to him. She said she also saw in him a lack of need to be taken care of, which was as far from her father as could be. Mama also said, which I thought was kind of funny, she liked that despite the fact that dad was tall and handsome, he wasn't full of himself. She said he wasn't particularly impressed nor intimidated by her good looks or height either.

So that was her explanation of how she could fall in love and make a life with someone like our father. She knew no one could ever understand why she ended up with Alan, but she loves Alan with all her heart and is in awe of how committed he is to his work. She also said that someday we will understand that he does the best he can to show love to us, but that he is simply not wired like the average person.

So that was about all of it, and I have to say, Ivy, it really does answer pretty much every question I have ever had when it comes to trying to understand our parents' strange relationship. Mama is certainly correct in Alan not being wired like others, but I am sure you agree, she shows us enough love to more than make up for our fathers shortcomings, right?

Love you, Ives!

Ivy sat curled up on the couch and finished reading her brother's journal entry for the third time in a row. She had learned so much in it. Suddenly, her phone buzzed and Ivy checked her text messages to find a message from Cathy.

Ivy,

This I'm sure will be as much of a shock to you as it was to me, but your father, Harry, and my husband and I will all be coming to watch your home volleyball match this Saturday afternoon. I am assuming we don't need to buy tickets beforehand, but if I am wrong please let me know and I will arrange accordingly.

Looking forward to seeing you play,
Cathy

Ivy's heart raced at the thought that her father would actually come and watch her play volleyball. It seemed so strange to her, and such a wonderful coincidence, after reading what Jake had said, that her father would suddenly decide to take an interest in her athletic career. Harry must have had something to do with it, Ivy thought. What would it be like to know her father was in the crowd watching her play? The thought made Ivy nervous.

Ivy looked at her watch and realized she was running a bit late. In ten minutes, the car service would be waiting to bring her to Brookline for the grand opening of the Phams' fifth Golden Dragon restaurant. Ivy jumped up to take a quick shower and change her clothes.

– 63 –

Lisa lay in a ball under the covers of her bed. With her hands and feet numb with pins, she clenched her fists tightly over both her ears as if to keep a monster from entering her head. She was having a full-blown panic attack.

"This fear is not logical, Lisa, just breathe. Lisa, it is not real, just breathe. This fear is not real and there is nothing to fear. It will pass like it has hundreds of times before, just breathe." She whispered to herself over and over, just as she had learned in rehab.

As the waves of anxiety and panic began to subside, Lisa recalled one of her happiest memories in order to keep her mind away from the monster. It was the time her mother came home with an old Monopoly game that she had bought at a yard sale. It was missing most of the money and only a few of the houses and hotels were still in the old taped up box. There were several Lego pieces of different shapes and colors that were included for what Lisa imagined to be substitutes for the car, shoe, bucket, and other figures she couldn't remember. She must have been nine or ten years old at the time and was the one and only time she could ever remember playing with her mother. Neither knew the rules of the game and of course there were no instructions included in the box. Regardless, they played their own made-up game for what must have been several hours. By then, her mother had finished off several bottles of wine and was dozing off at the table. Lisa quietly placed all the pieces and game board back in the box and left it on top of the old fridge in the kitchen, where it stayed until they were kicked out of the apartment.

Her breathing was calmer, her body more relaxed, and eventually Lisa closed her eyes. As she drifted off to sleep, she wondered where that old Monopoly game ended up.

– 64 –

As the town car drove up to the entrance of the newest Golden Dragon restaurant, Ivy was amazed at the sheer size of the building. It looked more like something from the Las Vegas strip than the outskirts of Boston.

Jimmy and Nancy were both greeting the local politicians, businessmen, friends, and workers from the many companies that had a hand in the construction of the building project. Both greeted Ivy warmly and ushered her into the restaurant, arm in arm. Ivy was struck by the ornate interior. She was fascinated by how the designers could create such an amazing and elaborate atmosphere. When Ivy spotted Sophie, she realized that her best friend was looking more grown up and more beautiful than she had ever seen her before. Sophie was dressed in a simple but elegant white dinner dress and suddenly, Ivy felt very underdressed.

Just as she was about to walk in Sophie's direction, she saw Eduardo, Jimmy's right-hand man, also walking towards Sophie. Ivy met Eduardo several times over the years, and she knew that Sophie had often baby-sat for him and his wife over the past months. However, Eduardo looked somehow different, Ivy thought to herself. Perhaps he had lost weight and gotten in better shape? She was certain he had changed his hair style to a modern, slicked back style. Whatever the changes, he looked years younger than the last time Ivy had seen him.

Then, unexpectedly, Ivy saw something secret pass between Eduardo and Sophie. It was fleeting but unmistakable; their hands brushed, briefly, and they shared a knowing, mischievous look. Ivy felt her face flush as she realized that her best friend was having an affair with a much older, married man who also happened to be her father's right-hand man. She felt sick.

As Eduardo turned his head, his eyes met Ivy's, and he immediately knew she had figured it out. Up until that moment, the affair had been the most exciting and alluring experience Eduardo had ever had, aside from getting married and moving to Boston. After so many years of dating countless beautiful young girls in Vegas, he and his wife had gone through years of hormone therapy, which meant engaging in sex only on specific dates and times when his wife's body was at its most fertile. Eduardo had come to feel like sex with his wife was more a chore or work than it was lovemaking. After three years and almost a hundred thousand dollars of hormone treatments, his wife got pregnant and gave birth to a healthy baby boy. If the sex before the pregnancy seemed like a chore to Eduardo, at the very least it was physical contact of some kind. Since the day his wife had received the news that her dreams had finally come true and she was indeed pregnant, the couple had not had any physical relationship of any kind.

When the baby was just over a year old, Eduardo's wife decided she was ready to once again go back to work as a nurse. They began interviewing nannies and babysitters for the weekends when they both needed to be at work, but none seemed a good fit. It wasn't until one day at the office when he was complaining to his boss Jimmy about their inability to find a sitter that both he and his wife trusted, that Jimmy suggested his daughter. The next day after school, Sophie went to their house to spend time with the baby and immediately took to the adorable little boy.

Every other week, Eduardo's wife worked the weekend shift. Sophie would come to the house at 4:00 p.m. and Eduardo would make sure she had everything she needed before driving to the restaurant farthest away from his home and working his way back towards his house. After doing his rounds at all four Golden Dragon restaurants, making sure everything was in order, he would race back to the house to take over for Sophie. Over the months, Eduardo found he truly enjoyed the short time he spent talking with Sophie until she left to bike the mile-and-a-half route back to her house. Though only fifteen years old, Eduardo felt like he and Sophie had a special connection, and unlike his wife, felt that Sophie actually listened to him when he talked.

As time went by, Eduardo found himself home earlier and earlier, and Sophie stayed later and later, often times watching a movie or TV together. It started out so innocently in Eduardo's mind, just laughing and flirting, until the night Sophie was complaining of muscle soreness in her back and shoulders from a particularly intense volleyball practice she had had earlier in the day. Eduardo offered her a back massage, and as she sat in front of him on the couch and he began massaging her, he could no longer stop the momentum of the emotions they were both feeling. That night they shared their first kiss and week after week things progressed until he began making love to his underage babysitter who just happened to be his boss's daughter.

Eduardo knew what he was doing was not only immoral, but illegal as well. Yet no matter how many times he told himself he had to end the relationship with Sophie, his heart simply wouldn't let him go through with it. Instead, he spent every waking minute of every day waiting for the next time Sophie was babysitting so they could spend time together.

Now, Eduardo saw the contempt in Ivy's eyes and in an instant, his heart sank to his knees. He saw himself in that look of disgust, and the truth came roaring to the surface. Not knowing how to react or what to do in such a public situation, Eduardo simply passed by Ivy woodenly, without making eye contact. He walked to the main entrance to join Jimmy and Nancy as they stood waiting for the mayor of Boston along with his assistant and his security detail, who were due to arrive any minute. His thoughts were racing and his heart was pounding.

Ivy too needed to take several deep breaths and to pull herself together. Every fiber in her body wanted to scream out that she knew what Eduardo was doing and that he was taking advantage of a young girl like Sophie. But Sophie looked so peaceful and happy, and it occurred to Ivy that Sophie had likely fallen in love with Eduardo.

Right or wrong, she was not going to be the one to turn her best friend's world upside down. Not today, anyway. Instead, Ivy took a deep breath and, sneaking up behind Sophie, gave her a big hug. She whispered in Sophie's ear, "When did my best friend get so damn sexy? That dress is more Hollywood than Boston!"

"Hey Ivy, I was hoping you'd be here. Do you really like the dress? It's a little too much for this event, but I figured why not? I don't exactly have the long legs like you, but I work with what I've got."

"Let's eat!" said Ivy with a big smile on her face.

– 65 –

After spending most of the day in the old VW van, Dennis had walked the five miles to the dealer that he trusted the most to give him at least half-way clean heroin. Dennis knew of dealers in Boston said to cut their heroin with all kinds of substances such as baking soda, starch, talcum powder, crushed ibuprofen tablets, laundry detergent, and in some cases even rat poison, but he had been lucky so far.

Dennis had already gone to the ATM and took out three hundred fifty dollars, which he figured would be enough to buy seven small plastic bags—five for himself and two for Olive. He didn't know it at the time, but only about twenty-five per cent of what he bought was actually heroin; the rest was cut with powdered sugar and laundry detergent. After he made his buy, Dennis stopped at a convenience store and bought a six-pack of Budweiser. In the parking lot, he pulled his dirty hoodie closer against himself to ward off the cold and headed back to the van.

He walked for what felt like forever when suddenly, he stopped in his tracks. Blue lights flickered and flashed, reflecting off car windows, pulsing through the trees—and shining on the VW van.

Dennis doubled back, hit the dirt and belly crawled behind some garbage cans. Three police cars surrounded the van. Tina sat in the back of one of them, her pale face streaked with mascara. Olive had his hands cuffed behind his back. It was over. No—it was worse than over, it was only beginning. Dennis closed his eyes. Tina was at most fifteen, but probably younger? He wasn't sure. But he knew she was underage and that he and Olive would serve serious time for that alone.

With his heart pounding and his hands caked with dirt, Dennis crawled deeper into the woods and leaned up against a big oak tree. Hungrily, he opened one of the bags of beef jerky he had bought and cracked a beer, and as he chewed, tried to figure out what his next move should be. The cops would be looking for him, he knew that much. Olive would sing like canary and the first place they'd check would be Lisa's apartment, so that was out. There were several abandoned warehouses he knew of, but they were full of junkies and runaways and too often, police with warrants. The judge had been very clear that he would cut Dennis a break only once, and only if he agreed to complete a long-term rehab program. If there was a next time, the judge told Dennis, he would be facing real prison time. On top of the original drug charges, Dennis figured he'd spend at least three to five years behind bars for having sex with a minor. Then he'd be officially in the system as a sex offender, which meant no more union work ever again. Dennis took another slug of the beer and crumpled the can. He began to weep and wiped his nose with the back of his sleeve.

Within fifteen minutes, he had cooked the contents of all seven of the bags and his syringe was almost completely full, something he had never seen before. It fascinated him to think what it would feel like to take a dose that large all at once. He tied a belt around his arm, found a vein, and pushed the full syringe of heroin into his bloodstream. The high was intense and reminded him of the first time he had shot heroin. Dennis leaned back against the tree and the open bag of chips on his lap tipped over into the leaves.

His breathing began to slow, leaving him taking only short shallow breaths. He couldn't stop smiling and hoped to himself the feeling would last forever. Slowly everything began to fade away as his central nervous system shut down, until no more oxygen reached his brain. He breathed one last breath, his brain cells dying by the millions, and a gurgling sound that was heard by no one escaped from his chest. Dennis's lips and fingernails turned blue, his body went limp, and slowly, he fell over onto his side with his face lying in the wet leaves.

It was several days before he was found.

– 66 –

Toots had spent over a decade sharing a cell with Otis Carlisle. Otis had been in and out of prison for petty theft and other non-violent petty crimes, until he took part in a botched robbery during which his partner had killed a convenience store clerk. Otis served nearly twenty-one years, before being released early for good behavior. For the majority of those years, he had worked as the prison barber for both the prisoners and the guards. It took a few months, but after his release, Otis eventually found a job at a barber shop in his old neighborhood. He had worked there for fifteen years when Toots arrived.

Otis loaned Toots two hundred fifty dollars to cover food, drink, and housing. For less than fifty dollars a month, Toots rented a dingy room in a hotel that housed mostly drug addicts and prostitutes. After calling a prison cell home for more than twenty years, to Toots, it was as if he had moved into a luxury apartment. He had his own toilet, shower, TV with remote control, and most importantly, he could come and go as he pleased.

Otis brought Toots to a second-hand shop in the neighborhood and together they bought old sheets, a blanket and pillow, and a bagful of old clothes, some of which fit and some that didn't. Toots was content, and although there never passed a night that he wasn't awakened at least once by shouting, gun shots, or a prostitute screaming in feigned pleasure for the sake of her client, he couldn't have been happier to call the rundown old hotel home. Within a few weeks, Otis found work for Toots cleaning and detailing cabs for a taxi company owned by a customer at the barber shop. Toots got a license and began covering shifts whenever his boss needed a driver. Eventually, that led to driving a Lincoln Town Car as the owner of the cab company began serving customers traveling to and from the airport.

After almost four years of living outside prison walls, Toots was content. What he cherished most though was his friendship with Otis, who in his mid-70s was still on his feet cutting hair six days a week and showing no signs of slowing down any time soon.

Aside from the occasional illness, the two met for breakfast every morning at 5:30 a.m. at a diner around the corner from the barber shop. The diner's owner Ernie came to work at 4:45 a.m. to prepare for the day. Minutes after Otis and Toots sat down, Ernie served them the same breakfast, every day: two eggs, sunny-side up, home fries, white toast with butter, and two sausage links.

Toots took his first sip of hot, black coffee before he shared with Otis his exciting news.

"Otis, you're not going to believe what I'm about to tell you." He blew on his coffee to cool it off.

"You picked up Tina Turner from her hotel and she asked you to marry her!" Otis said.

Toots laughed.

"No, no, listen, I picked up a man from a hospital just on the outskirts of D.C. yesterday. My boss warned me that this was some real important cat, a rich and famous lawyer of some sort. Mr. Miles is his name. He and I get to talking while I'm driving him to his private jet at an airport in Maryland and he tells me he just found out he got the cancer."

Otis made a sympathetic sound and put jam on his toast.

"He says he needs a driver and asks me if I'd be interested in the job," Toots continued. "But here's the part you are not gonna believe, Otis. I talked with his assistant from his office in Boston yesterday and she told me the job pays twenty-five hundred *per week* and it includes full medical and dental insurance."

Otis raised his eyebrows. "Say again?"

"You heard me," said Toots with a laugh. "What do you think?"

Otis put his fork down carefully before replying. With a twinkle in his eye, he said, "I think you need to bring this cat into the barber shop and I can charge him five hundred for a cut and a shave!" Otis laughed loud enough to startle Ernie, who had been lost in his own thoughts while standing in front of his old grill, turning a mountain of home fries over and over.

"I bet he just really liked you," Otis continued. "And if money doesn't mean anything to him, he probably figured the best way to make sure you take the job is to make you an offer you couldn't refuse."

"I feel like I hit the lottery!" Toots said, with a laugh. "Even after taxes, that's over fifteen hundred a *week*! I was thinking that maybe I can buy a little house. Wouldn't that be something, Otis, me owning my very own house?"

"I tell you what," said Otis, "you buy one of those multi-family buildings over near the projects off Main Street. You can live in one of the apartments and I'll live in the other. You can be my landlord. I sure as damn hell rather pay you every month rather than these damn slumlords that send in their goons to collect."

Toots grinned. "You've been so good to me since I've been on the outside, if can save enough to get my own place, we can split the taxes and whatever other costs like electricity and gas and you don't need to pay no rent. How's that sound?" Toots was happy at the prospect that he could finally in some way pay back his friend for all that he had done for him.

Otis raised his coffee cup and the two clinked.

– 67 –

Mr. C. contacted the school to let them know that he would not be able to work for the rest of the year. Thankfully, the principal told him to focus on his health, and promised him, much to his relief, that his job would be waiting for him the following school year.

Despite the warm and caring conversation he had had with the principal, Mr. C. felt sad; not one of his colleagues had bothered to call and check on him since he had missed work for the last week. He knew that he was not the most social person and blamed himself for not creating connections with others, but he also had the feeling that people had a pre-conceived notion of him because he was obese. He had often noticed the way his colleagues seemed embarrassed or uncomfortable around him and it felt to him as if they saw him as a weak, lumbering dumb person. In some ways he agreed with that sentiment, he was weak for not being able to control his eating, but dumb he was not.

Mr. C. turned his attention to calling the number of the transportation company he was hoping would get him to Boulder as soon as possible. Ed Dwyer, along with his wife, owned and operated a conversion van specially equipped for handicapped clients. Ed had taken over his father-in-law's food distribution company in the early 80s. At the time, it was a small business that delivered mostly frozen organic foods to the Colorado organic market. By the time he sold the business in 2008, Ed and his son had turned the business into a distribution and trucking giant, servicing fifteen states throughout the Midwest and reaching over a billion in gross sales. Ed was having the time of his life watching his only son George take the reins of the business, and was continuously impressed and amazed by George's natural leadership abilities.

One of the things that Ed loved and respected most about his son was the passion he had for all aspects of the business. At just twelve years old, George would sweep floors on the loading dock and watch and learn all that went on down in the heart of the operation. By the time he was fifteen, he was working every day after school and knew every step of the process, from the moment the inside salesgirls keyed in an order to when it was delivered to any one of the thousands of customers they served throughout the Midwest. By the time George was in his mid-30s, he was one of the most well-respected young leaders in the industry. Year after year, he took more responsibilities from his father, allowing his parents to spend more time in Naples, Florida, where they had their second home.

Then one day in 2007, a freak accident on the loading dock changed the Dwyer family and their business forever. George was giving the owner of a twenty-store chain of organic grocery markets a tour of the warehouse operations. George and his guest were out on the loading dock when a tractor trailer started backing in. Without thinking twice, George leaned his head out of the bay doors and began waving in the driver as he and every other person on the loading dock had done thousands of times before. But this time, something went terribly wrong. As the truck approached the dock, George turned his head away for a split second to check where the man he was leading around on the tour was standing. George's head became wedged between the metal frame of the loading door and the trailer that he was directing. His head was crushed and though he lived for another three years, he was brain dead from that moment on.

Ed and his wife spent every waking hour of those years caring for their beloved only child until the day his heart finally stopped beating. They had sold the business the year after the accident, when it was clear their son would never recover. Though they had more financial wealth than they could ever need, no amount of money could make George healthy again. The couple spent over a million dollars converting a bus containing all the machines needed to keep George breathing and alive for the trip to and from Naples, Florida and back to Boulder, Colorado.

Little did George's parents realize that they had found a new calling: since George's passing, they continued to offer the service of transporting severely handicapped people. By using the bus to help other families who have loved ones with handicaps such as their son George had, the couple somehow felt it kept their son closer in their hearts. As it turned out, they spent much of their time transporting morbidly obese patients to the many rehab facilities located in Boulder. After several years of doing this, they had found that obesity and food addictions were every bit as real and painful as any other handicap or illness. They had made many personal connections with patients for whom they had worked with over the last years, and in many cases continued to communicate and follow their progress.

Mr. C. arranged with Ed to be picked up the following week at his home outside Boston and brought to the Boulder Eating Recovery Center in Boulder, Colorado. He was feeling the pressure to get his life and the house in order. Ed was to arrive the following Friday between mid-morning and early afternoon, depending on the traffic.

He looked around the empty family home sadly, recalling how much life it had once held. His favorite memories were of Saturday mornings when he and his sisters would wake up and watch TV all morning, as their mother made lunch in the kitchen and their father cut the grass or worked in the garden. Those were the warmest and happiest times in his life. Often, he had a friend sleep over, and the two played video games into the early morning, long after the rest of the family had gone to sleep. He thought of reaching out to a few of those old friends that he had lost contact with, to see how their lives had turned out after all these years. But in the end, he decided to wait until after he came back from his time in Colorado, when he had his weight in control and didn't feel so ashamed of who he had become.

The house was messy and cluttered. He searched for a roll of plastic trash bags that he was sure was somewhere in the kitchen. But after only a few minutes, he was completely depleted of energy, and gave up on the cleaning mission. Slowly, he made his way into his computer room. He had put his computer back together on the desk the day before and aside from no longer having multiple screens, all was in working order.

He sat down in his oversized chair and with a few clicks of his mouse found his way to the grocery site from which he ordered all of his food. He was sure that all his favorite foods would be strictly off limits at the rehab and ordered twice the amount of junk food than was his normal. This was his last week of freedom, after all.

Chapter 68

Sitting in her last class of the day, Ivy kept thinking about Sophie. She wanted to believe that she had somehow misinterpreted what she had seen. But the more she thought about the way in which Sophie's fingers had interlocked with Eduardo's, the look the two had given each other in the seconds after, and the unmistakable look of terror and shame on Eduardo's face when he made eye contact with Ivy—well, it all added up. Ivy was positive that the two were having an affair and it was Eduardo that had gotten Sophie pregnant.

Ivy couldn't help but notice how happy and normal Sophie had been throughout the school day; it seemed completely counterintuitive to not be honest with her best friend and hide the fact that she knew she was having an affair with a married man old enough to be her father.

As was always the case on the day before a match, the volleyball team had only an hour of light practice so the coach could go through a basic game plan for their opponent the following day. Afterward, Ivy showered quickly and walked over to the baseball field to watch Stevie and the team practice.

Stevie was standing next to the backstop using a rubber resistance band that he had hooked to the metal fence as he did stretches. He had headphones in his ears and was totally focused. As she approached the field, Ivy noticed several of the players staring at her as she climbed up to the top bench and sat down on the metal stands. When she looked directly at her apparent admirers, they nervously looked away, which she found rather amusing.

Ivy shifted her focus to Stevie, his eyes squinting from the sun now hanging low in the sky. She wondered what he was thinking at that moment. She guessed it was most likely what had been weighing heavily on his mind lately, whether to take the money and begin his professional baseball career, or choose the scholarship to college for the education. Stevie had just switched the elastic band to his other hand when he spotted Ivy and took his headphones off, walking toward her. She descended the stands to meet him at the fence.

"A penny for your thoughts, Stevie," Ivy said as he reached with both hands above his head and grabbed the metal backstop fence in front of where Ivy was sitting.

"I suspect you know exactly what I am thinking about right now, and no, it's not sex," Stevie said, laughing. "Although now that I have seen you here freshly showered with your hair still wet and probably smelling like the vanilla shampoo you use, that may very well be the direction in which my thoughts begin to wander!"

Between the smile that reminded Ivy that Stevie was without a doubt the most handsome guy she had ever seen, and the mere mention of sex, she immediately felt the butterflies in her stomach and the heat in her cheeks.

Ivy gathered herself. "Well, I guess I'm flattered that you know which type of shampoo I use!" she said.

Stevie stuck a few fingers through the fence almost daintily and Ivy reached for them, sharing an affectionate half handshake.

"I am very impressed, Mr. Smith!" Ivy responded.

"I can't decide if you calling me Mr. Smith is the hottest thing I have ever heard a girl say to me because it makes me feel like a grown man, or the creepiest thing because it makes me think you're talking about my father."

"Well, maybe I'm just using you to get to your father. Did you ever think of that, Mr. Smith?" Ivy said, emphasizing the words Mr. Smith.

"Stop playing with my heart, I am a very fragile boy!" Stevie said.

Ivy grew serious. "I've been here a few minutes watching you while you were stretching and I could see you were deep in thought. Are you are still stressing about whether to turn pro or take the scholarship?"

"Yup, and it's making me a bit nuts, to be honest with you. I just keep going over and over the same things in my head, and in the end, I cannot come to any clear conclusion. It's exhausting!"

"How much longer do you practice today?" asked Ivy.

"In theory we have another forty-five minutes or so. But if given the opportunity to spend time with *the* Ivy S. Miles, I'm quite sure I can speak with my coach and be out of here in less than five minutes!" Stevie said, smiling again.

"Well, Mr. Smith, *the* Ivy S. Miles would very much like it if you would ask to leave practice early and drive me back to my place!"

Without another word, Stevie ran over to the batting cage where his coach was, leaving Ivy standing alone by the fence. She felt a pang of discomfort when the coach turned his head, looked at Ivy and waved. Stevie grabbed his bag and came jogging back over to where Ivy was standing.

"So, should I take a quick shower here or can I shower at your place?" Stevie asked.

Ivy immediately imagined Stevie walking out of the bathroom next to her bedroom after showering, shirtless with a towel wrapped around his waist, like from a scene from a movie.

"Sure, you can shower at the Omni," Ivy said quickly, composing herself and trying not to let her voice give away her thoughts.

"Okay, cool. Well, hopefully my old pickup will start and not break down during the drive to your place. I know you said you don't care, but it is really embarrassing to drive you around in that old truck. You are, after all, used to being driven around in brand new limos and fancy cars," said Stevie.

"Come on, Stevie, don't be silly. It's just a car. It wouldn't mean anymore to me if you had a Ferrari, I assure you!" Ivy said.

"Really?!" said Stevie.

"Really," said Ivy, and hugged him.

As Stevie and Ivy walked away, talking and laughing, the entire baseball team as well as both the coaches, turned to watch. They were a stunning couple.

– 69 –

On a normal day, Alan would be sitting at his desk in the office, working on whatever case happened to be of the highest priority. Instead, after having had several back-to-back meetings with money managers and lawyers to finalize his last will and testament, he was lying on the floor waiting for the pain meds he had taken fifteen minutes earlier to take effect.

Alan regretted the fact that he had agreed to join Harry and Cathy at Ivy's volleyball game. If it hadn't been for Harry talking him into staying, he would be on his way back to D.C. later that evening and could have rested all weekend before beginning the chemotherapy treatment. Faced with the stress of seeing his daughter and having to pretend everything was fine, he was tempted to order the jet himself and fly back to D.C. right away. But something told him that this would be the last time he would see Cathy, Harry, and his daughter, and he owed it to them all to keep his promise.

Alan stood up and felt the lightness in both his body and mind that told him the pain meds had begun to work their magic. Slowly, he walked to the dining room, where the now cold meal he had ordered for dinner was waiting. He removed the cover but the aroma of the food that wafted up turned his stomach. He took several deep breaths and was able to take a few small bites before covering the dish and making his way back to the sofa.

Gingerly, Alan lay down on the sofa and closed his eyes. Perhaps it was best, he thought, to skip treatment and face death without the discomfort of the vomiting and the weeks and months living in and out of the hospital. Not to mention losing his hair.

It was clear to Alan that he was not going to survive his illness, so why not embrace that reality and spend the last months of his life in London or Paris, in an apartment overlooking Big Ben or the Eiffel Tower? Perhaps his new employee Toots would accompany him. The thought of Toots brought a smile to Alan's face. What a curious and fascinating man he was. Not since his wife Clara had anyone affected him in the manner in which Toots had, somehow soothing and calming his mind and soul. As often was the case, his mind began drifting back to Clara and Jake and within a few minutes, Alan was fast asleep.

– 70 –

Stevie effortlessly and expertly worked the manual gearshift of the old pickup truck and Ivy was fascinated. Between the clutch, the gas pedal, the brake pedal, and of course the actual shifting of the gears, Ivy decided that she never wanted to even attempt to learn how to drive a stick shift.

"When you're on the field, do you still love the game?" Ivy asked, catching Stevie off guard. "Is the passion and the fire for baseball still burning in your heart when you're practicing or working out or watching video of a game?"

"Oh yeah, that's never changed," Stevie said, without hesitation. "I love the challenge and the constant striving to improve. There is still passion there, no doubt."

Ivy nodded and smiled, encouraging Stevie to go on.

"In fact, it may be that I love the game more now than I ever have because for the first time, I feel that I am playing for myself, and not for my father, like I felt when I was younger. So, it's not the lack of love for the game that worries me, it's the passion and love I also have for excelling in school, getting straight As, and learning in general. It's perhaps more this feeling of somehow giving up on this other gift I have been given and turning my back on my love of learning. Do you know what I mean?" Stevie concluded, looking at Ivy.

"Well, why not turn pro and work on your bachelor's degree at the same time?" asked Ivy.

Stevie nodded in vigorous agreement. "That would be the ideal situation, but the NCAA doesn't allow that option. The moment I take money for my sport, I lose my amateur status and can no longer accept a college scholarship or play college sports. Not to mention the fact that with all the traveling involved after signing a pro contract, taking college classes just isn't a reasonable option."

Ivy frowned. "Stevie, you know my parents both went to Harvard and so we get all the Harvard mail. Because they've always been on our coffee table and kitchen, I've read pretty much everything that's ever been printed since I was twelve years old. I know for a fact that Harvard is one of the world leaders in online learning and it's now possible to get a bachelor's degree from Harvard almost completely online."

"Really?" Stevie said, incredulous.

"If I remember correctly, in order to finish a bachelor's degree at Harvard online, you're required to take only four classes at the Boston campus and all of those are offered as weekend and three-week intensive classes offered during holidays."

Stevie nodded. "Really?!"

"Yes," said Ivy, emphatically. "Stevie, you certainly would be able to afford the tuition once you sign your professional contract, so why not turn pro *and* attend Harvard online?"

Ivy could see by the way Stevie's eyes lit up that he had not considered that option. It was as if a weight had lifted off his shoulders.

"Wait, wait, what?" asked Stevie, as if what he had just heard wasn't quite registering. "I can't believe it."

"Stevie Smith, focus!" Ivy laughed. "I am telling you that you at least have the option to play professional baseball *and* study for your degree at the same time."

"Wait, so you're saying I can get my bachelor's degree online regardless of where I am in the country? That would literally solve all my problems! I have been slowly dying inside thinking I had to choose one or the other...like literally dying inside!"

Ivy laughed. "Dying inside? Literally?"

Stevie laughed too and pulled his truck into the Omni parking lot. "Okay, maybe dying inside is a little dramatic, but sometimes it felt that way. If I can sign a pro contract directly out of high school and at the same time work towards a bachelor's degree at Harvard via the internet, that's exactly what I'm going to do."

Stevie put the truck in park, leaned over, and kissed Ivy passionately. She responded, and the moment went on for what felt like forever. Then Stevie pulled back. "Now there's only one problem I'm facing." Ivy's eyes widened.

Stevie looked at Ivy seriously. "I am falling in love with you, Ivy S. Miles."

– 71 –

Hello,

I am writing you all today to regretfully inform you that I must cancel both the bus transportation as well as the reservation at your rehab facility. I have once again been admitted to the hospital with a respiratory infection that I have been fighting for some time now. As soon as I am released from the hospital and the doctors give me the OK to once again travel, I will be in touch.

I hope to communicate soon and look forward to meeting you in the near future.

Mr. C. pressed the send button and felt both a tremendous relief and a shame deeper than he had ever felt before. He had the terrible feeling that the email he had just written, the lies he told to both the rehabilitation center and the owner of the transportation company, would in all likelihood lead to his death. It wasn't so much death itself that Mr. C. feared, it was dying alone. He thought of the stories he had read, about elderly people who had died and hadn't been found or noticed for months or years because they were alone in a world of seven billion people.

With the help of the walker that the hospital had provided upon his release, Mr. C. slowly made his way into the kitchen and took two family-size frozen lasagna dinners and three packages of frozen mozzarella sticks out of the freezer and put them into the oven. While he waited the twenty-four minutes for his dinner to heat up, Mr. C. finished off a canister of sour cream and onion Pringles and another container of original Pringles, plus a two-liter bottle of Mountain Dew. He decided that he would celebrate the fact that he wasn't going to Boulder and the fact that he wouldn't have to leave behind his one and only friend in this world, his food.

– 72 –

As Ivy and Stevie walked hand in hand through the Omni lobby and up to the elevator, Stevie couldn't keep the smile off his face. The concept of studying towards a degree from Harvard while playing professional baseball was something he thought could never happen. Stevie was so lost in his thoughts that the young couple hadn't spoken one word the entire walk from the parking lot. The question Ivy asked when the elevator doors shut to take them up to the apartment caught him completely off guard.

"When did you lose your virginity, Stevie?"

"When did I what now?" Stevie asked, blushing.

"How old were you when you lost your virginity?" Ivy bravely repeated the question with her cheeks now pink.

"Ms. Miles, a true gentleman never kisses and tells!" Stevie responded, causing them both to laugh. "What would make you ask me that out of nowhere?" Stevie asked.

"Well, I'm still a virgin as of course you are well aware, being that you and Sophie were having a full conversation about it in public earlier this week. At this point, I feel like the longer I stay a virgin the bigger deal it becomes. I can't seriously look at my virginity as a big deal, since there are over three billion women on the earth right now that all have or will have sex for the first time sooner or later. Of course, I want it to be with someone special, but I don't want to treat it like something it's not. You know what I mean?"

Stevie stared at Ivy for a long moment.

"Too much information?" she asked, laughing, to hide her embarrassment.

"No, not at all," said Stevie, taking Ivy's hand tenderly. "I get what you're saying."

"Phew," said Ivy, with a nervous laugh. "I guess it's obvious that I've thought about it—a lot!"

Steve smiled.

"What was your first time like?" Ivy asked, softly.

Stevie hesitated, then began to speak. "Well, my first time was as far from a big deal as you can possibly get."

"Tell me," Ivy encouraged, happy that she and Stevie were able to be so open with each other.

"I was at this guy Josh Hamilton's fifteenth birthday party at his house," Stevie continued. "It was a kind of pool party type thing during the summer after tenth grade. Josh's best friend Sherry lived next door and was also at the party. She was sixteen at that time, really cute, and super flirty."

Ivy gave a mock frown. "Hmmm... go on."

Stevie laughed. "Anyway, so we kind of hit it off and got to talking, and somehow it came up that I was still a virgin. Sherry was older than me, but she looked so young and seemed so sweet and innocent, I assumed she too was a virgin. Then she grabbed my hand, walked me out Josh's front door, and to her house next door. I asked her why we were leaving the party and that we should at least tell Josh, but she just ignored me and said we won't be long and to just trust her."

"Uh oh," Ivy chuckled, wanting yet not wanting to hear the rest of the story.

"No one was home at her house. She led me up to her room, we sat on her bed, and she started kissing me. I was only wearing a bathing suit and a t-shirt and she had on a bikini and an oversized t-shirt. Then she kind of pushed me back on the bed, and with no warning pulled my bathing suit down, pulled her bikini bottoms to the side, and sat down on me. It happened so fast and I was so not prepared or expecting anything like that to happen, it was almost like I was in some kind of movie."

Ivy didn't know where to look. She was embarrassed and yet curious.

"It is okay that I'm telling you this?" Stevie asked, sensing Ivy's discomfort.

"Yes. Please go on," said Ivy.

"Not long before, my mom had given me the talk about sex and condoms and how getting a girl pregnant would change my life and future forever. So after about ten seconds of shock and being mesmerized by the amazing new feeling I was experiencing, the reality of the situation hit me. First it was, *oh my god, I am having sex right now*, immediately followed by *holy shit, I am having sex without a condom and this girl is going to get pregnant and I will have to quit baseball and get a job at a fast food restaurant to support this baby*! I totally panicked, pushed her off me, pulled my bathing suit up, and told her we should get back to the party before they realized we were gone."

Ivy didn't know what to say. Stevie blushed at the memory.

"And that was it, that was the ten seconds of sex I had the day I lost my virginity."

Stevie and Ivy were standing at the door of her apartment in the Omni, which made Ivy feel braver, somehow. She was on her turf, and Stevie was being as open and honest as she could have hoped for.

"So just to recap, your first time having sex lasted ten seconds and you didn't like, you know..." Ivy paused, "orgasm or ejaculate?"

Stevie blushed. "Yes, it lasted approximately ten seconds and neither did I orgasm nor ejaculate." The two laughed.

"In the girlie magazines with all the sex advice and tips, they talk about the girl's first time often lasting only seconds because it's over for the boy very quickly. That's why I asked, just so you know," said Ivy.

"Oh, I have had my experiences like that too, just not this time," replied Stevie.

"Did you ever see her again?" asked Ivy as she turned to unlock the door to the apartment.

"Well, I saw her again a few times when she and Josh came to watch a few of my baseball games. She acted like it never happened, so I did the same. What's really weird is that Josh told me that she had done that with a bunch of different guys, including Josh. She told him she had some weird thing about being a guy's first because she will be forever remembered by them. Strange story, right?" Stevie asked.

"Yeah, that is really one of the strangest stories I could ever imagine, thanks for sharing it with me though. It's interesting to hear how not special your first was." Ivy laughed, suddenly very self-conscious.

Stevie shrugged.

"So that was how you officially lost your virginity." Ivy felt bolder after Stevie's honesty. "What was your real first, like the first time you really made love?"

"Well, I dated Leah Trainor throughout tenth and eleventh grade, until she moved to Ohio with her family. Do you remember her? She was a year ahead of me and was an awesome track and field athlete."

Ivy nodded. "Of course I remember Leah! Every girl in the school remembers her as the girl that got to date Stevie Smith!" she said.

"Come on, Ivy, you're making me blush," said Stevie. "Leah had dated the same guy since she was fourteen, but he had graduated the year before. As a result, she was very experienced when it came to anything and everything having to do with sex. Of course, I may have stretched the truth and made it seem that I too was quite experienced in all that goes on in the bedroom. Unfortunately, when the first time we had sex lasted maybe all of three seconds, I had no choice but to be more honest with her. She never let me forget that either, by the way."

"I read that the average newlywed couple between the ages of eighteen and twenty-eight have sex on average two to three times a week, which is another reason I don't want to make my first time into more than it is," said Ivy, with conviction. "It's like the first time I started a game for the varsity volleyball team my freshman year. It was such a big deal when coach told me I would be the starting outside hitter, that I threw up in the locker room before the game. Then I got out on that court for the first time, and of course it was really cool, but in the end was just another game. You know what I'm saying?" asked Ivy.

"To be honest, that's exactly how it is," Stevie said. "Don't get me wrong, sex is really, really, really fun, much more fun than playing baseball or volleyball, but the first time is definitely way overrated. Maybe we should just do it right here and now so you can get it over with and put it behind you. I am willing to voluntarily sacrifice my time and energy and be your partner. I know what you're going to say, that I am such a nice guy for being willing to do that for you. Hey what can I say, I will take one for the team for you on this one, Ivy!" Stevie said.

"Wow, you're quite a charmer...but wait, you will take one for the team? What team are you even talking about?" asked Ivy, laughing.

"Man, I almost thought I had you going for a second," Stevie said, pulling Ivy into him and passionately kissing her.

Ivy pulled her lips away from Stevie's and looked into his eyes. "I am not sure tonight is the night, but I am sure I want my first time to be with you, Stevie Smith."

Ivy looked at Stevie seriously. She was sure now that she was falling in love.

"It would be my honor, Ms. Miles," said Stevie, with a bow. "But do me a favor—when you decide you're ready, just give me enough time to prepare myself."

Ivy nodded solemnly. "For sure."

"I want your first time to last more than three and a half seconds. I'm aiming for at least ten seconds, minimum!" Stevie said, and the two laughed, hard.

"Okay, but for now," Ivy said, growing serious, "you can use the guest bathroom to shower and then we can hang out in my bedroom. Maybe you can teach me a few new things tonight."

– 73 –

When Lisa heard a knock on the door, she knew in her bones that it was bad news. She took a deep breath, opened the door, and saw two police officers standing in front of her, uncomfortably. Lisa knew at once that they had been assigned the unpleasant job of informing her that Dennis was dead.

"Good evening, ma'am. We are looking for friends or family of a Mr. Dennis Williams. According to our records, Mr. Williams listed this address as his current residence. Is that correct?"

"Is Dennis dead?" asked Lisa, with a cold feeling in the pit of her stomach.

"Yes, ma'am, I am sorry to inform you that his body was found earlier this morning in a park in the city. The coroner will perform an autopsy, which is required by law, but it seems very likely Mr. Williams died from a drug overdose."

Lisa hung her head. She felt like a stone was in her heart and it was hard to breathe.

"I am sorry for your loss, ma'am," said the officer, lamely.

Lisa was too numb and too angry to cry.

"Mr. Williams had no other next of kin listed in our records. Do you know if he had any living relatives that should be informed?" asked the officer.

Lisa choked on her next words. "No, Dennis had no one else in this world besides me." Then the tears began to flow.

"Is there anything we can do for you, ma'am? Are there any friends or family you can call so you don't have to be alone this evening?" asked the other officer, with obvious concern for Lisa's state.

"No, I don't need anybody. Thank you for your concern, but I have survived worse." The officers exchanged an uncomfortable look.

Lisa began to close the door. "Thank you for giving me this news, I don't have to worry about him anymore."

"Wait." The female officer handed Lisa a folder with some paperwork and explained to her where Dennis's body had been taken. She also told Lisa where she could go to retrieve the personal items that were found on his person. When the officers had left, Lisa walked to her sofa and collapsed into tears. It felt like her world had come apart. Again.

– 74 –

Ivy,

I am in more pain everyday now. In order for the pain meds to function and trick my brain into thinking there is no pain, I need to take such high doses that it zonks me out. So now I am sleeping pretty much all day and night, kind of like you used to when you were first born. Earlier today, I was thinking about when you were born, and you and Mama came home from the hospital for your first night here at the Omni. Everyone had been warning me how babies cry all night long and that I should get used to sleep deprivation. Needless to say, it was quite a pleasant surprise that first night when you slept six hours straight, woke up for your feeding from Mama, and went right back to sleep for another six hours. Everyone who met you said you were the happiest and easiest baby they had ever seen. Sometimes it seemed that you somehow knew that I was sick, and that Mama was already stressed out enough without adding sleep deprivation to the list. And so, you just chilled and never bothered anyone.

Mama would place you on my bed, and the three of us would just lie there, both of us content to watch you play with your baby toys. Then your eyes would start to get heavy and slowly they would close, and you would fall asleep in between the two of us. It was so nice just to watch you sleep. You were so beautiful and looked so peaceful.

As I get closer to the end, you're now spending more time at Nancy's house with your little best baby friend Sophie. Sophie is Nancy's daughter, the two of you are just a few months apart but she is about half your size. You are so damn cute together. I hope you stay in touch with Nancy and her family as you grow up, they have been so helpful taking care of you over the last months. Between Mama's headaches and my pain meds, it's best for everyone that you aren't around all the sad energy and negative atmosphere my illness is creating here at the apartment!

Unfortunately, I am running out of energy to continue this entry for much longer. The pain meds are starting to kick in and my eyes are begging to close so I will try and make this quick. When I am writing to you, I am of course focusing on my thoughts, what I want to write, and what I want to share with you. It's strange, but this journal is the only thing of any value that I feel I am leaving behind after my short stay here on earth. So, in these moments when I am communicating with you, I am content and it feels like I don't have a problem in the world. Even the pain is barely noticeable when I am lost in my thoughts, trying to decide which of the many pearls of wisdom I want to leave behind for my little sister. Okay, that was my attempt at a joke. I am not sure I have much wisdom to share with you, Ives. But I do know that when I am not focused, and not actively living in the moment, my mind starts to dwell on my impending and looming death, and that creates anxiety, sadness, anger, and all the other emotions that one might experience when facing death.

I began thinking about all the things that I used to worry about before I got sick. I try to imagine what normal people worry about, and stress about, and make themselves crazy about…and from that came this song. Unfortunately, I no longer have the energy, nor the strength to make a recording, but at least I can share with you the lyrics. Just think of it as a poem!

I love you, Ives!

Living In The Moment

I don't live my life jaded, I ain't weary or guarded
My mind ain't broken, I don't feel broken hearted
I ain't got no longings, no dreams or a wish list
Got no particular direction, ain't lethargic or listless

I'm too busy
Living in the moment
To be praying
For false atonement
I'm too busy
Living in the moment
To worry about you!

I ain't got no aspirations, no goals or ambitions
I don't contemplate the future, and I don't ever listen
I ain't got no worries, no particular objective
Don't offer no opinions, cause my hearing is selective

– 75 –

Sitting in the back of the town car riding to the volleyball match she'd be playing in just over two hours, Ivy was still buzzing from the time spent with Stevie the night before; the smile on her face wasn't exactly hiding this fact. Unfortunately, Stevie had meetings with several different agents in the afternoon and couldn't be at her game.

A little reluctantly, Ivy's thoughts switched to the prospect of her father coming to see her play for the first time. She hadn't allowed herself to get too excited, because some part of her didn't believe Alan would actually follow through with it. It was difficult for Ivy to imagine him sitting in the high school bleacher seats while surrounded by screaming students and fans. Ivy was well aware her father avoided anything that involved interacting with other humans, that is, if it wasn't directly related to the law. Ivy steeled herself not to be too disappointed if her father chose not to come; the last thing she wanted was for him to suffer on her account.

Her mind wandered back to Stevie and all the talk about her virginity, and sex, and how much fun they had had together in her bed the night before. Ivy knew for sure that Stevie was the one, but she was realistic. She knew he'd be leaving soon to pursue his dream of becoming a professional ball player when the school year ended in only a few months. They had spoken briefly earlier, and he had asked if they should meet later so they could continue from where they had left off the night before. Ivy felt the butterflies flutter in her stomach at the mere thought of finally shedding herself of the virgin label with the man she had fallen in love with. She had read enough articles in women's magazines to not expect fireworks the first time, but also knew it would quickly get better.

"Ms. Miles, you haven't stopped smiling since you got in that back seat," said the driver, startling Ivy, who was deep in her thoughts.

"Don't get me wrong," the driver continued, "I'm not complaining, you sure do have a beautiful smile, young lady." The driver, Carl, was a retired high school principal from one of the toughest inner-city public schools in Boston. He was a very pleasant man with a very grandfatherly quality about him. Ivy blushed at the thought that if Carl knew what was going through her mind he would likely be appalled.

"Thank you, Carl. Yes, today is an exciting day. Both Harry and my father have plans to come to my volleyball game to watch me play later this afternoon. That's quite unexpected, as you can probably imagine," said Ivy.

"I can see Harry attending your game, but your father, now that is a surprise to say the least!" Carl said, grinning. "I've been driving for this company for almost eight years now, and rarely have I brought your father anywhere but to the office or the airport."

Ivy nodded. "Sounds about right."

"I keep up with your high school volleyball career in the newspaper and read that you're having another wonderful season," Carl continued. "The next time I'm not working, I promise to come see you play, okay?"

"That would be great," Ivy said, smiling.

– 76 –

Lisa knew that sooner or later she would have to pack up Dennis's belongings and figure out what to do with them. Beginning with the stay at the rehabilitation facility, followed by Dennis moving into her apartment, Lisa had become accustomed to wearing her artificial leg from the moment she woke up until just before going to bed at night. No longer having to worry about Dennis seeing her without her prosthesis, Lisa grabbed her crutches and headed into the kitchen for her first cup of coffee of the morning.

For the past three mornings, she had prepared only half a pot of coffee. While waiting for the coffee to brew, Lisa had an unexpected thought. She wondered what had happened to the young girl that Dennis had brought into the apartment, and hoped she too hadn't overdosed. Then Lisa thought of something that Dennis had told her when they had first met in the rehab center. Dennis explained that no experienced drug addict had ever accidentally overdosed. It could happen to a new user, whose body was unaccustomed to a powerful narcotic being suddenly introduced into their bloodstream. Addicts, however, knew exactly how much they needed to get high and Dennis was very clear in his opinion that when an addict died of an overdose, it was done by choice. Lisa realized, with a sick feeling, that Dennis had been informing her early in their relationship that if he was ever to commit suicide, that was how he would choose to do it.

Lisa had never questioned whether Dennis loved her with all his heart; she had felt his love deep in her soul. But she also knew that once his addiction took its hold on him, he was no longer the man she had fallen in love with.

It was going to take a long time to heal from the loss, Lisa knew. But time was all she had.

– 77 –

Alan had arranged for the car service to pick him up early and now he waited awkwardly in the high school parking lot. The driver turned to let him know that Harry's car had just pulled into the lot and asked if he would like to be dropped off closer to the entrance of the sports auditorium. Before Alan had a chance to answer, he felt the rumbling of one of Harry's 600-plus horsepower sports car pull into the parking spot directly next to the limo. Harry revved the engine, knowing well that his partner despised his penchant for loud sports cars. Harry was still sitting in his car when Alan got out and impatiently knocked on the driver's side window. He shut off the engine, and up swung the driver-side door.

"Why in the hell would you possibly buy a car with goddamn doors that open up? What is the point of that design, Harry? You look foolish in this damn machine!" Alan grumbled.

"Now Alan, I am certainly no expert of design nor engineering, but I can make a calculated guess, the doors open up, because it looks cool. You are welcome to take her for a ride around the block, she's a blast to drive," said Harry, with an indulgent smile.

"Why must men refer to a machine as 'she'? Please tell me you haven't given this automobile a crass female name. Honestly, Harry, I expect more of you," said Alan.

"I don't yet have a name for her, but now that you mention it, I am thinking Betty has a nice ring to it."

Alan rolled his eyes, but Harry wasn't done. "How about Big Black Betty? That seems like a fitting name, wouldn't you agree?" He knew full well that Alan would ignore that last remark.

Slowly, Alan made his way toward the auditorium. Harry followed. "Alan, I don't want to be judgmental, but you really look like shit! You look like you're dying!"

Alan gave Harry a scathing look. "Too soon?" Harry asked.

There was a silence before Alan spoke again. "You know it's interesting, Harry. I haven't seen Ivy in over three months." Harry avoided Alan's look. "I didn't mean for it to be so, but some months ago I stopped spending nights at the Omni," Alan continued, almost to himself. "In some ways I think that I was aware of the tumors inside me and I was trying to distance myself from my daughter."

Harry stopped and stared at his friend of so many years.

"Distance yourself? Alan, I hate to break the news to you, but you might as well have been living in Siberia for the sixteen years that Ivy has been on this earth. I haven't ever heard you say more than three words to her in all her life. Perhaps you can speak with Elon Musk and get a spot on his ship going to Mars to put more distance between you and your daughter."

Alan continued walking, ignoring the comment.

"Ivy doesn't need me, just like her mother never needed me. Ivy can take care of herself."

The two friends and business associates were approaching the entrance to the gym, and people were beginning to crowd in to see the match.

"My, my, Alan, you sure are particularly unaware this morning," said Harry. "I can tell you with certainty that yes, you are indeed correct in saying that neither Ivy nor Clara ever needed you."

Alan looked at Harry with something between hurt and acceptance in his eyes.

Undaunted, Harry continued. "But that doesn't mean they wouldn't have wanted more of you in their lives. Clara certainly knew who and what you were before she chose you to be her husband and the father of her children. She married the man she wanted to marry, and I assure you that she never changed her mind. So yes, she didn't *need* you, but that's only because she loved you unconditionally and knew you loved her in your own strange and limited way."

Alan frowned at the words.

But Harry wasn't done. "The same holds true for your Ivy, who has certainly shown she does not *need* you in her life. But that is like saying I don't need to smoke a hundred-dollar Cuban cigar while drinking a glass of five-hundred-dollar Cabernet, or that I didn't need to spend over a million dollars on that sports car parked outside. Of course, I don't *need* any of those things, but they bring me joy and make me happy."

Alan only stared at his colleague as the crowd streamed around them. His pain was returning and he longed to go home and rest.

"Does it ever occur to you that you're the only family Ivy has in this world?" Harry asked. "And that you're not going to be around for much longer?

"I know I won't be around for much longer," Alan said, somberly. "But I don't know how to have a normal relationship with Ivy. I'm not—I'm not the same as other people, Harry. You must know that by now."

Harry put his arm around his friend.

"I know, Alan."

"I wouldn't have any idea what Ivy and I could possibly talk about," Alan continued.

"The first step is to change your plans and have the treatment here in Boston," Harry said as he let go of Alan and held open the gym door for his friend.

As they walked around the corner Alan caught sight of Ivy on the court warming up. He got goosebumps all over his body; Ivy was the spitting image of her mother. Alan had only ever seen Clara play the one time, but he never forgot how she looked in her Harvard Crimson uniform with her hair up in a braided ponytail. It seemed as if he had gone back in time and was back in the Harvard sports hall watching his wife-to-be about to start the match.

"Ivy sure is the spitting image of her mother, isn't that right, Alan?" said Harry, his hands crossed over his chest as he looked at Ivy in admiration and pride.

"It's uncanny," Alan said, from deep within a haze of unfamiliar emotions.

– 78 –

Stevie was seated at the breakfast table with the Harvard newsletter Ivy had given him. His mother was sitting next to him reading the newspaper and sipping her coffee, while his father finished cooking bacon and eggs.

His father approached Stevie with the frying pan and slid some eggs onto Stevie's plate.

"What's that you're reading, son?"

Stevie dug into his eggs. "Well, I've officially made my decision as to whether I'll turn pro or take the scholarship to a university." His parents looked at him expectantly.

"And?" his mother asked, putting the paper down.

"As you know, I've been struggling with this decision because as much as I love playing ball, I cannot imagine not continuing my education. I was talking about this with Ivy Miles last night, and she mentioned this program Harvard offers."

Stevie placed the Harvard newspaper in the middle of the table before continuing. "Dad, Mom, I don't have to choose one or the other. Harvard now offers a new program that allows students to attend online classes from anywhere in the world."

Stevie's parents peered at the newsletter, curiously. There was a long pause.

"Mom? Dad?" Stevie asked.

"I know this is hard for you to believe, son, but we have also been torn with the prospect of you turning your back on this other gift you have, the gift you inherited from your mother," said Stevie's dad.

"Now it seems you can have your cake and eat it too,." Stevie's mom beamed and put her hand on her husband's shoulder.

"How about we give those two agents a call this morning, Pops, and let them know that I'm officially ready to become a professional ball player," said Stevie.

His father grinned. "You got it."

Stevie looked at his mother. "Mama, will you sit with me and check out the Harvard website to see what degrees the online program offers?"

Stevie's mother smiled. "You betcha."

"And to celebrate this news, you get to wash the dishes this morning!" Stevie's father said, and playfully slugged his son's shoulder.

"Oh, how incredibly kind of you, Dad!" Stevie said, laughing.

– 79 –

By the time the game was about to begin, teachers, parents, family members, and students had filed in until there was standing room only in the gym. An older couple that Alan assumed to be grandparents of one of the players sat on his left. Harry sat on his right.

"Who are you here to watch today? Does your daughter play on one of the teams?" asked the older woman sitting next to Alan.

"My daughter, yes," said Alan, unused to normal conversation. Harry smiled to himself, noting his friend's discomfort.

The sport was much faster than Alan remembered and expected. The opponent served the first ball, which was received by a player who Alan recognized as Sophie Pham. Sophie passed the ball perfectly to the setter, who set a ball to the outside where Ivy was positioned. Ivy jumped easily over both the opponent's blockers' outstretched hands, and hit the ball with tremendous force straight down, for her team's first point. The crowd roared to life, and only then did it dawn on Alan that most of the people in the stands had come to see one of the best high school volleyball players in the country. Alan smiled and swelled with pride for a brief moment, but the feeling was immediately replaced by shame. Alan had allowed his daughter's entire childhood to pass by without ever attempting to be a part of it.

The crowd roared in anticipation, interrupting Alan's thoughts. Ivy walked to the service line for her first serve of the game. When the referee's whistle blew, Ivy bounced the ball three times with both hands, spun it in her right hand, threw it up ten feet in the air, took three powerful strides, jumped and smashed a serve that landed on the opponent's side of the court before any of their players even had time to react.

The crowd chanted Ivy's name, waiting for another jump serve ace. The whistle sounded, Ivy again went through her pre-serve routine, and pounded another ace in virtually the same spot as the first. Alan thought of Clara and how proud she would be to see her daughter on the court and how much fun they would have had sharing the sport they both loved.

An hour and a half later, Ivy's team had easily won three straight sets to win the match. Alan watched as Ivy and the rest of the team jumped with joy, all with smiles on their young faces. The fans came down from the bleachers to interact with the players, converging on Ivy with their congratulations.

"Boy, she is something else," Harry said, beaming. "If there is a heaven, Clara must be looking down smiling from ear to ear!"

"It's nice to think Clara might be able to see how her daughter turned out," said Alan, almost to himself.

"*Your* daughter, Alan." Harry put his hand on his friend's thin shoulder. "Ivy is your daughter, too."

Alan looked lost in thought.

"So," Harry said after an awkward moment, "are you feeling up to inviting Ivy to join us for a bite to eat?"

"I don't have much of an appetite, so I'm going to have to pass. But please don't change your plans on my behalf," said Alan, apologetically.

Harry looked at his friend with concern. Alan was noticeably thinner.

As Ivy walked toward her father, she too noticed that Alan had lost a significant amount of weight. Not only that, his skin had a waxy, unhealthy pallor and he seemed a bit bent at the waist, making him appear much shorter than his normal height of 6'5".

"Did you enjoy watching the game, Ala...uhm...Dad?"

Harry peered at Alan, wondering how he would respond.

"I once watched your mother play a game when we were at Harvard."

As Alan said these words, he realized it was the first time he had ever spoken to his daughter about Clara. This fact wasn't lost on Ivy, who looked momentarily taken aback at the mention of the mother she could barely remember but had only recently gotten to know in Jake's journals.

"Well, I'm glad you came tonight," Ivy said. "I know it isn't your cup of tea." Alan avoided Ivy's eyes and looked at his feet.

"To be fair, Ivy, other than lawyering, Alan doesn't really have a cup of tea!" said Harry, laughing.

Fans and teammates kept patting Ivy on the back and congratulating her.

"I hate to do this, but I have to join the team for a kind of post-match meeting we do with our coach. Do either of you have plans for this evening?" asked Ivy, hoping they could spend more time together.

"Harry, would you excuse us? I would like to have a minute alone with Ivy."

"Of course," said Harry and left the two alone.

Immediately, Ivy knew something was not right. It struck her that the man she had always thought of as both physically and emotionally intimidating was now, due to his strange posture, essentially her same height. She had always dreamed of her father coming to one of her games, and of having some sort of normal father-daughter conversations, yet here they stood, and seeing the pain and discomfort in his eyes, Ivy knew this was the last place on earth her father wanted to be.

Ivy so badly wanted her father to know that she was no longer a child and that everything was okay. She yearned to explain how Jake's journal helped her understand that her mother loved Alan not in spite of his emotional shortcomings, but as a result of them. She needed to tell him how, with all the information Jake had provided, she too had changed the way she viewed her father and no longer felt any resentment towards him. Most importantly, she yearned to tell her father that she appreciated him for the person that he was, strong, stoic, intense, and unflappable.

Still staring at the gym floor, Alan was unable to find a way to explain his prognosis to his daughter, nor of his plan to move to Washington to die alone.

Ivy broke the silence. "Alan, it's okay...whatever it is that you need to say, it's okay. I'm sixteen years old and I'll soon be off to college. I'm not a child anymore. I've had a wonderful life with all the opportunities a girl could ever ask for. You don't need to worry about me, I'm okay."

Alan finally looked into his daughter's eyes and saw not the child that he had failed, but a young woman who, despite his shortcomings as a father, had grown up to be an incredible young woman. Ivy, like her mother, was in many ways stronger than he himself could ever be.

Father and daughter looked in each other's eyes and held a gaze that seemed to last forever. Ivy felt a sense of understanding, and maybe even closure. The crowd was draining out of the gym now and Ivy's teammates were gathered near the coach. She knew she had to join them, and soon.

"I'll be moving to Washington D.C. for the next year or so. If you ever need me to be here, I will of course do everything in my power to make the trip back as soon as possible."

Ivy looked at Alan with questions in her eyes.

"Harry will take care of all the inheritance issues until you feel comfortable with handling it yourself, if—when something should happen to me," Alan added. He gathered strength before continuing.

"Your mother would be so proud of the woman you have become. You are every bit as strong and independent as Clara was." He paused as if he had more to say.

Instead, he turned and slowly walked away from his daughter and out of the gym to his waiting car. Alan knew it would be the last conversation they would have, and he should have shared more, but simply couldn't find the strength.

Ivy watched Alan walk away. Not quite understanding what had just transpired between the two of them, she debated whether or not to run after him. Just then, several of her teammates called to tell her coach was waiting for her to start the meeting. Ivy wiped her eyes with the sleeve of her jersey, turned and jogged to the locker room.

– 80 –

Less than six months later, Ivy was standing at the funeral home with Stevie by her side. He had flown in from southern Florida, where his baseball team was located. Ivy was astonished to see hundreds of people who had flown in from all over the country and the world, to pay their respects to her father—Alan Miles.

Ivy often thought back to the last conversation she had with her father. In retrospect, she knew that it would be the last time she would ever see him alive, although she didn't acknowledge the fact at the time. It had been too much, too emotional. But now he was gone and Ivy was in a state of acceptance and perhaps even peace. Jake's journals had helped her face this moment, she realized, and she smiled at the thought of the brother she never knew, yet had come to know so well.

Many of the guests shared with Ivy their memories of her father, and it warmed her heart to learn what a profound effect he'd had on so many people. She would never have imagined the role that Alan had played in the lives of so many.

Ivy hoped that wherever he was, Alan also realized how he was remembered by the people at the service. He had, after all, taught Ivy to be the well-adjusted, strong, independent, fearless, and driven woman that she was.

Ivy and Stevie walked out of the building hand in hand. She thought to herself, perhaps her family—Clara, Alan, and Jake, were all together once again. With Jake's songs playing in her mind, Ivy looked up to the sky, and smiled.

About the Author

Carlos Knowlton Baker was born and raised in Providence, Rhode Island. He grew up in Rehoboth, Massachusetts with his American father, Bolivian mother, and his brother Michael. Upon graduating in 1996 with a business degree from the University of Hartford, he continued his studies for two years at the Hartt School of Music.

At 12 years old, Carlos was diagnosed with osteogenic sarcoma (a type of bone cancer) in his left knee that spread to his lungs. After multiple surgeries and chemotherapy at Boston Children's Hospital / Dana Farber Cancer Institute / The Jimmy Fund, he was cancer-free. His left leg, however, was beyond repair and was amputated at the middle of his thigh.

In 1992, he met Bianca, a German volleyball scholarship athlete at the University of Hartford. Bianca is the love of his life. In 2002, they married and settled down in Rhode Island where they had three children, Fiona, Kaia, and Damian. In 2009, they moved to her home town in northern Germany where their fourth child Logan was born and they reside today.

For the last decade in Germany, Carlos has lived life as a stay-at-home father, author, singer/songwriter, and bass player.

"Songs for Ivy" is the title of his first album as well as his debut novel.